THE TALES OF CHEKHOV
VOLUME 6

.

THE WITCH
AND OTHER STORIES

THE TALES OF CHEKHOV

THE WITCH

AND OTHER STORIES

By
ANTON CHEKHOV

Translated By
CONSTANCE GARNETT

The Ecco Press
New York

The Ecco Press logo by Ahmed Yacoubi

Library of Congress Cataloging in Publication Data
Chekhov, Anton Pavlovich, 1860–1904.
The witch and other stories.
(The tales of Chekhov; vol. 6)
Reprint. Originally published: New York: Macmillan, 1918.
Contents: The witch–Peasant wives–The post–[etc.]
1. Chekhov, Anton Pavlovich, 1860–1904   –Translations, English.
I. Title. II. Series: Chekhov, Anton Pavlovich, 1860–1904.
Short stories. English; vol. 6
PG3456.A15G3   1984   vol. 6   891.73'3s   84-13649
ISBN 0-88001-053-3 (pbk.)   [891.73'3]

SECOND PRINTING, 1988

CONTENTS

THE WITCH

THE TALES OF CHEKHOV

THE WITCH

IT was approaching nightfall. The sexton, Savély Gykin, was lying in his huge bed in the hut adjoining the church. He was not asleep, though it was his habit to go to sleep at the same time as the hens. His coarse red hair peeped from under one end of the greasy patchwork quilt, made up of coloured rags, while his big unwashed feet stuck out from the other. He was listening. His hut adjoined the wall that encircled the church and the solitary window in it looked out upon the open country. And out there a regular battle was going on. It was hard to say who was being wiped off the face of the earth, and for the sake of whose destruction nature was being churned up into such a ferment; but, judging from the unceasing malignant roar, someone was getting it very hot. A victorious force was in full chase over the fields, storming in the forest and on the church roof, battering spitefully with its fists upon the windows, raging and tearing, while something vanquished was howling and wailing. . . . A plaintive lament sobbed at the window, on the roof, or in the stove. It sounded not like a call for help, but like a cry of misery, a consciousness that it was too late, that there was no salvation. The snowdrifts were covered with a thin coating of ice; tears quivered on them and on the trees; a dark slush of mud and melting snow flowed along the roads and paths. In short, it was thawing, but through the dark night the heavens failed to see it, and flung flakes of fresh snow upon the melting earth at a terrific rate. And the wind staggered like a drunkard. It would not let the snow settle on the ground, and whirled it round in the darkness at random.

Savély listened to all this din and frowned. The fact was that he knew, or at any rate suspected, what all this racket outside the window was tending to and whose handiwork it was.

" I know! " he muttered, shaking his finger menacingly under the bedclothes; " I know all about it."

On a stool by the window sat the sexton's wife, Raïssa Nilovna. A tin lamp standing on another stool, as though timid and distrustful of its powers, shed a dim and flickering light on her broad shoulders, on the handsome, tempting-looking contours of her person, and on her thick plait, which reached to the floor. She was making sacks out of coarse hempen stuff. Her hands moved nimbly, while her whole body, her eyes, her eyebrows, her full lips, her white neck were as still as though they were asleep, absorbed in the monotonous, mechanical toil. Only from time to time she raised her head to rest her weary neck, glanced for a moment towards the window, beyond which the snowstorm was raging, and bent again over her sacking. No desire, no joy, no grief, nothing was expressed by her handsome face with its turned-up nose and its dimples. So a beautiful fountain expresses nothing when it is not playing.

But at last she had finished a sack. She flung it aside, and, stretching luxuriously, rested her motion-less, lack-lustre eyes on the window. The panes were swimming with drops like tears, and white with short-lived snowflakes which fell on the window, glanced at Raïssa, and melted. . . .

" Come to bed ! " growled the sexton. Raïssa re-mained mute. But suddenly her eyelashes flickered and there was a gleam of attention in her eye. Savély, all the time watching her expression from under the quilt, put out his head and asked:

" What is it ? "

" Nothing. . . . I fancy someone's coming," she answered quietly.

The sexton flung the quilt off with his arms and legs, knelt up in bed, and looked blankly at his wife. The timid light of the lamp illuminated his hirsute, pock-marked countenance and glided over his rough matted hair.

" Do you hear ? " asked his wife.

Through the monotonous roar of the storm he caught a scarcely audible thin and jingling monotone like the shrill note of a gnat when it wants to settle on one's cheek and is angry at being prevented.

" It's the post," muttered Savély, squatting on his heels.

Two miles from the church ran the posting road. In windy weather, when the wind was blowing from the road to the church, the inmates of the hut caught the sound of bells.

"Lord! fancy people wanting to drive about in such weather," sighed Raïssa.

"It's government work.   You've to go whether you like or not."

The murmur hung in the air and died away.

"It has driven by," said Savély, getting into bed.

But before he had time to cover himself up with the bedclothes he heard a distinct sound of the bell. The sexton looked anxiously at his wife, leapt out of bed and walked, waddling, to and fro by the stove. The bell went on ringing for a little, then died away again as though it had ceased.

"I don't hear it," said the sexton, stopping and looking at his wife with his eyes screwed up.

But at that moment the wind rapped on the window and with it floated a shrill jingling note. Savély turned pale, cleared his throat, and flopped about the floor with his bare feet again.

"The postman is lost in the storm," he wheezed out glancing malignantly at his wife.   "Do you hear?   The postman has lost his way! . . . I . . . I know!   Do you suppose I . . . don't understand?" he muttered.   "I know all about it, curse you!"

"What do you know?" Raïssa asked quietly, keeping her eyes fixed on the window.

"I know that it's all your doing, you she-devil! Your doing, damn you!   This snowstorm and the post going wrong, you've done it all — you!"

"You're mad, you silly," his wife answered calmly.

"I've been watching you for a long time past and

I've seen it. From the first day I married you I noticed that you'd bitch's blood in you! "

" Tfoo! " said Raïssa, surprised, shrugging her shoulders and crossing herself. " Cross yourself, you fool! "

" A witch is a witch," Savély pronounced in a hollow, tearful voice, hurriedly blowing his nose on the hem of his shirt; " though you are my wife, though you are of a clerical family, I'd say what you are even at confession. . . . Why, God have mercy upon us! Last year on the Eve of the Prophet Daniel and the Three Young Men there was a snowstorm, and what happened then? The mechanic came in to warm himself. Then on St. Alexey's Day the ice broke on the river and the district policeman turned up, and he was chatting with you all night . . . the damned brute! And when he came out in the morning and I looked at him, he had rings under his eyes and his cheeks were hollow! Eh? During the August fast there were two storms and each time the huntsman turned up. I saw it all, damn him! Oh, she is redder than a crab now, aha! "

" You didn't see anything."

" Didn't I! And this winter before Christmas on the Day of the Ten Martyrs of Crete, when the storm lasted for a whole day and night — do you remember? — the marshal's clerk was lost, and turned up here, the hound. . . . Tfoo! To be tempted by the clerk! It was worth upsetting God's weather for him! A drivelling scribbler, not a foot from the ground, pimples all over his mug and his

neck awry! If he were good-looking, anyway —
but he, tfoo! he is as ugly as Satan!"

The sexton took breath, wiped his lips and listened. The bell was not to be heard, but the wind
banged on the roof, and again there came a tinkle
in the darkness.

"And it's the same thing now!" Savély went on.
"It's not for nothing the postman is lost! Blast
my eyes if the postman isn't looking for you! Oh,
the devil is a good hand at his work; he is a fine
one to help! He will turn him round and round and
bring him here. I know, I see! You can't conceal
it, you devil's bauble, you heathen wanton! As
soon as the storm began I knew what you were up
to."

"Here's a fool!" smiled his wife. "Why, do
you suppose, you thick-head, that I make the
storm?"

"H'm! . . . Grin away! Whether it's your
doing or not, I only know that when your blood's on
fire there's sure to be bad weather, and when there's
bad weather there's bound to be some crazy fellow
turning up here. It happens so every time! So it
must be you!"

To be more impressive the sexton put his finger
to his forehead, closed his left eye, and said in a sing-
song voice:

"Oh, the madness! oh, the unclean Judas! If
you really are a human being and not a witch, you
ought to think what if he is not the mechanic, or the
clerk, or the huntsman, but the devil in their form!
Ah! You'd better think of that!"

"Why, you are stupid, Savély," said his wife, looking at him compassionately. "When father was alive and living here, all sorts of people used to come to him to be cured of the ague: from the village, and the hamlets, and the Armenian settlement. They came almost every day, and no one called them devils. But if anyone once a year comes in bad weather to warm himself, you wonder at it, you silly, and take all sorts of notions into your head at once."

His wife's logic touched Savély. He stood with his bare feet wide apart, bent his head, and pondered. He was not firmly convinced yet of the truth of his suspicions, and his wife's genuine and unconcerned tone quite disconcerted him. Yet after a moment's thought he wagged his head and said:

"It's not as though they were old men or bandy-legged cripples; it's always young men who want to come for the night. . . . Why is that? And if they only wanted to warm themselves —— But they are up to mischief. No, woman; there's no creature in this world as cunning as your female sort! Of real brains you've not an ounce, less than a starling, but for devilish slyness — oo-oo-oo! The Queen of Heaven protect us! There is the postman's bell! When the storm was only beginning I knew all that was in your mind. That's your witchery, you spider!"

"Why do you keep on at me, you heathen?" His wife lost her patience at last. "Why do you keep sticking to it like pitch?"

"I stick to it because if anything — God forbid

— happens to-night . . . do you hear? . . . if anything happens to-night, I'll go straight off to-morrow
morning to Father Nikodim and tell him all about
it. 'Father Nikodim,' I shall say, 'graciously excuse me, but she is a witch.' 'Why so?' 'H'm!
do you want to know why?' 'Certainly. . . .'
And I shall tell him. And woe to you, woman!
Not only at the dread Seat of Judgment, but in your
earthly life you'll be punished, too! It's not for
nothing there are prayers in the breviary against
your kind!"

Suddenly there was a knock at the window, so
loud and unusual that Savély turned pale and almost
dropped backwards with fright. His wife jumped
up, and she, too, turned pale.

"For God's sake, let us come in and get warm!"
they heard in a trembling deep bass. "Who lives
here? For mercy's sake! We've lost our way."

"Who are you?" asked Raïssa, afraid to look at
the window.

"The post," answered a second voice.

"You've succeeded with your devil's tricks," said
Savély with a wave of his hand. "No mistake; I
am right! Well, you'd better look out!"

The sexton jumped on to the bed in two skips,
stretched himself on the feather mattress, and sniffing
angrily, turned with his face to the wall. Soon he
felt a draught of cold air on his back. The door
creaked and the tall figure of a man, plastered over
with snow from head to foot, appeared in the doorway. Behind him could be seen a second figure as
white.

"Am I to bring in the bags?" asked the second in a hoarse bass voice.

"You can't leave them there." Saying this, the first figure began untying his hood, but gave it up, and pulling it off impatiently with his cap, angrily flung it near the stove. Then taking off his great-coat, he threw that down beside it, and, without saying good-evening, began pacing up and down the hut.

He was a fair-haired, young postman wearing a shabby uniform and black rusty-looking high boots. After warming himself by walking to and fro, he sat down at the table, stretched out his muddy feet towards the sacks and leaned his chin on his fist. His pale face, reddened in places by the cold, still bore vivid traces of the pain and terror he had just been through. Though distorted by anger and bearing traces of recent suffering, physical and moral, it was handsome in spite of the melting snow on the eyebrows, moustaches, and short beard.

"It's a dog's life!" muttered the postman, looking round the walls and seeming hardly able to believe that he was in the warmth. "We were nearly lost! If it had not been for your light, I don't know what would have happened. Goodness only knows when it will all be over! There's no end to this dog's life! Where have we come?" he asked, dropping his voice and raising his eyes to the sexton's wife.

"To the Gulyaevsky Hill on General Kalinovsky's estate," she answered, startled and blushing.

"Do you hear, Stepan?" The postman turned

to the driver, who was wedged in the doorway with a huge mail-bag on his shoulders. " We've got to Gulyaevsky Hill."

" Yes . . . we're a long way out." Jerking out these words like a hoarse sigh, the driver went out and soon after returned with another bag, then went out once more and this time brought the postman's sword on a big belt, of the pattern of that long flat blade with which Judith is portrayed by the bedside of Holofernes in cheap woodcuts. Laying the bags along the wall, he went out into the outer room, sat down there and lighted his pipe.

" Perhaps you'd like some tea after your journey? " Raïssa inquired.

" How can we sit drinking tea? " said the postman, frowning. " We must make haste and get warm, and then set off, or we shall be late for the mail train. We'll stay ten minutes and then get on our way. Only be so good as to show us the way."

" What an infliction it is, this weather! " sighed Raïssa.

" H'm, yes. . . . Who may you be? "

" We? We live here, by the church. . . . We belong to the clergy. . . . There lies my husband. Savély, get up and say good-evening! This used to be a separate parish till eighteen months ago. Of course, when the gentry lived here there were more people, and it was worth while to have the services. But now the gentry have gone, and I need not tell you there's nothing for the clergy to live on. The nearest village is Markovka, and that's over three miles away. Savély is on the retired list now, and has got the watchman's job; he has to look after the church. . . ."

And the postman was immediately informed that if Savély were to go to the General's lady and ask her for a letter to the bishop, he would be given a good berth. "But he doesn't go to the General's lady because he is lazy and afraid of people. We belong to the clergy all the same . . ." added Raïssa.

"What do you live on?" asked the postman.

"There's a kitchen garden and a meadow belonging to the church. Only we don't get much from that," sighed Raïssa. "The old skinflint, Father Nikodim, from the next village celebrates here on St. Nicolas' Day in the winter and on St. Nicolas' Day in the summer, and for that he takes almost all the crops for himself. There's no one to stick up for us!"

"You are lying," Savély growled hoarsely. "Father Nikodim is a saintly soul, a luminary of the Church; and if he does take it, it's the regulation!"

"You've a cross one!" said the postman, with a grin. "Have you been married long?"

"It was three years ago the last Sunday before Lent. My father was sexton here in the old days, and when the time came for him to die, he went to the Consistory and asked them to send some unmarried man to marry me that I might keep the place. So I married him."

"Aha, so you killed two birds with one stone!"

said the postman, looking at Savély's back. "Got wife and job together."

Savély wriggled his leg impatiently and moved closer to the wall. The postman moved away from the table, stretched, and sat down on the mail-bag. After a moment's thought he squeezed the bags with his hands, shifted his sword to the other side, and lay down with one foot touching the floor.

"It's a dog's life," he muttered, putting his hands behind his head and closing his eyes. "I wouldn't wish a wild Tatar such a life."

Soon everything was still. Nothing was audible except the sniffing of Savély and the slow, even breathing of the sleeping postman, who uttered a deep prolonged "h-h-h" at every breath. From time to time there was a sound like a creaking wheel in his throat, and his twitching foot rustled against the bag.

Savély fidgeted under the quilt and looked round slowly. His wife was sitting on the stool, and with her hands pressed against her cheeks was gazing at the postman's face. Her face was immovable, like the face of some one frightened and astonished.

"Well, what are you gaping at?" Savély whispered angrily.

"What is it to you? Lie down!" answered his wife without taking her eyes off the flaxen head.

Savély angrily puffed all the air out of his chest and turned abruptly to the wall. Three minutes later he turned over restlessly again, knelt up on the bed, and with his hands on the pillow looked

askance at his wife. She was still sitting motionless, staring at the visitor. Her cheeks were pale
and her eyes were glowing with a strange fire. The
sexton cleared his throat, crawled on his stomach off
the bed, and going up to the postman, put a handkerchief over his face.

" What's that for? " asked his wife.

" To keep the light out of his eyes."

" Then put out the light! "

Savély looked distrustfully at his wife, put out
his lips towards the lamp, but at once thought better
of it and clasped his hands.

" Isn't that devilish cunning? " he exclaimed.
" Ah! Is there any creature slyer than women-
kind? "

" Ah, you long-skirted devil! " hissed his wife,
frowning with vexation. " You wait a bit! "

And settling herself more comfortably, she stared
at the postman again.

It did not matter to her that his face was covered.
She was not so much interested in his face as in his
whole appearance, in the novelty of this man. His
chest was broad and powerful, his hands were slender
and well formed, and his graceful, muscular legs
were much comelier than Savély's stumps. There
could be no comparison, in fact.

" Though I am a long-skirted devil," Savély said
after a brief interval, " they've no business to sleep
here. . . . It's government work; we shall have to
answer for keeping them. If you carry the letters,
carry them, you can't go to sleep. . . . Hey! you! "
Savély shouted into the outer room. " You, driver.

. . . What's your name? Shall I show you the way? Get up; postmen mustn't sleep!"

And Savély, thoroughly roused, ran up to the postman and tugged him by the sleeve.

"Hey, your honour, if you must go, go; and if you don't, it's not the thing. . . . Sleeping won't do."

The postman jumped up, sat down, looked with blank eyes round the hut, and lay down again.

"But when are you going?" Savély pattered away. "That's what the post is for — to get there in good time, do you hear? I'll take you."

The postman opened his eyes. Warmed and relaxed by his first sweet sleep, and not yet quite awake, he saw as through a mist the white neck and the immovable, alluring eyes of the sexton's wife. He closed his eyes and smiled as though he had been dreaming it all.

"Come, how can you go in such weather!" he heard a soft feminine voice; "you ought to have a sound sleep and it would do you good!"

"And what about the post?" said Savély anxiously. "Who's going to take the post? Are you going to take it, pray, you?"

The postman opened his eyes again, looked at the play of the dimples on Raïssa's face, remembered where he was, and understood Savély. The thought that he had to go out into the cold darkness sent a chill shudder all down him, and he winced.

"I might sleep another five minutes," he said, yawning. "I shall be late, anyway. . . ."

"We might be just in time," came a voice from

the outer room. "All days are not alike; the train may be late for a bit of luck."

The postman got up, and stretching lazily began putting on his coat.

Savély positively neighed with delight when he saw his visitors were getting ready to go.

"Give us a hand," the driver shouted to him as he lifted up a mail-bag.

The sexton ran out and helped him drag the post-bags into the yard. The postman began undoing the knot in his hood. The sexton's wife gazed into his eyes, and seemed trying to look right into his soul.

"You ought to have a cup of tea . . ." she said.

"I wouldn't say no . . . but, you see, they're getting ready," he assented. "We are late, anyway."

"Do stay," she whispered, dropping her eyes and touching him by the sleeve.

The postman got the knot undone at last and flung the hood over his elbow, hesitating. He felt it comfortable standing by Raïssa.

"What a . . . neck you've got! . . ." And he touched her neck with two fingers. Seeing that she did not resist, he stroked her neck and shoulders.

"I say, you are . . ."

"You'd better stay . . . have some tea."

"Where are you putting it?" The driver's voice could be heard outside. "Lay it crossways."

"You'd better stay. . . . Hark how the wind howls."

And the postman, not yet quite awake, not yet

quite able to shake off the intoxicating sleep of youth
and fatigue, was suddenly overwhelmed by a desire
for the sake of which mail-bags, postal trains . . .
and all things in the world, are forgotten. He
glanced at the door in a frightened way, as though
he wanted to escape or hide himself, seized Raïssa
round the waist, and was just bending over the lamp
to put out the light, when he heard the tramp of
boots in the outer room, and the driver appeared in
the doorway. Savély peeped in over his shoulder.
The postman dropped his hands quickly and stood
still as though irresolute.

"It's all ready," said the driver. The postman
stood still for a moment, resolutely threw up his
head as though waking up completely, and followed
the driver out. Raïssa was left alone.

"Come, get in and show us the way!" she heard.

One bell sounded languidly, then another, and the
jingling notes in a long delicate chain floated away
from the hut.

When little by little they had died away, Raïssa
got up and nervously paced to and fro. At first
she was pale, then she flushed all over. Her face
was contorted with hate, her breathing was tremulous, her eyes gleamed with wild, savage anger, and,
pacing up and down as in a cage, she looked like a
tigress menaced with red-hot iron. For a moment
she stood still and looked at her abode. Almost
half of the room was filled up by the bed, which
stretched the length of the whole wall and consisted
of a dirty feather-bed, coarse grey pillows, a quilt,
and nameless rags of various sorts. The bed was

a shapeless ugly mass which suggested the shock of
hair that always stood up on Savély's head whenever
it occurred to him to oil it. From the bed to the
door that led into the cold outer room stretched the
dark stove surrounded by pots and hanging clouts.
Everything, including the absent Savély himself, was
dirty, greasy, and smutty to the last degree, so that
it was strange to see a woman's white neck and deli·
cate skin in such surroundings.

Raïssa ran up to the bed, stretched out her hands
as though she wanted to fling it all about, stamp
it underfoot, and tear it to shreds. But then, as
though frightened by contact with the dirt, she leapt
back and began pacing up and down again.

When Savély returned two hours later, worn out
and covered with snow, she was undressed and in
bed. Her eyes were closed, but from the slight
tremor that ran over her face he guessed that she
was not asleep. On his way home he had vowed
inwardly to wait till next day and not to touch her,
but he could not resist a biting taunt at her.

" Your witchery was all in vain: he's gone off,"
he said, grinning with malignant joy.

His wife remained mute, but her chin quivered.
Savély undressed slowly, clambered over his wife,
and lay down next to the wall.

" To-morrow I'll let Father Nikodim know what
sort of wife you are! " he muttered, curling himself
up.

Raïssa turned her face to him and her eyes
gleamed.

" The job's enough for you, and you can look for

a wife in the forest, blast you!" she said. "I am no wife for you, a clumsy lout, a slug-a-bed, God forgive me!"

"Come, come . . . go to sleep!"

"How miserable I am!" sobbed his wife. "If it weren't for you, I might have married a merchant or some gentleman! If it weren't for you, I should love my husband now! And you haven't been buried in the snow, you haven't been frozen on the highroad, you Herod!"

Raïssa cried for a long time. At last she drew a deep sigh and was still. The storm still raged without. Something wailed in the stove, in the chimney, outside the walls, and it seemed to Savély that the wailing was within him, in his ears. This evening had completely confirmed him in his suspicions about his wife. He no longer doubted that his wife, with the aid of the Evil One, controlled the winds and the post sledges. But to add to his grief, this mysteriousness, this supernatural, weird power gave the woman beside him a peculiar, incomprehensible charm of which he had not been conscious before. The fact that in his stupidity he unconsciously threw a poetic glamour over her made her seem, as it were, whiter, sleeker, more unapproachable.

"Witch!" he muttered indignantly. "Tfoo, horrid creature!"

Yet, waiting till she was quiet and began breathing evenly, he touched her head with his finger . . . held her thick plait in his hand for a minute. She did not feel it. Then he grew bolder and stroked her neck.

"Leave off!" she shouted, and prodded him on the nose with her elbow with such violence that he saw stars before his eyes.

The pain in his nose was soon over, but the torture in his heart remained.

1886

PEASANT WIVES

PEASANT WIVES

In the village of Reybuzh, just facing the church, stands a two-storeyed house with a stone foundation and an iron roof. In the lower storey the owner himself, Filip Ivanov Kashin, nicknamed Dyudya, lives with his family, and on the upper floor, where it is apt to be very hot in summer and very cold in winter, they put up government officials, merchants, or landowners, who chance to be travelling that way. Dyudya rents some bits of land, keeps a tavern on the highroad, does a trade in tar, honey, cattle, and jackdaws, and has already something like eight thousand roubles put by in the bank in the town.

His elder son, Fyodor, is head engineer in the factory, and, as the peasants say of him, he has risen so high in the world that he is quite out of reach now. Fyodor's wife, Sofya, a plain, ailing woman, lives at home at her father-in-law's. She is for ever crying, and every Sunday she goes over to the hospital for medicine. Dyudya's second son, the hunchback Alyoshka, is living at home at his father's. He has only lately been married to Varvara, whom they singled out for him from a poor family. She is a handsome young woman, smart and buxom. When officials or merchants put up at the house, they always insist on having Varvara to bring in the samovar and make their beds.

One June evening when the sun was setting and the air was full of the smell of hay, of steaming dung-heaps and new milk, a plain-looking cart drove into Dyudya's yard with three people in it: a man of about thirty in a canvas suit, beside him a little boy of seven or eight in a long black coat with big bone buttons, and on the driver's seat a young fellow in a red shirt.

The young fellow took out the horses and led them out into the street to walk them up and down a bit, while the traveller washed, said a prayer, turning towards the church, then spread a rug near the cart and sat down with the boy to supper. He ate without haste, sedately, and Dyudya, who had seen a good many travellers in his time, knew him from his manners for a businesslike man, serious and aware of his own value.

Dyudya was sitting on the step in his waistcoat without a cap on, waiting for the visitor to speak first. He was used to hearing all kinds of stories from the travellers in the evening, and he liked listening to them before going to bed. His old wife, Afanasyevna, and his daughter-in-law Sofya, were milking in the cowshed. The other daughter-in-law, Varvara, was sitting at the open window of the upper storey, eating sunflower seeds.

" The little chap will be your son, I'm thinking? " Dyudya asked the traveller.

" No; adopted. An orphan. I took him for my soul's salvation."

They got into conversation. The stranger seemed to be a man fond of talking and ready of speech, and Dyudya learned from him that he was from the town, was of the tradesman class, and had a house of his own, that his name was Matvey Savitch, that he was on his way now to look at some gardens that he was renting from some German colonists, and that the boy's name was Kuzka. The evening was hot and close, no one felt inclined for sleep. When it was getting dark and pale stars began to twinkle here and there in the sky, Matvey Savitch began to tell how he had come by Kuzka. Afanasyevna and Sofya stood a little way off, listening. Kuzka had gone to the gate.

"It's a complicated story, old man," began Matvey Savitch, "and if I were to tell you all just as it happened, it would take all night and more. Ten years ago in a little house in our street, next door to me, where now there's a tallow and oil factory, there was living an old widow, Marfa Semyonovna Kapluntsev, and she had two sons: one was a guard on the railway, but the other, Vasya, who was just my own age, lived at home with his mother. Old Kapluntsev had kept five pair of horses and sent carriers all over the town; his widow had not given up the business, but managed the carriers as well as her husband had done, so that some days they would bring in as much as five roubles from their rounds.

"The young fellow, too, made a trifle on his own account. He used to breed fancy pigeons and sell them to fanciers; at times he would stand for hours on the roof, waving a broom in the air and whistling; his pigeons were right up in the clouds, but it wasn't enough for him, and he'd want them to go higher yet. Siskins and starlings, too, he used to catch, and he made cages for sale. All trifles, but, mind you, he'd pick up some ten roubles a month over such trifles. Well, as time went on, the old lady lost the use of her legs and took to her bed. In consequence of which event the house was left without a woman to look after it, and that's for all the world like a man without an eye. The old lady bestirred herself and made up her mind to marry Vasya. They called in a matchmaker at once, the women got to talking of one thing and another, and Vasya went off to have a look at the girls. He picked out Mashenka, a widow's daughter. They made up their minds without loss of time and in a week it was all settled. The girl was a little slip of a thing, seventeen, but fair-skinned and pretty-looking, and like a lady in all her ways; and a decent dowry with her, five hundred roubles, a cow, a bed. . . . Well, the old lady — it seemed as though she had known it was coming — three days after the wedding, departed to the Heavenly Jerusalem where is neither sickness nor sighing. The young people gave her a good funeral and began their life together. For just six months they got on splendidly, and then all of a sudden another misfortune. It never rains but it pours: Vasya was summoned to the recruiting office to draw lots for the service. He was taken, poor chap, for a soldier, and not even granted exemption. They shaved his head and packed him off to Poland. It was God's will; there was nothing to be done. When he said good-bye to his wife in the yard, he bore it all right; but as he glanced up at the hay-loft and his pigeons for the last time, he burst out crying. It was pitiful to see him.

"At first Mashenka got her mother to stay with her, that she mightn't be dull all alone; she stayed till the baby — this very Kuzka here — was born, and then she went off to Oboyan to another married daughter's and left Mashenka alone with the baby. There were five peasants — the carriers — a drunken saucy lot; horses, too, and dray-carts to see to, and then the fence would be broken or the soot afire in the chimney — jobs beyond a woman, and through our being neighbours, she got into the way of turning to me for every little thing. . . . Well, I'd go over, set things to rights, and give advice. . . . Naturally, not without going indoors, drinking a cup of tea and having a little chat with her. I was a young fellow, intellectual, and fond of talking on all sorts of subjects; she, too, was well-bred and educated. She was always neatly dressed, and in summer she walked out with a sunshade. Sometimes I would begin upon religion or politics with her, and she was flattered and would entertain me with tea and jam. . . . In a word, not to make a long story of it, I must tell you, old man, a year had not passed before the Evil One, the enemy of all mankind, confounded me. I began to notice that any day I didn't go to see her, I seemed out of sorts and dull. And I'd be continually making up something that I must see her about: 'It's high time,' I'd say to myself, 'to put the double windows in for the winter,' and the whole day I'd idle away over at her place putting in the windows and take good care to leave a couple of them over for the next day too.

" 'I ought to count over Vasya's pigeons, to see none of them have strayed,' and so on. I used always to be talking to her across the fence, and in the end I made a little gate in the fence so as not to have to go so far round. From womankind comes much evil into the world and every kind of abomination. Not we sinners only; even the saints themselves have been led astray by them. Mashenka did not try to keep me at a distance. Instead of thinking of her husband and being on her guard, she fell in love with me. I began to notice that she was dull without me, and was always walking to and fro by the fence looking into my yard through the cracks.

" My brains were going round in my head in a sort of frenzy. On Thursday in Holy Week I was going early in the morning — it was scarcely light — to market. I passed close by her gate, and the Evil One was by me — at my elbow. I looked — she had a gate with open trellis work at the top — and there she was, up already, standing in the middle of the yard, feeding the ducks. I could not restrain myself, and I called her name. She came up and looked at me through the trellis. . . . Her little face was white, her eyes soft and sleepy-looking. . . . I liked her looks immensely, and I began paying her compliments, as though we were not at the gate, but just as one does on namedays, while she blushed, and laughed, and kept looking straight into my eyes without winking. . . . I lost all sense and began to declare my love to her. . . . She opened the gate, and from that morning we began to live as man and wife. . . ."

The hunchback Alyoshka came into the yard from the street and ran out of breath into the house, not looking at any one. A minute later he ran out of the house with a concertina. Jingling some coppers in his pocket, and cracking sunflower seeds as he ran, he went out at the gate.

"And who's that, pray?" asked Matvey Savitch.

"My son Alexey," answered Dyudya. "He's off on a spree, the rascal. God has afflicted him with a hump, so we are not very hard on him."

"And he's always drinking with the other fellows, always drinking," sighed Afanasyevna. "Before Carnival we married him, thinking he'd be steadier, but there! he's worse than ever."

"It's been no use. Simply keeping another man's daughter for nothing," said Dyudya.

Somewhere behind the church they began to sing a glorious, mournful song. The words they could not catch and only the voices could be heard — two tenors and a bass. All were listening; there was complete stillness in the yard. . . . Two voices suddenly broke off with a loud roar of laughter, but the third, a tenor, still sang on, and took so high a note that every one instinctively looked upwards, as though the voice had soared to heaven itself.

Varvara came out of the house, and screening her eyes with her hand, as though from the sun, she looked towards the church.

" It's the priest's sons with the schoolmaster," she said.

Again all the three voices began to sing together. Matvey Savitch sighed and went on:

"Well, that's how it was, old man. Two years later we got a letter from Vasya from Warsaw. He wrote that he was being sent home sick. He was ill. By that time I had put all that foolishness out of my head, and I had a fine match picked out all ready for me, only I didn't know how to break it off with my sweetheart. Every day I'd make up my mind to have it out with Mashenka, but I didn't know how to approach her so as not to have a woman's screeching about my ears. The letter freed my hands. I read it through with Mashenka; she turned white as a sheet, while I said to her: ' Thank God; now,' says I, ' you'll be a married woman again.' But says she: ' I'm not going to live with him.' ' Why, isn't he your husband?' said I. ' Is it an easy thing? . . . I never loved him and I married him not of my own free will. My mother made me.' ' Don't try to get out of it, silly,' said I, ' but tell me this: were you married to him in church or not?' ' I was married,' she said, ' but it's you that I love, and I will stay with you to the day of my death. Folks may jeer. I don't care. . . .' ' You're a Christian woman,' said I, ' and have read the Scriptures; what is written there?' "

"Once married, with her husband she must live," said Dyudya.

" ' Man and wife are one flesh. We have sinned,' I said, ' you and I, and it is enough; we must repent

and fear God. We must confess it all to Vasya,'
said I; ' he's a quiet fellow and soft — he won't kill
you. And indeed,' said I, ' better to suffer torments
in this world at the hands of your lawful master than
to gnash your teeth at the dread Seat of Judgment.'
The wench wouldn't listen; she stuck to her silly,
' It's you I love!' and nothing more could I get out
of her.

" Vasya came back on the Saturday before Trinity,
early in the morning. From my fence I could see
everything; he ran into the house, and came back a
minute later with Kuzka in his arms, and he was
laughing and crying all at once; he was kissing Kuzka
and looking up at the hay-loft, and hadn't the heart
to put the child down, and yet he was longing to go
to his pigeons. He was always a soft sort of chap
— sentimental. That day passed off very well, all
quiet and proper. They had begun ringing the
church bells for the evening service, when the thought
struck me: ' To-morrow's Trinity Sunday; how is
it they are not decking the gates and the fence with
green? Something's wrong,' I thought. I went
over to them. I peeped in, and there he was, sitting
on the floor in the middle of the room, his eyes staring like a drunken man's, the tears streaming down
his cheeks and his hands shaking; he was pulling
cracknels, necklaces, gingerbread nuts, and all sorts
of little presents out of his bundle and flinging them
on the floor. Kuzka — he was three years old —
was crawling on the floor, munching the ginger-
breads, while Mashenka stood by the stove, white
and shivering all over, muttering: ' I'm not your

wife; I can't live with you,' and all sorts of foolishness.   I bowed down at Vasya's feet, and said:
' We have sinned against you, Vassily Maximitch;
forgive us, for Christ's sake!'   Then I got up and
spoke to Mashenka: 'You, Marya Semyonovna,
ought now to wash Vassily Maximitch's feet and
drink the water.   Do you be an obedient wife to him,
and pray to God for me, that He in His mercy may
forgive my transgression.'   It came to me like an
inspiration from an angel of Heaven; I gave her sol-
emn counsel and spoke with such feeling that my own
tears flowed too.   And so two days later Vasya
comes to me: ' Matyusha,' says he, ' I forgive you
and my wife; God have mercy on you!   She was a
soldier's wife, a young thing all alone; it was hard
for her to be on her guard.   She's not the first, nor
will she be the last.   Only,' he says, ' I beg you to
behave as though there had never been anything between you, and to make no sign, while I,' says he,
' will do my best to please her in every way, so that
she may come to love me again.'   He gave me his
hand on it, drank a cup of tea, and went away more
cheerful.

" ' Well,' thought I, ' thank God!' and I did feel
glad that everything had gone off so well.   But no
sooner had Vasya gone out of the yard, when in came
Mashenka.   Ah!   What I had to suffer!   She hung
on my neck, weeping and praying: ' For God's
sake, don't cast me off; I can't live without you!'"

" The vile hussy!" sighed Dyudya.

" I swore at her, stamped my foot, and dragging
her into the passage, I fastened the door with the

hook. 'Go to your husband,' I cried. 'Don't shame me before folks. Fear God!' And every day there was a scene of that sort.

"One morning I was standing in my yard near the stable cleaning a bridle. All at once I saw her running through the little gate into my yard, with bare feet, in her petticoat, and straight towards me; she clutched at the bridle, getting all smeared with the pitch, and shaking and weeping, she cried: 'I can't stand him; I loathe him; I can't bear it! If you don't love me, better kill me!' I was angry, and I struck her twice with the bridle, but at that instant Vasya ran in at the gate, and in a despairing voice he shouted: 'Don't beat her! Don't beat her!' But he ran up himself, and waving his arms, as though he were mad, he let fly with his fists at her with all his might, then flung her on the ground and kicked her. I tried to defend her, but he snatched up the reins and thrashed her with them, and all the while, like a colt's whinny, he went: 'He — he — he!'"

"I'd take the reins and let you feel them," muttered Varvara, moving away; "murdering our sister, the damned brutes! . . ."

"Hold your tongue, you jade!" Dyudya shouted at her.

"'He — he — he!'" Matvey Savitch went on. "A carrier ran out of his yard; I called to my workman, and the three of us got Mashenka away from him and carried her home in our arms. The disgrace of it! The same day I went over in the evening to see how things were. She was lying in bed, all wrapped up in bandages, nothing but her eyes and nose to be seen; she was looking at the ceiling.   I said: 'Good-evening, Marya Semyonovna!' She did not speak.   And Vasya was sitting in the next room, his head in his hands, crying and saying: 'Brute that I am!   I've ruined my life!   O God, let me die!'   I sat for half an hour by Mashenka and gave her a good talking-to.   I tried to frighten her a bit.   'The righteous,' said I, 'after this life go to Paradise, but you will go to a Gehenna of fire, like all adulteresses.   Don't strive against your husband, go and lay yourself at his feet.'   But never a word from her; she didn't so much as blink an eyelid, for all the world as though I were talking to a post. The next day Vasya fell ill with something like cholera, and in the evening I heard that he was dead. Well, so they buried him, and Mashenka did not go to the funeral; she didn't care to show her shameless face and her bruises.   And soon there began to be talk all over the district that Vasya had not died a natural death, that Mashenka had made away with him.   It got to the ears of the police; they had Vasya dug up and cut open, and in his stomach they found arsenic.   It was clear he had been poisoned; the police came and took Mashenka away, and with her the innocent Kuzka.   They were put in prison. . . . The woman had gone too far — God punished her. . . . Eight months later they tried her.   She sat, I remember, on a low stool, with a little white kerchief on her head, wearing a grey gown, and she was so thin, so pale, so sharp-eyed it made one sad to look at her.   Behind her stood a soldier with a gun. She would not confess her guilt. Some in the court said she had poisoned her husband and others declared he had poisoned himself for grief. I was one of the witnesses. When they questioned me, I told the whole truth according to my oath. ' Hers,' said I, ' is the guilt. It's no good to conceal it; she did not love her husband, and she had a will of her own. . . .' The trial began in the morning and towards night they passed this sentence: to send her to hard labour in Siberia for thirteen years. After that sentence Mashenka remained three months longer in prison. I went to see her, and from Christian charity I took her a little tea and sugar. But as soon as she set eyes on me she began to shake all over, wringing her hands and muttering: ' Go away! go away!' And Kuzka she clasped to her as though she were afraid I would take him away. ' See,' said I, ' what you have come to! Ah, Masha, Masha! you would not listen to me when I gave you good advice, and now you must repent it. You are yourself to blame,' said I; ' blame yourself!' I was giving her good counsel, but she: ' Go away, go away!' huddling herself and Kuzka against the wall, and trembling all over.

" When they were taking her away to the chief town of our province, I walked by the escort as far as the station and slipped a rouble into her bundle for my soul's salvation. But she did not get as far as Siberia. . . . She fell sick of fever and died in prison."

" Live like a dog and you must die a dog's death," said Dyudya.

" Kuzka was sent back home. . . . I thought it over and took him to bring up.　After all — though a convict's child — still he was a living soul, a Christian. . . . I was sorry for him.　I shall make him my clerk, and if I have no children of my own, I'll make a merchant of him.　Wherever I go now, I take him with me; let him learn his work."

All the while Matvey Savitch had been telling his story, Kuzka had sat on a little stone near the gate. His head propped in both hands, he gazed at the sky, and in the distance he looked in the dark like a stump of wood.

" Kuzka, come to bed," Matvey Savitch bawled to him.

" Yes, it's time," said Dyudya, getting up; he yawned loudly and added:

" Folks will go their own way, and that's what comes of it."

Over the yard the moon was floating now in the heavens; she was moving one way, while the clouds beneath moved the other way; the clouds were disappearing into the darkness, but still the moon could be seen high above the yard.

Matvey Savitch said a prayer, facing the church, and saying good-night, he lay down on the ground near his cart.　Kuzka, too, said a prayer, lay down in the cart, and covered himself with his little overcoat; he made himself a little hole in the hay so as to be more comfortable, and curled up so that his elbows looked like knees.　From the yard Dyudya could be seen lighting a candle in his room below, putting on his spectacles and standing in the corner with a book. He was a long while reading and crossing himself.

The travellers fell asleep. Afanasyevna and Sofya came up to the cart and began looking at Kuzka.

" The little orphan's asleep," said the old woman. " He's thin and frail, nothing but bones. No mother and no one to care for him properly."

" My Grishutka must be two years older," said Sofya. " Up at the factory he lives like a slave without his mother. The foreman beats him, I dare say. When I looked at this poor mite just now, I thought of my own Grishutka, and my heart went cold within me."

A minute passed in silence.

" Doesn't remember his mother, I suppose," said the old woman.

" How could he remember? "

And big tears began dropping from Sofya's eyes.

" He's curled himself up like a cat," she said, sobbing and laughing with tenderness and sorrow. . . . " Poor motherless mite ! "

Kuzka started and opened his eyes. He saw before him an ugly, wrinkled, tear-stained face, and beside it another, aged and toothless, with a sharp chin and hooked nose, and high above them the infinite sky with the flying clouds and the moon. He cried out in fright, and Sofya, too, uttered a cry; both were answered by the echo, and a faint stir passed over the stifling air; a watchman tapped

somewhere near, a dog barked. Matvey Savitch
muttered something in his sleep and turned over on
the other side.

Late at night when Dyudya and the old woman
and the neighbouring watchman were all asleep,
Sofya went out to the gate and sat down on the
bench. She felt stifled and her head ached from
weeping. The street was a wide and long one; it
stretched for nearly two miles to the right and as far
to the left, and the end of it was out of sight. The
moon was now not over the yard, but behind the
church. One side of the street was flooded with
moonlight, while the other side lay in black shadow.
The long shadows of the poplars and the starling-
cotes stretched right across the street, while the
church cast a broad shadow, black and terrible that
enfolded Dyudya's gates and half his house. The
street was still and deserted. From time to time
the strains of music floated faintly from the end of
the street — Alyoshka, most likely, playing his concertina.

Someone moved in the shadow near the church enclosure, and Sofya could not make out whether it
were a man or a cow, or perhaps merely a big bird
rustling in the trees. But then a figure stepped out
of the shadow, halted, and said something in a
man's voice, then vanished down the turning by the
church. A little later, not three yards from the
gate, another figure came into sight; it walked
straight from the church to the gate and stopped
short, seeing Sofya on the bench.

" Varvara, is that you? " said Sofya.

" And if it were? "

It was Varvara. She stood still a minute, then came up to the bench and sat down.

" Where have you been? " asked Sofya.

Varvara made no answer.

" You'd better mind you don't get into trouble with such goings-on, my girl," said Sofya. " Did you hear how Mashenka was kicked and lashed with the reins? You'd better look out, or they'll treat you the same."

" Well, let them! "

Varvara laughed into her kerchief and whispered:

" I have just been with the priest's son."

" Nonsense! "

" I have! "

" It's a sin! " whispered Sofya.

" Well, let it be. . . . What do I care? If it's a sin, then it is a sin, but better be struck dead by thunder than live like this. I'm young and strong, and I've a filthy crooked hunchback for a husband, worse than Dyudya himself, curse him! When I was a girl, I hadn't bread to eat, or a shoe to my foot, and to get away from that wretchedness I was tempted by Alyoshka's money, and got caught like a fish in a net, and I'd rather have a viper for my bedfellow than that scurvy Alyoshka. And what's your life? It makes me sick to look at it. Your Fyodor sent you packing from the factory and he's taken up with another woman. They have robbed you of your boy and made a slave of him. You work like a horse, and never hear a kind word. I'd rather pine all my days an old maid, I'd rather get half a rouble from the priest's son, I'd rather beg my bread, or throw myself into the well. . . ."

" It's a sin! " whispered Sofya again.

" Well, let it be."

Somewhere behind the church the same three voices, two tenors and a bass, began singing again a mournful song. And again the words could not be distinguished.

" They are not early to bed," Varvara said, laughing.

And she began telling in a whisper of her midnight walks with the priest's son, and of the stories he had told her, and of his comrades, and of the fun she had with the travellers who stayed in the house. The mournful song stirred a longing for life and freedom. Sofya began to laugh; she thought it sinful and terrible and sweet to hear about, and she felt envious and sorry that she, too, had not been a sinner when she was young and pretty.

In the churchyard they heard twelve strokes beaten on the watchman's board.

" It's time we were asleep," said Sofya, getting up, " or, maybe, we shall catch it from Dyudya."

They both went softly into the yard.

" I went away without hearing what he was telling about Mashenka," said Varvara, making herself a bed under the window.

" She died in prison, he said. She poisoned her husband."

Varvara lay down beside Sofya a while, and said softly:

" I'd make away with my Alyoshka and never regret it."

" You talk nonsense; God forgive you."

When Sofya was just dropping asleep, Varvara, coming close, whispered in her ear:

" Let us get rid of Dyudya and Alyoshka ! "

Sofya started and said nothing. Then she opened her eyes and gazed a long while steadily at the sky.

" People would find out," she said.

" No, they wouldn't. Dyudya's an old man, it's time he did die; and they'd say Alyoshka died of drink."

" I'm afraid . . . God would chastise us."

" Well, let Him. . . ."

Both lay awake thinking in silence.

" It's cold," said Sofya, beginning to shiver all over. " It will soon be morning. . . . Are you asleep? "

" No. . . . Don't you mind what I say, dear," whispered Varvara; " I get so mad with the damned brutes, I don't know what I do say. Go to sleep, or it will be daylight directly. . . . Go to sleep."

Both were quiet and soon they fell asleep.

Earlier than all woke the old woman. She waked up Sofya and they went together into the cowshed to milk the cows. The hunchback Alyoshka came in hopelessly drunk without his con= certina; his breast and knees had been in the dust and straw — he must have fallen down in the road. Staggering, he went into the cowshed, and without undressing he rolled into a sledge and began to snore at once. When first the crosses on the church and then the windows were flashing in the light of the rising sun, and shadows stretched across the yard over the dewy grass from the trees and the top of the well, Matvey Savitch jumped up and began hurrying about:

"Kuzka! get up!" he shouted. "It's time to put in the horses! Look sharp!"

The bustle of morning was beginning. A young Jewess in a brown gown with flounces led a horse into the yard to drink. The pulley of the well creaked plaintively, the bucket knocked as it went down. . . .

Kuzka, sleepy, tired, covered with dew, sat up in the cart, lazily putting on his little overcoat, and listening to the drip of the water from the bucket into the well as he shivered with the cold.

"Auntie!" shouted Matvey Savitch to Sofya, "tell my lad to hurry up and to harness the horses!"

And Dyudya at the same instant shouted from the window:

"Sofya, take a farthing from the Jewess for the horse's drink! They're always in here, the mangy creatures!"

In the street sheep were running up and down, baaing; the peasant women were shouting at the shepherd, while he played his pipes, cracked his whip, or answered them in a thick sleepy bass. Three sheep strayed into the yard, and not finding the gate again, pushed at the fence.

Varvara was waked by the noise, and bundling her bedding up in her arms, she went into the house.

" You might at least drive the sheep out ! " the old woman bawled after her, " my lady ! "

" I dare say ! As if I were going to slave for you Herods ! " muttered Varvara, going into the house.

Dyudya came out of the house with his accounts in his hands, sat down on the step, and began reckoning how much the traveller owed him for the night's lodging, oats, and watering his horses.

" You charge pretty heavily for the oats, my good man," said Matvey Savitch.

" If it's too much, don't take them. There's no compulsion, merchant."

When the travellers were ready to start, they were detained for a minute. Kuzka had lost his cap.

" Little swine, where did you put it? " Matvey Savitch roared angrily. " Where is it? "

Kuzka's face was working with terror; he ran up and down near the cart, and not finding it there, ran to the gate and then to the shed. The old woman and Sofya helped him look.

" I'll pull your ears off ! " yelled Matvey Savitch. " Dirty brat ! "

The cap was found at the bottom of the cart.

Kuzka brushed the hay off it with his sleeve, put it on, and timidly he crawled into the cart, still with an expression of terror on his face as though he were afraid of a blow from behind.

Matvey Savitch crossed himself. The driver gave a tug at the reins and the cart rolled out of the yard.

1891

THE POST

THE POST

IT was three o'clock in the night. The postman, ready to set off, in his cap and his coat, with a rusty sword in his hand, was standing near the door, waiting for the driver to finish putting the mail bags into the cart which had just been brought round with three horses. The sleepy postmaster sat at his table, which was like a counter; he was filling up a form and saying:

"My nephew, the student, wants to go to the station at once. So look here, Ignatyev, let him get into the mail cart and take him with you to the station: though it is against the regulations to take people with the mail, what's one to do? It's better for him to drive with you free than for me to hire horses for him."

"Ready!" they heard a shout from the yard.

"Well, go then, and God be with you," said the postmaster. "Which driver is going?"

"Semyon Glazov."

"Come, sign the receipt."

The postman signed the receipt and went out. At the entrance of the post-office there was the dark outline of a cart and three horses. The horses were standing still except that one of the tracehorses kept uneasily shifting from one leg to the other and tossing its head, making the bell clang from time to

49

time. The cart with the mail bags looked like a
patch of darkness. Two silhouettes were moving
lazily beside it: the student with a portmanteau in
his hand and a driver. The latter was smoking a
short pipe; the light of the pipe moved about in
the darkness, dying away and flaring up again; for
an instant it lighted up a bit of a sleeve, then a
shaggy moustache and big copper-red nose, then
stern-looking, overhanging eyebrows. The postman
pressed down the mail bags with his hands, laid his
sword on them and jumped into the cart. The student clambered irresolutely in after him, and accidentally touching him with his elbow, said timidly
and politely: " I beg your pardon."

The pipe went out. The postmaster came out
of the post-office just as he was, in his waistcoat and
slippers; shrinking from the night dampness and
clearing his throat, he walked beside the cart and
said:

" Well, God speed! Give my love to your
mother, Mihailo. Give my love to them all. And
you, Ignatyev, mind you don't forget to give the
parcel to Bystretsov. . . . Off ! "

The driver took the reins in one hand, blew his
nose, and, arranging the seat under himself, clicked
to the horses.

" Give them my love," the postmaster repeated.

The big bell clanged something to the little bells,
the little bells gave it a friendly answer. The cart
squeaked, moved. The big bell lamented, the little
bells laughed. Standing up in his seat the driver
lashed the restless tracehorse twice, and the cart

rumbled with a hollow sound along the dusty road.
The little town was asleep. Houses and trees stood
black on each side of the broad street, and not a light
was to be seen. Narrow clouds stretched here and
there over the star-spangled sky, and where the
dawn would soon be coming there was a narrow
crescent moon; but neither the stars, of which there
were many, nor the half-moon, which looked white,
lighted up the night air. It was cold and damp,
and there was a smell of autumn.

The student, who thought that politeness required
him to talk affably to a man who had not refused to
let him accompany him, began:

" In summer it would be light at this time, but
now there is not even a sign of the dawn. Summer
is over! "

The student looked at the sky and went on:

" Even from the sky one can see that it is autumn.
Look to the right. Do you see three stars side by
side in a straight line? That is the constellation of
Orion, which, in our hemisphere, only becomes visible in September."

The postman, thrusting his hands into his sleeves
and retreating up to his ears into his coat collar, did
not stir and did not glance at the sky. Apparently
the constellation of Orion did not interest him. He
was accustomed to see the stars, and probably he
had long grown weary of them. The student
paused for a while and then said:

" It's cold! It's time for the dawn to begin.
Do you know what time the sun rises? "

" What? "

" What time does the sun rise now? "

" Between five and six," said the driver.

The mail cart drove out of the town.   Now nothing could be seen on either side of the road but the fences of kitchen gardens and here and there a solitary willow-tree; everything in front of them was shrouded in darkness.   Here in the open country the half-moon looked bigger and the stars shone more brightly.   Then came a scent of dampness; the postman shrank further into his collar, the student felt an unpleasant chill first creeping about his feet, then over the mail bags, over his hands and his face. The horses moved more slowly; the bell was mute as though it were frozen.   There was the sound of the splash of water, and stars reflected in the water danced under the horses' feet and round the wheels.

But ten minutes later it became so dark that neither the stars nor the moon could be seen.   The mail cart had entered the forest.   Prickly pine branches were continually hitting the student on his cap and a spider's web settled on his face.   Wheels and hoofs knocked against huge roots, and the mail cart swayed from side to side as though it were drunk.

" Keep to the road," said the postman angrily. " Why do you run up the edge?   My face is scratched all over by the twigs!   Keep more to the right! "

But at that point there was nearly an accident. The cart suddenly bounded as though in the throes of a convulsion, began trembling, and, with a creak, lurched heavily first to the right and then to the left,

and at a fearful pace dashed along the forest track.
The horses had taken fright at something and
bolted.

"Wo! wo!" the driver cried in alarm. "Wo
. . . you devils!"

The student, violently shaken, bent forward and
tried to find something to catch hold of so as to keep
his balance and save himself from being thrown out,
but the leather mail bags were slippery, and the
driver, whose belt the student tried to catch at, was
himself tossed up and down and seemed every moment on the point of flying out. Through the rattle
of the wheels and the creaking of the cart they heard
the sword fall with a clank on the ground, then a
little later something fell with two heavy thuds behind the mail cart.

"Wo!" the driver cried in a piercing voice,
bending backwards. "Stop!"

The student fell on his face and bruised his forehead against the driver's seat, but was at once tossed
back again and knocked his spine violently against
the back of the cart.

"I am falling!" was the thought that flashed
through his mind, but at that instant the horses
dashed out of the forest into the open, turned
sharply to the right, and rumbling over a bridge of
logs, suddenly stopped dead, and the suddenness of
this halt flung the student forward again.

The driver and the student were both breathless.
The postman was not in the cart. He had been
thrown out, together with his sword, the student's
portmanteau, and one of the mail bags.

"Stop, you rascal! Sto-op!" they heard him shout from the forest. "You damned black-guard!" he shouted, running up to the cart, and there was a note of pain and fury in his tearful voice. "You anathema, plague take you!" he roared, dashing up to the driver and shaking his fist at him.

"What a to-do! Lord have mercy on us!" muttered the driver in a conscience-stricken voice, setting right something in the harness at the horses' heads. "It's all that devil of a tracehorse. Cursed filly; it is only a week since she has run in harness. She goes all right, but as soon as we go down hill there is trouble! She wants a touch or two on the nose, then she wouldn't play about like this. . . . Stea-eady! Damn!"

While the driver was setting the horses to rights and looking for the portmanteau, the mail bag, and the sword on the road, the postman in a plaintive voice shrill with anger ejaculated oaths. After re-placing the luggage the driver for no reason what-ever led the horses for a hundred paces, grumbled at the restless tracehorse, and jumped up on the box.

When his fright was over the student felt amused and good-humoured. It was the first time in his life that he had driven by night in a mail cart, and the shaking he had just been through, the postman's hav-ing been thrown out, and the pain in his own back struck him as interesting adventures. He lighted a cigarette and said with a laugh:

"Why you know, you might break your neck like that! I very nearly flew out, and I didn't even notice you had been thrown out. I can fancy what it is like driving in autumn! "

The postman did not speak.

" Have you been going with the post for long? " the student asked.

" Eleven years."

" Oho; every day? "

" Yes, every day. I take this post and drive back again at once. Why? "

Making the journey every day, he must have had a good many interesting adventures in eleven years. On bright summer and gloomy autumn nights, or in winter when a ferocious snowstorm whirled howling round the mail cart, it must have been hard to avoid feeling frightened and uncanny. No doubt more than once the horses had bolted, the mail cart had stuck in the mud, they had been attacked by highwaymen, or had lost their way in the blizzard. . . .

" I can fancy what adventures you must have had in eleven years! " said the student. " I expect it must be terrible driving? "

He said this and expected that the postman would tell him something, but the latter preserved a sullen silence and retreated into his collar. Meanwhile it began to get light. The sky changed colour imperceptibly; it still seemed dark, but by now the horses and the driver and the road could be seen. The crescent moon looked bigger and bigger, and the cloud that stretched below it, shaped like a cannon in a gun-carriage, showed a faint yellow on its lower edge. Soon the postman's face was visible. It was wet with dew, grey and rigid as the face of a corpse. An expression of dull, sullen anger was set upon it, as though the postman were still in pain and still angry with the driver.

"Thank God it is daylight!" said the student, looking at his chilled and angry face. "I am quite frozen. The nights are cold in September, but as soon as the sun rises it isn't cold. Shall we soon reach the station?"

The postman frowned and made a wry face.

"How fond you are of talking, upon my word!" he said. "Can't you keep quiet when you are travelling?"

The student was confused, and did not approach him again all the journey. The morning came on rapidly. The moon turned pale and melted away into the dull grey sky, the cloud turned yellow all over, the stars grew dim, but the east was still cold-looking and the same colour as the rest of the sky, so that one could hardly believe the sun was hidden in it.

The chill of the morning and the surliness of the postman gradually infected the student. He looked apathetically at the country around him, waited for the warmth of the sun, and thought of nothing but how dreadful and horrible it must be for the poor trees and the grass to endure the cold nights. The sun rose dim, drowsy, and cold. The tree-tops were not gilded by the rays of the rising sun, as usually described, the sunbeams did not creep over the earth and there was no sign of joy in the flight of the sleepy birds. The cold remained just the same now that the sun was up as it had been in the night.

The student looked drowsily and ill-humouredly at the curtained windows of a mansion by which the mail cart drove. Behind those windows, he thought, people were most likely enjoying their soundest morning sleep not hearing the bells, nor feeling the cold, nor seeing the postman's angry face; and if the bell did wake some young lady, she would turn over on the other side, smile in the fulness of her warmth and comfort, and, drawing up her feet and putting her hand under her cheek, would go off to sleep more soundly than ever.

The student looked at the pond which gleamed near the house and thought of the carp and the pike which find it possible to live in cold water. . . .

" It's against the regulations to take anyone with the post. . . ." the postman said unexpectedly. " It's not allowed! And since it is not allowed, people have no business . . . to get in. . . . Yes. It makes no difference to me, it's true, only I don't like it, and I don't wish it."

" Why didn't you say so before, if you don't like it? "

The postman made no answer but still had an unfriendly, angry expression. When, a little later, the horses stopped at the entrance of the station the student thanked him and got out of the cart. The mail train had not yet come in. A long goods train stood in a siding; in the tender the engine driver and his assistant, with faces wet with dew, were drinking tea from a dirty tin teapot. The carriages, the

platforms, the seats were all wet and cold.   Until
the train came in the student stood at the buffet
drinking tea while the postman, with his hands thrust
up his sleeves and the same look of anger still on
his face, paced up and down the platform in solitude, staring at the ground under his feet.

With whom was he angry?   Was it with people,
with poverty, with the autmn nights?

1887

THE NEW VILLA

THE NEW VILLA

I

Two miles from the village of Obrutchanovo a huge
bridge was being built. From the village, which
stood up high on the steep river-bank, its trellis-like
skeleton could be seen, and in foggy weather and on
still winter days, when its delicate iron girders and
all the scaffolding around was covered with hoar
frost, it presented a picturesque and even fantastic
spectacle. Kutcherov, the engineer who was building the bridge, a stout, broad-shouldered, bearded
man in a soft crumpled cap drove through the village in his racing droshky or his open carriage.
Now and then on holidays navvies working on the
bridge would come to the village; they begged for
alms, laughed at the women, and sometimes carried
off something. But that was rare; as a rule the days
passed quietly and peacefully as though no bridge-
building were going on, and only in the evening,
when camp fires gleamed near the bridge, the wind
faintly wafted the songs of the navvies. And by
day there was sometimes the mournful clang of
metal, don-don-don.

It happened that the engineer's wife came to see
him. She was pleased with the river-banks and
the gorgeous view over the green valley with trees,

churches, flocks, and she began begging her husband to buy a small piece of ground and to build them a cottage on it. Her husband agreed. They bought sixty acres of land, and on the high bank in a field, where in earlier days the cows of Obrutchanovo used to wander, they built a pretty house of two storeys with a terrace and a verandah, with a tower and a flagstaff on which a flag fluttered on Sundays — they built it in about three months, and then all the winter they were planting big trees, and when spring came and everything began to be green there were already avenues to the new house, a gardener and two labourers in white aprons were digging near it, there was a little fountain, and a globe of looking-glass flashed so brilliantly that it was painful to look at. The house had already been named the New Villa.

On a bright, warm morning at the end of May two horses were brought to Obrutchanovo to the village blacksmith, Rodion Petrov. They came from the New Villa. The horses were sleek, graceful beasts, as white as snow, and strikingly alike.

" Perfect swans! " said Rodion, gazing at them with reverent admiration.

His wife Stepanida, his children and grandchildren came out into the street to look at them. By degrees a crowd collected. The Lytchkovs, father and son, both men with swollen faces and entirely beardless, came up bareheaded. Kozov, a tall, thin old man with a long, narrow beard, came up leaning on a stick with a crook handle: he kept winking with his crafty eyes and smiling ironically as though he knew something.

" It's only that they are white; what is there in them? " he said. " Put mine on oats, and they will be just as sleek. They ought to be in a plough and with a whip, too. . . ."

The coachman simply looked at him with disdain, but did not utter a word. And afterwards, while they were blowing up the fire at the forge, the coachman talked while he smoked cigarettes. The peasants learned from him various details: his employers were wealthy people; his mistress, Elena Ivanovna, had till her marriage lived in Moscow in a poor way as a governess; she was kind-hearted, compassionate, and fond of helping the poor. On the new estate, he told them, they were not going to plough or to sow, but simply to live for their pleasure, live only to breathe the fresh air. When he had finished and led the horses back a crowd of boys followed him, the dogs barked, and Kozov, looking after him, winked sarcastically.

" Landowners, too-oo! " he said. " They have built a house and set up horses, but I bet they are nobodies — landowners, too-oo."

Kozov for some reason took a dislike from the first to the new house, to the white horses, and to the handsome, well-fed coachman. Kozov was a solitary man, a widower; he had a dreary life (he was prevented from working by a disease which he sometimes called a rupture and sometimes worms); he was maintained by his son, who worked at a confectioner's in Harkov and sent him money; and from early morning till evening he sauntered at leisure about the river or about the village; if he saw, for

Instance, a peasant carting a log, or fishing, he would say: "That log's dry wood — it is rotten," or, "They won't bite in weather like this." In times of drought he would declare that there would not be a drop of rain till the frost came; and when the rains came he would say that everything would rot in the fields, that everything was ruined. And as he said these things he would wink as though he knew something.

At the New Villa they burned Bengal lights and sent up fireworks in the evenings, and a sailing-boat with red lanterns floated by Obrutchanovo. One morning the engineer's wife, Elena Ivanovna, and her little daughter drove to the village in a carriage with yellow wheels and a pair of dark bay ponies; both mother and daughter were wearing broad-brimmed straw hats, bent down over their ears.

This was exactly at the time when they were carting manure, and the blacksmith Rodion, a tall, gaunt old man, bareheaded and barefooted, was standing near his dirty and repulsive-looking cart and, flustered, looked at the ponies, and it was evident by his face that he had never seen such little horses before.

" The Kutcherov lady has come ! " was whispered around. " Look, the Kutcherov lady has come ! "

Elena Ivanovna looked at the huts as though she were selecting one, and then stopped at the very poorest, at the windows of which there were so many children's heads — flaxen, red, and dark. Stepanida, Rodion's wife, a stout woman, came running out of the hut; her kerchief slipped off her grey head;

she looked at the carriage facing the sun, and her face smiled and wrinkled up as though she were blind.

" This is for your children," said Elena Ivanovna, and she gave her three roubles.

Stepanida suddenly burst into tears and bowed down to the ground. Rodion, too, flopped to the ground, displaying his brownish bald head, and as he did so he almost caught his wife in the ribs with the fork. Elena Ivanovna was overcome with confusion and drove back.

II

The Lytchkovs, father and son, caught in their meadows two cart-horses, a pony, and a broad-faced Aalhaus bull-calf, and with the help of red-headed Volodka, son of the blacksmith Rodion, drove them to the village. They called the village elder, collected witnesses, and went to look at the damage.

" All right, let 'em! " said Kozov, winking, " le-et 'em! Let them get out of it if they can, the engineers! Do you think there is no such thing as law? All right! Send for the police inspector, draw up a statement! . . ."

" Draw up a statement," repeated Volodka.

" I don't want to let this pass! " shouted the younger Lytchkov. He shouted louder and louder, and his beardless face seemed to be more and more swollen. " They've set up a nice fashion! Leave them free, and they will ruin all the meadows! You've no sort of right to ill-treat people! We are not serfs now! "

" We are not serfs now! " repeated Volodka.

" We got on all right without a bridge," said the elder Lytchkov gloomily; " we did not ask for it. What do we want a bridge for? We don't want it! "

" Brothers, good Christians, we cannot leave it like this! "

" All right, let 'em! " said Kozov, winking. " Let them get out of it if they can! Landowners, indeed! "

They went back to the village, and as they walked the younger Lytchkov beat himself on the breast with his fist and shouted all the way, and Volodka shouted, too, repeating his words. And meanwhile quite a crowd had gathered in the village round the thoroughbred bull-calf and the horses. The bull-calf was embarrassed and looked up from under his brows, but suddenly lowered his muzzle to the ground and took to his heels, kicking up his hind legs; Kozov was frightened and waved his stick at him, and they all burst out laughing. Then they locked up the beasts and waited.

In the evening the engineer sent five roubles for the damage, and the two horses, the pony and the bull-calf, without being fed or given water, returned home, their heads hanging with a guilty air as though they were convicted criminals.

On getting the five roubles the Lytchkovs, father and son, the village elder and Volodka, punted over the river in a boat and went to a hamlet on the other side where there was a tavern, and there had a long carousal. Their singing and the shouting of the younger Lytchkov could be heard from the village. Their women were uneasy and did not sleep all night. Rodion did not sleep either.

" It's a bad business," he said, sighing and turning from side to side. " The gentleman will be angry, and then there will be trouble. . . . They have insulted the gentleman. . . . Oh, they've insulted him. It's a bad business. . . ."

It happened that the peasants, Rodion amongst them, went into their forest to divide the clearings for mowing, and as they were returning home they were met by the engineer. He was wearing a red cotton shirt and high boots; a setter dog with its long tongue hanging out, followed behind him.

" Good-day, brothers," he said.

The peasants stopped and took off their hats.

" I have long wanted to have a talk with you, friends," he went on. " This is what it is. Ever since the early spring your cattle have been in my copse and garden every day. Everything is trampled down; the pigs have rooted up the meadow, are ruining everything in the kitchen garden, and all the undergrowth in the copse is destroyed. There is no getting on with your herdsmen; one asks them civilly, and they are rude. Damage is done on my estate every day and I do nothing — I don't fine you or make a complaint; meanwhile you impounded my horses and my bull calf and exacted five roubles. Was that right? Is that neighbourly?" he went on, and his face was so soft and persuasive, and his expression was not forbidding. " Is that the way decent people behave? A week ago one of your people cut down two oak saplings in my copse. You have dug up the road to Eresnevo, and now I have to go two miles round. Why do you injure me at every step? What harm have I done you? For God's sake, tell me! My wife and I do our utmost to live with you in peace and harmony; we help the peasants as we can. My wife is a kind, warm-hearted woman; she never refuses you help. That is her dream — to be of use to you and your children. You reward us with evil for our good. You are unjust, my friends. Think of that. I ask you earnestly to think it over. We treat you humanely; repay us in the same coin."

He turned and went away. The peasants stood a little longer, put on their caps and walked away. Rodion, who always understood everything that was said to him in some peculiar way of his own, heaved a sigh and said:

"We must pay. 'Repay in coin, my friends' . . . he said."

They walked to the village in silence. On reaching home Rodion said his prayer, took off his boots, and sat down on the bench beside his wife. Stepanida and he always sat side by side when they were at home, and always walked side by side in the street; they ate and they drank and they slept always together, and the older they grew the more they loved one another. It was hot and crowded in their hut, and there were children everywhere — on the floors, in the windows, on the stove. . . . In spite of her advanced years Stepanida was still bearing children, and now, looking at the crowd of children, it was hard to distinguish which were Rodion's and which were Volodka's. Volodka's wife, Lukerya, a plain young woman with prominent eyes and a nose like the beak of a bird, was kneading dough in a tub; Volodka was sitting on the stove with his legs hanging.

"On the road near Nikita's buckwheat . . . the engineer with his dog . . ." Rodion began, after a rest, scratching his ribs and his elbow. "'You must pay,' says he . . . 'coin,' says he. . . . Coin or no coin, we shall have to collect ten kopecks from every hut. We've offended the gentleman very much. I am sorry for him. . . ."

"We've lived without a bridge," said Volodka, not looking at anyone, "and we don't want one."

"What next; the bridge is a government business."

"We don't want it."

"Your opinion is not asked. What is it to you?"

"'Your opinion is not asked,'" Volodka mimicked him. "We don't want to drive anywhere; what do we want with a bridge? If we have to, we can cross by the boat."

Someone from the yard outside knocked at the window so violently that it seemed to shake the whole hut.

"Is Volodka at home?" he heard the voice of the younger Lytchkov. "Volodka, come out, come along."

Volodka jumped down off the stove and began looking for his cap.

" Don't go, Volodka," said Rodion diffidently.
" Don't go with them, son. You are foolish, like
a little child; they will teach you no good; don't
go ! "

" Don't go, son," said Stepanida, and she blinked
as though about to shed tears. " I bet they are
calling you to the tavern."

" ' To the tavern,' " Volodka mimicked.

" You'll come back drunk again, you currish
Herod," said Lukerya, looking at him angrily.
" Go along, go along, and may you burn up with
vodka, you tailless Satan ! "

" You hold your tongue," shouted Volodka.

" They've married me to a fool, they've ruined
me, a luckless orphan, you red-headed drunkard
. . ." wailed Lukerya, wiping her face with a hand
covered with dough. " I wish I had never set eyes
on you."

Volodka gave her a blow on the ear and went off.

III

Elena Ivanovna and her little daughter visited
the village on foot. They were out for a walk. It
was a Sunday, and the peasant women and girls were
walking up and down the street in their brightly-col-
oured dresses. Rodion and Stepanida, sitting side
by side at their door, bowed and smiled to Elena
Ivanovna and her little daughter as to acquaintances.
From the windows more than a dozen children
stared at them; their faces expressed amazement
and curiosity, and they could be heard whispering:

" The Kutcherov lady has come! The Kutcherov lady! "

" Good-morning," said Elena Ivanovna, and she stopped; she paused, and then asked: " Well, how are you getting on? "

" We get along all right, thank God," answered Rodion, speaking rapidly. " To be sure we get along."

" The life we lead! " smiled Stepanida. " You can see our poverty yourself, dear lady! The family is fourteen souls in all, and only two bread-winners. We are supposed to be blacksmiths, but when they bring us a horse to shoe we have no coal, nothing to buy it with. We are worried to death, lady," she went on, and laughed. " Oh, oh, we are worried to death."

Elena Ivanovna sat down at the entrance and, putting her arm round her little girl, pondered something, and judging from the little girl's expression, melancholy thoughts were straying through her mind, too; as she brooded she played with the sumptuous lace on the parasol she had taken out of her mother's hands.

" Poverty," said Rodion, " a great deal of anxiety — you see no end to it. Here, God sends no rain . . . our life is not easy, there is no denying it."

" You have a hard time in this life," said Elena Ivanovna, " but in the other world you will be happy."

Rodion did not understand her, and simply coughed into his clenched hand by way of reply. Stepanida said:

" Dear lady, the rich men will be all right in the next world, too. The rich put up candles, pay for services; the rich give to beggars, but what can the poor man do? He has no time to make the sign of the cross. He is the beggar of beggars himself; how can he think of his soul? And many sins come from poverty; from trouble we snarl at one another like dogs, we haven't a good word to say to one another, and all sorts of things happen, dear lady — God forbid! It seems we have no luck in this world nor the next. All the luck has fallen to the rich."

She spoke gaily; she was evidently used to talking of her hard life. And Rodion smiled, too; he was pleased that his old woman was so clever, so ready of speech.

" It is only on the surface that the rich seem to be happy," said Elena Ivanovna. " Every man has his sorrow. Here my husband and I do not live poorly, we have means, but are we happy? I am young, but I have had four children; my children are always being ill. I am ill, too, and constantly being doctored."

" And what is your illness? " asked Rodion.

" A woman's complaint. I get no sleep; a continual headache gives me no peace. Here I am sitting and talking, but my head is bad, I am weak all over, and I should prefer the hardest labour to such a condition. My soul, too, is troubled; I am in continual fear for my children, my husband. Every family has its own trouble of some sort; we have ours. I am not of noble birth. My grand-

father was a simple peasant, my father was a tradesman in Moscow; he was a plain, uneducated man,
too, while my husband's parents were wealthy and
distinguished. They did not want him to marry me,
but he disobeyed them, quarrelled with them, and
they have not forgiven us to this day. That worries
my husband; it troubles him and keeps him in con-
stant agitation; he loves his mother, loves her dearly.
So I am uneasy, too, my soul is in pain."

Peasants, men and women, were by now standing
round Rodion's hut and listening. Kozov came up,
too, and stood twitching his long, narrow beard.
The Lytchkovs, father and son, drew near.

" And say what you like, one cannot be happy and
satisfied if one does not feel in one's proper place."
Elena Ivanovna went on. " Each of you has his
strip of land, each of you works and knows what he
is working for; my husband builds bridges — in
short, everyone has his place, while I, I simply walk
about. I have not my bit to work. I don't work,
and feel as though I were an outsider. I am saying
all this that you may not judge from outward ap-
pearances; if a man is expensively dressed and has
means it does not prove that he is satisfied with his
life."

She got up to go away and took her daughter by
the hand.

" I like your place here very much," she said, and
smiled, and from that faint, diffident smile one could
tell how unwell she really was, how young and how
pretty; she had a pale, thinnish face with dark eyebrows and fair hair. And the little girl was just

such another as her mother: thin, fair, and slender.
There was a fragrance of scent about them.

"I like the river and the forest and the village,"
Elena Ivanovna went on; "I could live here all my
life, and I feel as though here I should get strong
and find my place. I want to help you — I want to
dreadfully — to be of use, to be a real friend to you.
I know your need, and what I don't know I feel, my
heart guesses. I am sick, feeble, and for me perhaps it is not possible to change my life as I would.
But I have children. I will try to bring them up
that they may be of use to you, may love you. I
shall impress upon them continually that their life
does not belong to them, but to you. Only I beg you
earnestly, I beseech you, trust us, live in friendship
with us. My husband is a kind, good man. Don't
worry him, don't irritate him. He is sensitive to
every trifle, and yesterday, for instance, your cattle
were in our vegetable garden, and one of your
people broke down the fence to the bee-hives, and
such an attitude to us drives my husband to despair.
I beg you," she went on in an imploring voice, and
she clasped her hands on her bosom — "I beg you
to treat us as good neighbours; let us live in peace!
There is a saying, you know, that even a bad peace
is better than a good quarrel, and, 'Don't buy property, but buy neighbours.' I repeat my husband is
a kind man and good; if all goes well we promise to
do everything in our power for you; we will mend
the roads, we will build a school for your children.
I promise you."

"Of course we thank you humbly, lady," said

Lytchkov the father, looking at the ground; "you are educated people; it is for you to know best. Only, you see, Voronov, a rich peasant at Eresnevo, promised to build a school; he, too, said, ' I will do this for you,' ' I will do that for you,' and he only put up the framework and refused to go on. And then they made the peasants put the roof on and finish it; it cost them a thousand roubles. Voronov did not care; he only stroked his beard, but the peasants felt it a bit hard."

"That was a crow, but now there's a rook, too," said Kozov, and he winked.

There was the sound of laughter.

"We don't want a school," said Volodka sullenly. "Our children go to Petrovskoe, and they can go on going there; we don't want it."

Elena Ivanovna seemed suddenly intimidated; her face looked paler and thinner, she shrank into herself as though she had been touched with something coarse, and walked away without uttering another word. And she walked more and more quickly, without looking round.

"Lady," said Rodion, walking after her, "lady, wait a bit; hear what I would say to you."

He followed her without his cap, and spoke softly as though begging.

"Lady, wait and hear what I will say to you."

They had walked out of the village, and Elena Ivanovna stopped beside a cart in the shade of an old mountain ash.

"Don't be offended, lady," said Rodion. "What does it mean? Have patience. Have pa-

tience for a couple of years.   You will live here, you
will have patience, and it will all come round.   Our
folks are good and peaceable; there's no harm in
them; it's God's truth I'm telling you.   Don't mind
Kozov and the Lytchkovs, and don't mind Volodka.
He's a fool; he listens to the first that speaks.   The
others are quiet folks; they are silent.   Some would
be glad, you know, to say a word from the heart and
to stand up for themselves, but cannot.   They have
a heart and a conscience, but no tongue.   Don't be
offended . . . have patience. . . . What does it
matter? "

Elena Ivanovna looked at the broad, tranquil
river, pondering, and tears flowed down her cheeks.
And Rodion was troubled by those tears; he almost
cried himself.

"Never mind . . ." he muttered.   "Have patience for a couple of years.   You can have the
school, you can have the roads, only not all at once.
If you went, let us say, to sow corn on that mound
you would first have to weed it out, to pick out all
the stones, and then to plough, and work and work
. . . and with the people, you see, it is the same . . .
you must work and work until you overcome them."

The crowd had moved away from Rodion's hut,
and was coming along the street towards the mountain ash.   They began singing songs and playing the
concertina, and they kept coming closer and
closer. . . .

"Mamma, let us go away from here," said the
little girl, huddling up to her mother, pale and shaking all over; " let us go away, mamma ! "

" Where ? "

" To Moscow. . . . Let us go, mamma."

The child began crying.

Rodion was utterly overcome; his face broke into profuse perspiration; he took out of his pocket a little crooked cucumber, like a half-moon, covered with crumbs of rye bread, and began thrusting it into the little girl's hands.

" Come, come," he muttered, scowling severely; "take the little cucumber, eat it up. . . . You mustn't cry. Mamma will whip you. . . . She'll tell your father of you when you get home. Come, come. . . ."

They walked on, and he still followed behind them, wanting to say something friendly and persuasive to them. And seeing that they were both absorbed in their own thoughts and their own griefs, and not noticing him, he stopped and, shading his eyes from the sun, looked after them for a long time till they disappeared into their copse.

IV

The engineer seemed to grow irritable and petty, and in every trivial incident saw an act of robbery or outrage. His gate was kept bolted even by day, and at night two watchmen walked up and down the garden beating a board; and they gave up employing anyone from Obrutchanovo as a labourer. As ill-luck would have it someone (either a peasant or one of the workmen) took the new wheels off the cart and replaced them by old ones, then soon afterwards two bridles and a pair of pincers were carried off, and murmurs arose even in the village. People began to say that a search should be made at the Lytchkovs' and at Volodka's, and then the bridles and the pincers were found under the hedge in the engineer's garden; someone had thrown them down there.

It happened that the peasants were coming in a crowd out of the forest, and again they met the engineer on the road. He stopped, and without wishing them good-day he began, looking angrily first at one, then at another:

" I have begged you not to gather mushrooms in the park and near the yard, but to leave them for my wife and children, but your girls come before daybreak and there is not a mushroom left. . . . Whether one asks you or not it makes no difference. Entreaties, and friendliness, and persuasion I see are all useless."

He fixed his indignant eyes on Rodion and went on:

" My wife and I behaved to you as human beings, as to our equals, and you? But what's the use of talking! It will end by our looking down upon you. There is nothing left! "

And making an effort to restrain his anger, not to say too much, he turned and went on.

On getting home Rodion said his prayer, took off his boots, and sat down beside his wife.

" Yes . . ." he began with a sigh. " We were walking along just now, and Mr. Kutcherov met us. . . . Yes. . . . He saw the girls at daybreak.

. . . ' Why don't they bring mushrooms,' he said
. . . ' to my wife and children?' he said. . . . And
then he looked at me and he said: ' I and my
wife will look after you,' he said. I wanted to
fall down at his feet, but I hadn't the courage. . . .
God give him health. . . . God bless him! . . ."

Stephania crossed herself and sighed.

"They are kind, simple-hearted people," Rodion
went on. " ' We shall look after you.' . . . He
promised me that before everyone. In our old age
. . . it wouldn't be a bad thing. . . . I should
always pray for them. . . . Holy Mother, bless
them. . . ."

The Feast of the Exaltation of the Cross, the
fourteenth of September, was the festival of the
village church. The Lytchkovs, father and son,
went across the river early in the morning and returned to dinner drunk; they spent a long time going about the village, alternately singing and swearing; then they had a fight and went to the New Villa
to complain. First Lytchkov the father went into
the yard with a long ashen stick in his hands. He
stopped irresolutely and took off his hat. Just at
that moment the engineer and his family were sitting
on the verandah, drinking tea.

"What do you want?" shouted the engineer.

"Your honour . . ." Lytchkov began, and burst
into tears. "Show the Divine mercy, protect me
. . . my son makes my life a misery . . . your
honour. . . ."

Lytchkov the son walked up, too; he, too, was
bareheaded and had a stick in his hand; he stopped

and fixed his drunken senseless eyes on the verandah.

" It is not my business to settle your affairs," said the engineer. " Go to the rural captain or the police officer."

" I have been everywhere. . . . I have lodged a petition . . .." said Lytchkov the father, and he sobbed. " Where can I go now? He can kill me now, it seems. He can do anything. Is that the way to treat a father? A father? "

He raised his stick and hit his son on the head; the son raised his stick and struck his father just on his bald patch such a blow that the stick bounced back. The father did not even flinch, but hit his son again and again on the head. And so they stood and kept hitting one another on the head, and it looked not so much like a fight as some sort of a game. And peasants, men and women, stood in a crowd at the gate and looked into the garden, and the faces of all were grave. They were the peasants who had come to greet them for the holi-day, but seeing the Lytchkovs, they were ashamed and did not go in.

The next morning Elena Ivanovna went with the children to Moscow. And there was a rumour that the engineer was selling his house. . . .

V

The peasants had long ago grown used to the sight of the bridge, and it was difficult to imagine the river at that place without a bridge. The heap

of rubble left from the building of it had long been
overgrown with grass, the navvies were forgotten,
and instead of the strains of the " Dubinushka "
that they used to sing, the peasants heard almost
every hour the sounds of a passing train.

The New Villa has long ago been sold; now it
belongs to a government clerk who comes here from
the town for the holidays with his family, drinks
tea on the terrace, and then goes back to the town
again. He wears a cockade on his cap; he talks
and clears his throat as though he were a very important official, though he is only of the rank of a
collegiate secretary, and when the peasants bow he
makes no response.

In Obrutchanovo everyone has grown older;
Kozov is dead. In Rodion's hut there are even
more children. Volodka has grown a long red
beard. They are still as poor as ever.

In the early spring the Obrutchanovo peasants
were sawing wood near the station. And after
work they were going home; they walked without
haste one after the other. Broad saws curved over
their shoulders; the sun was reflected in them. The
nightingales were singing in the bushes on the bank,
larks were trilling in the heavens. It was quiet at
the New Villa; there was not a soul there, and only
golden pigeons — golden because the sunlight was
streaming upon them — were flying over the house.
All of them — Rodion, the two Lytchkovs, and
Volodka — thought of the white horses, the little
ponies, the fireworks, the boat with the lanterns;
they remembered how the engineer's wife, so beauti-

ful and so grandly dressed, had come into the village and talked to them in such a friendly way. And it seemed as though all that had never been; it was like a dream or a fairy-tale.

They trudged along, tired out, and mused as they went. . . . In their village, they mused, the people were good, quiet, sensible, fearing God, and Elena Ivanovna, too, was quiet, kind, and gentle; it made one sad to look at her, but why had they not got on together? Why had they parted like enemies? How was it that some mist had shrouded from their eyes what mattered most, and had let them see nothing but damage done by cattle, bridles, pincers, and all those trivial things which now, as they remembered them, seemed so nonsensical? How was it that with the new owner they lived in peace, and yet had been on bad terms with the engineer?

And not knowing what answer to make to these questions they were all silent except Volodka, who muttered something.

"What is it?" Rodion asked.

"We lived without a bridge . . ." said Volodka gloomily. "We lived without a bridge, and did not ask for one . . . and we don't want it. . . ."

No one answered him and they walked on in silence with drooping heads.

1899

DREAMS

DREAMS

Two peasant constables — one a stubby, black-bearded individual with such exceptionally short legs that if you looked at him from behind it seemed as though his legs began much lower down than in other people; the other, long, thin, and straight as a stick, with a scanty beard of dark reddish colour — were escorting to the district town a tramp who refused to remember his name. The first waddled along, looking from side to side, chewing now a straw, now his own sleeve, slapping himself on the haunches and humming, and altogether had a careless and frivolous air; the other, in spite of his lean face and narrow shoulders, looked solid, grave, and substantial; in the lines and expression of his whole figure he was like the priests among the Old Believers, or the warriors who are painted on old-fashioned ikons. " For his wisdom God had added to his forehead "— that is, he was bald — which increased the resemblance referred to. The first was called Andrey Ptaha, the second Nikandr Sapozhnikov.

The man they were escorting did not in the least correspond with the conception everyone has of a tramp. He was a frail little man, weak and sickly-looking, with small, colourless, and extremely indefinite features. His eyebrows were scanty, his ex-

pression mild and submissive; he had scarcely a
trace of a moustache, though he was over thirty.
He walked along timidly, bent forward, with his
hands thrust into his sleeves. The collar of his
shabby cloth overcoat, which did not look like a
peasant's, was turned up to the very brim of his
cap, so that only his little red nose ventured to peep
out into the light of day. He spoke in an ingratiat-
ing tenor, continually coughing. It was very, very
difficult to believe that he was a tramp concealing
his surname. He was more like an unsuccessful
priest's son, stricken by God and reduced to beggary;
a clerk discharged for drunkenness; a merchant's
son or nephew who had tried his feeble powers in
a theatrical career, and was now going home to play
the last act in the parable of the prodigal son; perhaps, judging by the dull patience with which he
struggled with the hopeless autumn mud, he might
have been a fanatical monk, wandering from one
Russian monastery to another, continually seeking
" a peaceful life, free from sin," and not finding
it. . . .
    The travellers had been a long while on their
way, but they seemed to be always on the same
small patch of ground. In front of them there
stretched thirty feet of muddy black-brown mud, behind them the same, and wherever one looked
further, an impenetrable wall of white fog. They
went on and on, but the ground remained the same,
the wall was no nearer, and the patch on which
they walked seemed still the same patch. They
got a glimpse of a white, clumsy-looking stone, a

small ravine, or a bundle of hay dropped by a passer-by, the brief glimmer of a great muddy puddle, or, suddenly, a shadow with vague outlines would come into view ahead of them; the nearer they got to it the smaller and darker it became; nearer still, and there stood up before the way-farers a slanting milestone with the number rubbed off, or a wretched birch-tree drenched and bare like a wayside beggar. The birch-tree would whisper something with what remained of its yellow leaves, one leaf would break off and float lazily to the ground. . . . And then again fog, mud, the brown grass at the edges of the road. On the grass hung dingy, unfriendly tears. They were not the tears of soft joy such as the earth weeps at welcoming the summer sun and parting from it, and such as she gives to drink at dawn to the corncrakes, quails, and graceful, long-beaked crested snipes. The travel-lers' feet stuck in the heavy, clinging mud. Every step cost an effort.

Andrey Ptaha was somewhat excited. He kept looking round at the tramp and trying to under-stand how a live, sober man could fail to remember his name.

" You are an orthodox Christian, aren't you? " he asked.

" Yes," the tramp answered mildly.

" H'm . . . then you've been christened? "

" Why, to be sure! I'm not a Turk. I go to church and to the sacrament, and do not eat meat when it is forbidden. And I observe my religious duties punctually. . . ."

" Well, what are you called, then? "

" Call me what you like, good man."

Ptaha shrugged his shoulders and slapped himself on the haunches in extreme perplexity. The other constable, Nikandr Sapozhnikov, maintained a staid silence. He was not so naïve as Ptaha, and apparently knew very well the reasons which might induce an orthodox Christian to conceal his name from other people. His expressive face was cold and stern. He walked apart and did not condescend to idle chatter with his companions, but, as it were, tried to show everyone, even the fog, his sedateness and discretion.

" God knows what to make of you," Ptaha persisted in addressing the tramp. " Peasant you are not, and gentleman you are not, but some sort of a thing between. . . . The other day I was washing a sieve in the pond and caught a reptile — see, as long as a finger, with gills and a tail. The first minute I thought it was a fish, then I looked — and, blow it! if it hadn't paws. It was not a fish, it was a viper, and the deuce only knows what it was. . . . So that's like you. . . . What's your calling? "

" I am a peasant and of peasant family," sighed the tramp. " My mamma was a house serf. I don't look like a peasant, that's true, for such has been my lot, good man. My mamma was a nurse with the gentry, and had every comfort, and as I was of her flesh and blood, I lived with her in the master's house. She petted and spoiled me, and did her best to take me out of my humble class and make a gentleman of me. I slept in a bed, every

day I ate a real dinner, I wore breeches and shoes
like a gentleman's child. What my mamma ate I
was fed on, too; they gave her stuffs as a present,
and she dressed me up in them. . . . We lived
well! I ate so many sweets and cakes in my childish
years that if they could be sold now it would be
enough to buy a good horse. Mamma taught me
to read and write, she instilled the fear of God in
me from my earliest years, and she so trained me
that now I can't bring myself to utter an unrefined
peasant word. And I don't drink vodka, my lad,
and am neat in my dress, and know how to behave
with decorum in good society. If she is still living,
God give her health; and if she is dead, then, O
Lord, give her soul peace in Thy Kingdom, wherein
the just are at rest."

The tramp bared his head with the scanty hair
standing up like a brush on it, turned his eyes up-
ward and crossed himself twice.

"Grant her, O Lord, a verdant and peaceful rest-
ing-place," he said in a drawling voice, more like
an old woman's than a man's. "Teach Thy servant Xenia Thy justifications, O Lord! If it had
not been for my beloved mamma I should have been
a peasant with no sort of understanding! Now,
young man, ask me about anything and I understand it all: the holy Scriptures and profane writ-
ings, and every prayer and catechism. I live according to the Scriptures. . . . I don't injure anyone, I keep my flesh in purity and continence, I observe the fasts, I eat at fitting times. Another man
will take no pleasure in anything but vodka and lewd

talk, but when I have time I sit in a corner and read a book. I read and I weep and weep. . . ."

" What do you weep for? "

" They write so pathetically! For some books one gives but a five-kopeck piece, and yet one weeps and sighs exceedingly over it."

" Is your father dead? " asked Ptaha.

" I don't know, good man. I don't know my parent; it is no use concealing it. I judge that I was mamma's illegitimate son. My mamma lived all her life with the gentry, and did not want to marry a simple peasant. . . ."

" And so she fell into the master's hands," laughed Ptaha.

" She did transgress, that's true. She was pious, God-fearing, but she did not keep her maiden purity. It is a sin, of course, a great sin, there's no doubt about it, but to make up for it there is, maybe, noble blood in me. Maybe I am only a peasant by class, but in nature a noble gentleman."

The " noble gentleman " uttered all this in a soft, sugary tenor, wrinkling up his narrow forehead and emitting creaking sounds from his red, frozen little nose. Ptaha listened and looked askance at him in wonder, continually shrugging his shoulders.

After going nearly five miles the constables and the tramp sat down on a mound to rest.

" Even a dog knows his name," Ptaha muttered. " My name is Andryushka, his is Nikandr; every man has his holy name, and it can't be forgotten. Nohow."

" Who has any need to know my name? " sighed
the tramp, leaning his cheek on his fist. " And
what advantage would it be to me if they did know
it? If I were allowed to go where I would — but
it would only make things worse. I know the law,
Christian brothers. Now I am a tramp who doesn't
remember his name, and it's the very most if they
send me to Eastern Siberia and give me thirty or
forty lashes; but if I were to tell them my real name
and description they would send me back to hard
labour, I know! "

" Why, have you been a convict? "

" I have, dear friend. For four years I went
about with my head shaved and fetters on my legs."

" What for? "

" For murder, my good man! When I was still
a boy of eighteen or so, my mamma accidentally
poured arsenic instead of soda and acid into my
master's glass. There were boxes of all sorts in
the storeroom, numbers of them; it was easy to
make a mistake over them."

The tramp sighed, shook his head, and said:

" She was a pious woman, but, who knows? another man's soul is a slumbering forest! It may
have been an accident, or maybe she could not endure the affront of seeing the master prefer another
servant. . . . Perhaps she put it in on purpose, God
knows! I was young then, and did not understand
it all . . . now I remember that our master had
taken another mistress and mamma was greatly disturbed. Our trial lasted nearly two years. . . .

Mamma was condemned to penal servitude for twenty years, and I, on account of my youth, only to seven."

" And why were you sentenced? "

" As an accomplice. I handed the glass to the master. That was always the custom. Mamma prepared the soda and I handed it to him. Only I tell you all this as a Christian, brothers, as I would say it before God. Don't you tell anybody. . . ."

" Oh, nobody's going to ask us," said Ptaha. " So you've run away from prison, have you? "

" I have, dear friend. Fourteen of us ran away. Some folks, God bless them! ran away and took me with them. Now you tell me, on your conscience, good man, what reason have I to disclose my name? They will send me back to penal servitude, you know! And I am not fit for penal servitude! I am a refined man in delicate health. I like to sleep and eat in cleanliness. When I pray to God I like to light a little lamp or a candle, and not to have a noise around me. When I bow down to the ground I like the floor not to be dirty or spat upon. And I bow down forty times every morning and evening, praying for mamma."

The tramp took off his cap and crossed himself.

" And let them send me to Eastern Siberia," he said; " I am not afraid of that."

" Surely that's no better? "

" It is quite a different thing. In penal servitude you are like a crab in a basket: crowding, crushing, jostling, there's no room to breathe; it's downright hell — such hell, may the Queen of Heaven keep us from it! You are a robber and treated like a robber — worse than any dog. You can't sleep, you can't eat or even say your prayers. But it's not like that in a settlement. In a settlement I shall be a member of a commune like other people. The authorities are bound by law to give me my share . . . ye-es! They say the land costs nothing, no more than snow; you can take what you like! They will give me corn land and building land and garden. . . . I shall plough my fields like other people, sow seed. I shall have cattle and stock of all sorts, bees, sheep, and dogs. . . . A Siberian cat, that rats and mice may not devour my goods. . . . I will put up a house, I shall buy ikons. . . . Please God, I'll get married, I shall have children. . . ."

The tramp muttered and looked, not at his listeners, but away into the distance. Naïve as his dreams were, they were uttered in such a genuine and heartfelt tone that it was difficult not to believe in them. The tramp's little mouth was screwed up in a smile. His eyes and little nose and his whole face were fixed and blank with blissful anticipation of happiness in the distant future. The constables listened and looked at him gravely, not without sympathy. They, too, believed in his dreams.

"I am not afraid of Siberia," the tramp went on muttering. "Siberia is just as much Russia and has the same God and Tsar as here. They are just as orthodox Christians as you and I. Only there is more freedom there and people are better off. Everything is better there. Take the rivers there, for instance; they are far better than those here.

There's no end of fish; and all sorts of wild fowl. And my greatest pleasure, brothers, is fishing. Give me no bread to eat, but let me sit with a fish-hook. Yes, indeed! I fish with a hook and with a wire line, and set creels, and when the ice comes I catch with a net. I am not strong to draw up the net, so I shall hire a man for five kopecks. And, Lord, what a pleasure it is! You catch an eel-pout or a roach of some sort and are as pleased as though you had met your own brother. And would you believe it, there's a special art for every fish: you catch one with a live bait, you catch another with a grub, the third with a frog or a grasshopper. One has to understand all that, of course! For example, take the eel-pout. It is not a delicate fish — it will take a perch; and a pike loves a gudgeon, the *shilishper* likes a butterfly. If you fish for a roach in a rapid stream there is no greater pleasure. You throw the line of seventy feet without lead, with a butterfly or a beetle, so that the bait floats on the surface; you stand in the water without your trousers and let it go with the current, and tug! the roach pulls at it! Only you have got to be artful that he doesn't carry off the bait, the damned rascal. As soon as he tugs at your line you must whip it up; it's no good waiting. It's wonderful what a lot of fish I've caught in my time. When we were running away the other convicts would sleep in the forest; I could not sleep, but I was off to the river. The rivers there are wide and rapid, the banks are steep — awfully! It's all slumbering forests on the bank. The trees are so tall that if you look to the top it makes you dizzy. Every pine would be worth ten roubles by the prices here."

In the overwhelming rush of his fancies, of artistic images of the past and sweet presentiments of happiness in the future, the poor wretch sank into silence, merely moving his lips as though whispering to himself. The vacant, blissful smile never left his lips. The constables were silent. They were pondering with bent heads. In the autumn stillness, when the cold, sullen mist that rises from the earth lies like a weight on the heart, when it stands like a prison wall before the eyes, and reminds man of the limitation of his freedom, it is sweet to think of the broad, rapid rivers, with steep banks wild and luxuriant, of the impenetrable forests, of the boundless steppes. Slowly and quietly the fancy pictures how early in the morning, before the flush of dawn has left the sky, a man makes his way along the steep deserted bank like a tiny speck: the ancient, mast-like pines rise up in terraces on both sides of the torrent, gaze sternly at the free man and murmur menacingly; rocks, huge stones, and thorny bushes bar his way, but he is strong in body and bold in spirit, and has no fear of the pine-trees, nor stones, nor of his solitude, nor of the reverberating echo which repeats the sound of every footstep that he takes.

The peasants called up a picture of a free life such as they had never lived; whether they vaguely recalled the images of stories heard long ago or whether notions of a free life had been handed down to them with their flesh and blood from far-off free ancestors, God knows!

The first to break the silence was Nikandr Sapozhnikov, who had not till then let fall a single word. Whether he envied the tramp's transparent happiness, or whether he felt in his heart that dreams of happiness were out of keeping with the grey fog and the dirty brown mud — anyway, he looked sternly at the tramp and said:

" It's all very well, to be sure, only you won't reach those plenteous regions, brother. How could you? Before you'd gone two hundred miles you'd give up your soul to God. Just look what a weak-ling you are! Here you've hardly gone five miles and you can't get your breath."

The tramp turned slowly toward Nikandr, and the blissful smile vanished from his face. He looked with a scared and guilty air at the peasant's staid face, apparently remembered something, and bent his head. A silence followed again. . . . All three were pondering. The peasants were racking their brains in the effort to grasp in their imagina-tion what can be grasped by none but God — that is, the vast expanse dividing them from the land of freedom. Into the tramp's mind thronged clear and distinct pictures more terrible than that expanse. Before him rose vividly the picture of the long legal delays and procrastinations, the temporary and per-manent prisons, the convict boats, the wearisome stoppages on the way, the frozen winters, illnesses, deaths of companions. . . .

The tramp blinked guiltily, wiped the tiny drops of sweat from his forehead with his sleeve, drew a deep breath as though he had just leapt out of a very hot bath, then wiped his forehead with the other sleeve and looked round fearfully.

"That's true; you won't get· there!" Ptaha agreed. "You are not much of a walker! Look at you — nothing but skin and bone! You'll die, brother!"

"Of course he'll die! What could he do?" said Nikandr. "He's fit for the hospital now. . . . For sure!"

The man who had forgotten his name looked at the stern, unconcerned faces of his sinister companions, and without taking off his cap, hurriedly crossed himself, staring with wide-open eyes. . . . He trembled, his head shook, and he began twitching all over, like a caterpillar when it is stepped upon. . . .

"Well, it's time to go," said Nikandr, getting up; "we've had a rest."

A minute later they were stepping along the muddy road. The tramp was more bent than ever, and he thrust his hands further up his sleeves. Ptaha was silent.

1886

THE PIPE

THE PIPE

MELITON SHISHKIN, a bailiff from the Dementyev farm, exhausted by the sultry heat of the fir-wood and covered with spiders' webs and pine-needles, made his way with his gun to the edge of the wood. His Damka — a mongrel between a yard dog and a setter — an extremely thin bitch heavy with young, trailed after her master with her wet tail between her legs, doing all she could to avoid pricking her nose. It was a dull, overcast morning. Big drops dripped from the bracken and from the trees that were wrapped in a light mist; there was a pungent smell of decay from the dampness of the wood.

There were birch-trees ahead of him where the wood ended, and between their stems and branches he could see the misty distance. Beyond the birch-trees someone was playing on a shepherd's rustic pipe. The player produced no more than five or six notes, dragged them out languidly with no attempt at forming a tune, and yet there was something harsh and extremely dreary in the sound of the piping.

As the copse became sparser, and the pines were interspersed with young birch-trees, Meliton saw a herd. Hobbled horses, cows, and sheep were wandering among the bushes and, snapping the dry branches, sniffed at the herbage of the copse. A lean old shepherd, bareheaded, in a torn grey smock, stood leaning against the wet trunk of a birch-tree. He stared at the ground, pondering something, and played his pipe, it seemed, mechanically.

"Good-day, grandfather! God help you!" Meliton greeted him in a thin, husky voice which seemed incongruous with his huge stature and big, fleshy face. "How cleverly you are playing your pipe! Whose herd are you minding?"

"The Artamonovs'," the shepherd answered reluctantly, and he thrust the pipe into his bosom.

"So I suppose the wood is the Artamonovs' too?" Meliton inquired, looking about him. "Yes, it is the Artamonovs'; only fancy . . . I had completely lost myself. I got my face scratched all over in the thicket."

He sat down on the wet earth and began rolling up a bit of newspaper into a cigarette.

Like his voice, everything about the man was small and out of keeping with his height, his breadth, and his fleshy face: his smiles, his eyes, his buttons, his tiny cap, which would hardly keep on his big, closely-cropped head. When he talked and smiled there was something womanish, timid, and meek about his puffy, shaven face and his whole figure.

"What weather! God help us!" he said, and he turned his head from side to side. "Folk have not carried the oats yet, and the rain seems as though it had been taken on for good, God bless it."

The shepherd looked at the sky, from which a

drizzling rain was falling, at the wood, at the bailiff's wet clothes, pondered, and said nothing.

"The whole summer has been the same," sighed Meliton. "A bad business for the peasants and no pleasure for the gentry."

The shepherd looked at the sky again, thought a moment, and said deliberately, as though chewing each word:

"It's all going the same way. . . . There is nothing good to be looked for."

"How are things with you here?" Meliton inquired, lighting his cigarette. "Haven't you seen any coveys of grouse in the Artamonovs' clearing?"

The shepherd did not answer at once. He looked again at the sky and to right and left, thought a little, blinked. . . . Apparently he attached no little significance to his words, and to increase their value tried to pronounce them with deliberation and a certain solemnity. The expression of his face had the sharpness and staidness of old age, and the fact that his nose had a saddle-shaped depression across the middle and his nostrils turned upwards gave him a sly and sarcastic look.

"No, I believe I haven't," he said. "Our huntsman Eryomka was saying that on Elijah's Day he started one covey near Pustoshye, but I dare say he was lying. There are very few birds."

"Yes, brother, very few. . . . Very few everywhere! The shooting here, if one is to look at it with common sense, is good for nothing and not worth having. There is no game at all, and what there is is not worth dirtying your hands over — it is not full-grown. It is such poor stuff that one is ashamed to look at it."

Meliton gave a laugh and waved his hands.

" Things happen so queerly in this world that it is simply laughable and nothing else. Birds nowadays have become so unaccountable: they sit late on their eggs, and there are some, I declare, that have not hatched them by St. Peter's Day! "

" It's all going the same way," said the shepherd, turning his face upwards. " There was little game last year, this year there are fewer birds still, and in another five years, mark my words, there will be none at all. As far as I can see there will soon be not only no game, but no birds at all."

" Yes," Meliton assented, after a moment's thought. " That's true."

The shepherd gave a bitter smile and shook his head.

" It's a wonder," he said, " what has become of them all! I remember twenty years ago there used to be geese here, and cranes and ducks and grouse — clouds and clouds of them! The gentry used to meet together for shooting, and one heard nothing but pouf-pouf-pouf! pouf-pouf-pouf! There was no end to the woodcocks, the snipe, and the little teals, and the water-snipe were as common as starlings, or let us say sparrows — lots and lots of them! And what has become of them all? We don't even see the birds of prey. The eagles, the hawks, and the owls have all gone. . . . There are fewer of every sort of wild beast, too. Nowadays, brother, even the wolf and the fox have grown rare, let alone the bear or the otter. And you know in old days there were even elks! For forty years I have been observing the works of God from year to year, and it is my opinion that everything is going the same way."

"What way?"

"To the bad, young man. To ruin, we must suppose. . . . The time has come for God's world to perish."

The old man put on his cap and began gazing at the sky.

"It's a pity," he sighed, after a brief silence. "O God, what a pity! Of course it is God's will; the world was not created by us, but yet it is a pity, brother. If a single tree withers away, or let us say a single cow dies, it makes one sorry, but what will it be, good man, if the whole world crumbles into dust? Such blessings, Lord Jesus! The sun, and the sky, and the forest, and the rivers, and the creatures — all these have been created, adapted, and adjusted to one another. Each has been put to its appointed task and knows its place. And all that must perish."

A mournful smile gleamed on the shepherd's face, and his eyelids quivered.

"You say — the world is perishing," said Meliton, pondering. "It may be that the end of the world is near at hand, but you can't judge by the birds. I don't think the birds can be taken as a sign."

"Not the birds only," said the shepherd. "It's the wild beasts, too, and the cattle, and the bees, and the fish. . . . If you don't believe me ask the old people; every old man will tell you that the fish are not at all what they used to be. In the seas, in the lakes, and in the rivers, there are fewer fish from year to year. In our Pestchanka, I remember, pike used to be caught a yard long, and there were eel-pouts, and roach, and bream, and every fish had a presentable appearance; while nowadays, if you catch a wretched little pikelet or perch six inches long you have to be thankful. There are not any gudgeon even worth talking about. Every year it is worse and worse, and in a little while there will be no fish at all. And take the rivers now . . . the rivers are drying up, for sure."

"It is true; they are drying up."

"To be sure, that's what I say. Every year they are shallower and shallower, and there are not the deep holes there used to be. And do you see the bushes yonder?" the old man asked, pointing to one side. "Beyond them is an old river-bed; it's called a backwater. In my father's time the Pestchanka flowed there, but now look; where have the evil spirits taken it to? It changes its course, and, mind you, it will go on changing till such time as it has dried up altogether. There used to be marshes and ponds beyond Kurgasovo, and where are they now? And what has become of the streams? Here in this very wood we used to have a stream flowing, and such a stream that the peasants used to set creels in it and caught pike; wild ducks used to spend the winter by it, and nowadays there is no water in it worth speaking of, even at the spring floods. Yes,

brother, look where you will, things are bad everywhere. Everywhere! "

A silence followed. Meliton sank into thought,
with his eyes fixed on one spot. He wanted to
think of some one part of nature as yet untouched
by the all-embracing ruin. Spots of light glistened
on the mist and the slanting streaks of rain as
though on opaque glass, and immediately died away
again — it was the rising sun trying to break through
the clouds and peep at the earth.

" Yes, the forests, too . . ." Meliton muttered.

" The forests, too," the shepherd repeated.
" They cut them down, and they catch fire, and they
wither away, and no new ones are growing. Whatever does grow up is cut down at once; one day it
shoots up and the next it has been cut down — and
so on without end till nothing's left. I have kept
the herds of the commune ever since the time of
Freedom, good man; before the time of Freedom I
was shepherd of the master's herds. I have watched
them in this very spot, and I can't remember a summer day in all my life that I have not been here.
And all the time I have been observing the works
of God. I have looked at them in my time till I
know them, and it is my opinion that all things growing are on the decline. Whether you take the rye,
or the vegetables, or flowers of any sort, they are
all going the same way."

" But people have grown better," observed the
bailiff.

" In what way better? "

" Cleverer."

" Cleverer, maybe, that's true, young man; but what's the use of that? What earthly good is cleverness to people on the brink of ruin? One can perish without cleverness. What's the good of cleverness to a huntsman if there is no game? What I think is that God has given men brains and taken away their strength. People have grown weak, exceedingly weak. Take me, for instance . . . I am not worth a halfpenny, I am the humblest peasant in the whole village, and yet, young man, I have strength. Mind you, I am in my seventies, and I tend my herd day in and day out, and keep the night watch, too, for twenty kopecks, and I don't sleep, and I don't feel the cold; my son is cleverer than I am, but put him in my place and he would ask for a rise next day, or would be going to the doctors. There it is. I eat nothing but bread, for ' Give us this day our daily bread,' and my father ate nothing but bread, and my grandfather; but the peasant nowadays must have tea and vodka and white loaves, and must sleep from sunset to dawn, and he goes to the doctor and pampers himself in all sorts of ways. And why is it? He has grown weak; he has not the strength to endure. If he wants to stay awake, his eyes close — there is no doing anything."

" That's true," Meliton agreed; " the peasant is good for nothing nowadays."

" It's no good hiding what is wrong; we get worse from year to year. And if you take the gentry into consideration, they've grown feebler even more than the peasants have. The gentleman nowadays has mastered everything; he knows what he ought not to know, and what is the sense of it? It makes you feel pitiful to look at him. . . . He is a thin, puny little fellow, like some Hungarian or Frenchman; there is no dignity nor air about him; it's only in name he is a gentleman. There is no place for him, poor dear, and nothing for him to do, and there is no making out what he wants. Either he sits with a hook catching fish, or he lolls on his back reading, or trots about among the peasants saying all sorts of things to them, and those that are hungry go in for being clerks. So he spends his life in vain. And he has no notion of doing something real and useful. The gentry in old days were half of them generals, but nowadays they are — a poor lot."

"They are badly off nowadays," said Meliton.

"They are poorer because God has taken away their strength. You can't go against God."

Meliton stared at a fixed point again. After thinking a little he heaved a sigh as staid, reasonable people do sigh, shook his head, and said:

"And all because of what? We have sinned greatly, we have forgotten God . . . and it seems that the time has come for all to end. And, after all, the world can't last for ever — it's time to know when to take leave."

The shepherd sighed and, as though wishing to cut short an unpleasant conversation, he walked away from the birch-tree and began silently reckoning over the cows.

"Hey-hey-hey!" he shouted. "Hey-hey-hey! Bother you, the plague take you! The devil has taken you into the thicket. Tu-lu-lu!"

With an angry face he went into the bushes to collect his herd. Meliton got up and sauntered slowly along the edge of the wood. He looked at the ground at his feet and pondered; he still wanted to think of something which had not yet been touched by death. Patches of light crept upon the slanting streaks of rain again; they danced on the tops of the trees and died away among the wet leaves. Damka found a hedgehog under a bush, and wanting to attract her master's attention to it, barked and howled.

" Did you have an eclipse or not? " the shepherd called from the bushes.

" Yes, we had," answered Meliton.

" Ah! Folks are complaining all about that there was one. It shows there is disorder even in the heavens! It's not for nothing. . . . Hey-hey-hey! Hey! "

Driving his herd together to the edge of the wood, the shepherd leaned against the birch-tree, looked up at the sky, without haste took his pipe from his bosom and began playing. As before, he played mechanically and took no more than five or six notes; as though the pipe had come into his hands for the first time, the sounds floated from it uncertainly, with no regularity, not blending into a tune, but to Meliton, brooding on the destruction of the world, there was a sound in it of something very depressing and revolting which he would much rather not have heard. The highest, shrillest notes, which quivered and broke, seemed to be weeping disconsolately, as though the pipe were sick and frightened, while the lowest notes for some reason reminded him of the mist, the dejected trees, the grey sky. Such music seemed in keeping with the weather, the old man and his sayings.

Meliton wanted to complain. He went up to the old man and, looking at his mournful, mocking face and at the pipe, muttered:

" And life has grown worse, grandfather. It is utterly impossible to live. Bad crops, want. . . . Cattle plague continually, diseases of all sorts. . . . We are crushed by poverty."

The bailiff's puffy face turned crimson and took a dejected, womanish expression. He twirled his fingers as though seeking words to convey his vague feeling and went on:

" Eight children, a wife . . . and my mother still living, and my whole salary ten roubles a month and to board myself. My wife has become a Satan from poverty. . . . I go off drinking myself. I am a sensible, steady man; I have education. I ought to sit at home in peace, but I stray about all day with my gun like a dog because it is more than I can stand; my home is hateful to me! "

Feeling that his tongue was uttering something quite different from what he wanted to say, the bailiff waved his hand and said bitterly:

" If the world's going to end I wish it would make haste about it. There's no need to drag it out and make folks miserable for nothing. . . ."

The old man took the pipe from his lips and,

screwing up one eye, looked into its little opening. His face was sad and covered with thick drops like tears. He smiled and said:

" It's a pity, my friend! My goodness, what a pity! The earth, the forest, the sky, the beasts of all sorts — all this has been created, you know, adapted; they all have their intelligence. It is all going to ruin. And most of all I am sorry for people."

There was the sound in the wood of heavy rain coming nearer. Meliton looked in the direction of the sound, did up all his buttons, and said:

" I am going to the village. Good-bye, grandfather. What is your name?"

" Luka the, Poor."

" Well, good-bye, Luka! Thank you for your good words. Damka, ici!"

After parting from the shepherd Meliton made his way along the edge of the wood, and then down hill to a meadow which by degrees turned into a marsh. There was a squelch of water under his feet, and the rusty marsh sedge, still green and juicy, drooped down to the earth as though afraid of being trampled underfoot. Beyond the marsh, on the bank of the Pestchanka, of which the old man had spoken, stood a row of willows, and beyond the willows a barn looked dark blue in the mist. One could feel the approach of that miserable, utterly inevitable season, when the fields grow dark and the earth is muddy and cold, when the weeping willow seems still more mournful and tears trickle down its stem, and only the cranes fly away from the general misery, and even they, as though afraid of insulting dispirited nature by the expression of their happiness, fill the air with their mournful, dreary notes.

Meliton plodded along to the river, and heard the sounds of the pipe gradually dying away behind him. He still wanted to complain. He looked dejectedly about him, and he felt insufferably sorry for the sky and the earth and the sun and the woods and his Damka, and when the highest drawn-out note of the pipe floated quivering in the air, like a voice weeping, he felt extremely bitter and resentful of the impropriety in the conduct of nature.

The high note quivered, broke off, and the pipe was silent.

1887

AGAFYA

AGAFYA

DURING my stay in the district of S. I often used
to go to see the watchman Savva Stukatch, or simply
Savka, in the kitchen gardens of Dubovo. These
kitchen gardens were my favorite resort for so-called
" mixed " fishing, when one goes out without knowing what day or hour one may return, taking with
one every sort of fishing tackle as well as a store of
provisions. To tell the truth, it was not so much
the fishing that attracted me as the peaceful stroll,
the meals at no set time, the talk with Savka, and
being for so long face to face with the calm summer
nights. Savka was a young man of five-and-twenty,
well grown and handsome, and as strong as a flint.
He had the reputation of being a sensible and reasonable fellow. He could read and write, and very
rarely drank, but as a workman this strong and
healthy young man was not worth a farthing. A
sluggish, overpowering sloth was mingled with the
strength in his muscles, which were strong as cords.
Like everyone else in his village, he lived in his own
hut, and had his share of land, but neither tilled it
nor sowed it, and did not work at any sort of trade.
His old mother begged alms at people's windows and
he himself lived like a bird of the air; he did not
know in the morning what he would eat at midday.

It was not that he was lacking in will, or energy, or feeling for his mother; it was simply that he felt no inclination for work and did not recognize the advantage of it. His whole figure suggested unruffled serenity, an innate, almost artistic passion for living carelessly, never with his sleeves tucked up. When Savka's young, healthy body had a physical craving for muscular work, the young man abandoned himself completely for a brief interval to some free but nonsensical pursuit, such as sharpening skates not wanted for any special purpose, or racing about after the peasant women. His favorite attitude was one of concentrated immobility. He was capable of standing for hours at a stretch in the same place with his eyes fixed on the same spot without stirring. He never moved except on impulse, and then only when an occasion presented itself for some rapid and abrupt action: catching a running dog by the tail, pulling off a woman's kerchief, or jumping over a big hole. It need hardly be said that with such parsimony of movement Savka was as poor as a mouse and lived worse than any homeless outcast. As time went on, I suppose he accumulated arrears of taxes and, young and sturdy as he was, he was sent by the commune to do an old man's job — to be watchman and scarecrow in the kitchen gardens. However much they laughed at him for his premature senility he did not object to it. This position, quiet and convenient for motionless contemplation, exactly fitted his temperament.

It happened I was with this Savka one fine May evening. I remember I was lying on a torn and dirty sackcloth cover close to the shanty from which came a heavy, fragrant scent of hay. Clasping my hands under my head I looked before me. At my feet was lying a wooden fork. Behind it Savka's dog Kutka stood out like a black patch, and not a dozen feet from Kutka the ground ended abruptly in the steep bank of the little river. Lying down I could not see the river; I could only see the tops of the young willows growing thickly on the nearer bank, and the twisting, as it were gnawed away, edges of the opposite bank. At a distance beyond the bank on the dark hillside the huts of the village in which Savka lived lay huddling together like frightened young partridges. Beyond the hill the afterglow of sunset still lingered in the sky. One pale crimson streak was all that was left, and even that began to be covered by little clouds as a fire with ash.

A copse with alder-trees, softly whispering, and from time to time shuddering in the fitful breeze, lay, a dark blur, on the right of the kitchen gardens; on the left stretched the immense plain. In the distance, where the eye could not distinguish between the sky and the plain, there was a bright gleam of light. A little way off from me sat Savka. With his legs tucked under him like a Turk and his head hanging, he looked pensively at Kutka. Our hooks with live bait on them had long been in the river, and we had nothing left to do but to abandon ourselves to repose, which Savka, who was never exhausted and always rested, loved so much. The glow had not yet quite died away, but the summer night was already enfolding nature in its caressing, soothing embrace.

Everything was sinking into its first deep sleep except some night bird unfamiliar to me, which indolently uttered a long, protracted cry in several distinct notes like the phrase, " Have you seen Ni-ki-ta ? " and immediately answered itself, " Seen him, seen him, seen him ! "

" Why is it the nightingales aren't singing to-night ? " I asked Savka.

He turned slowly towards me. His features were large, but his face was open, soft, and expressive as a woman's. Then he gazed with his mild, dreamy eyes at the copse, at the willows, slowly pulled a whistle out of his pocket, put it in his mouth and whistled the note of a hen-nightingale. And at once, as though in answer to his call, a landrail called on the opposite bank.

" There's a nightingale for you . . ." laughed Savka. " Drag-drag ! drag-drag ! just like pulling at a hook, and yet I bet he thinks he is singing, too."

" I like that bird," I said. " Do you know, when the birds are migrating the landrail does not fly, but runs along the ground ? It only flies over the rivers and the sea, but all the rest it does on foot."

" Upon my word, the dog . . ." muttered Savka, looking with respect in the direction of the calling landrail.

Knowing how fond Savka was of listening, I told him all I had learned about the landrail from sportsman's books. From the landrail I passed imperceptibly to the migration of the birds. Savka listened attentively, looking at me without blinking, and smiling all the while with pleasure.

"And which country is most the bird's home? Ours or those foreign parts?" he asked.

"Ours, of course. The bird itself is hatched here, and it hatches out its little ones here in its native country, and they only fly off there to escape being frozen."

"It's interesting," said Savka. "Whatever one talks about it is always interesting. Take a bird now, or a man . . . or take this little stone; there's something to learn about all of them. . . . Ah, sir, if I had known you were coming I wouldn't have told a woman to come here this evening. . . . She asked to come to-day."

"Oh, please don't let me be in your way," I said. "I can lie down in the wood. . . ."

"What next! She wouldn't have died if she hadn't come till to-morrow. . . . If only she would sit quiet and listen, but she always wants to be slobbering. . . . You can't have a good talk when she's here."

"Are you expecting Darya?" I asked, after a pause.

"No . . . a new one has asked to come this evening . . . Agafya, the signalman's wife."

Savka said this in his usual passionless, somewhat hollow voice, as though he were talking of tobacco or porridge, while I started with surprise. I knew Agafya. . . . She was quite a young peasant woman of nineteen or twenty, who had been married not more than a year before to a railway signalman, a

fine young fellow.   She lived in the village, and· her
husband came home there from the line every night.

"Your goings on with the women will lead to
trouble, my boy," said I.

"Well, may be, . . ."

And after a moment's thought Savka added:

"I've said so to the women; they won't heed me.
. . . They don't trouble about it, the silly things!"

Silence followed. . . . Meanwhile the darkness
was growing thicker and thicker, and objects began
to lose their contours.   The streak behind the hill
had completely died away, and the stars were growing brighter and more luminous. . . . The mournfully monotonous chirping of the grasshoppers, the
call of the landrail, and the cry of the quail did
not destroy the stillness of the night, but, on the
contrary, gave it an added monotony.   It seemed as
though the soft sounds that enchanted the ear came,
not from birds or insects, but from the stars looking
down upon us from the sky. . . .

Savka was the first to break the silence.   He
slowly turned his eyes from black Kutka and said:

"I see you are dull, sir.   Let's have supper."

And without waiting for my consent he crept on
his stomach into the shanty, rummaged about there,
making the whole edifice tremble like a leaf; then
he crawled back and set before me my vodka and an
earthenware bowl; in the bowl there were baked
eggs, lard scones made of rye, pieces of black bread,
and something else. . . . We had a drink from
a little crooked glass that wouldn't stand, and then
we fell upon the food. . . . Coarse grey salt, dirty,

greasy cakes, eggs tough as india-rubber, but how nice it all was!

" You live all alone, but what lots of good things you have," I said, pointing to the bowl. " Where do you get them from? "

" The women bring them," mumbled Savka.

" What do they bring them to you for? "

" Oh . . . from pity."

Not only Savka's menu, but his clothing, too, bore traces of feminine " pity." Thus I noticed that he had on, that evening, a new woven belt and a crimson ribbon on which a copper cross hung round his dirty neck. I knew of the weakness of the fair sex for Savka, and I knew that he did not like talking about it, and so I did not carry my inquiries any further. Besides there was not time to talk. . . . Kutka, who had been fidgeting about near us and patiently waiting for scraps, suddenly pricked up his ears and growled. We heard in the distance repeated splashing of water.

" Someone is coming by the ford," said Savka.

Three minutes later Kutka growled again and made a sound like a cough.

" Shsh! " his master shouted at him.

In the darkness there was a muffled thud of timid footsteps, and the silhouette of a woman appeared out of the copse. I recognized her, although it was dark — it was Agafya. She came up to us diffidently and stopped, breathing hard. She was breathless, probably not so much from walking as from fear and the unpleasant sensation everyone experiences in wading across a river at night. Seeing near the shanty not one but two persons, she uttered a faint cry and fell back a step.

"Ah . . . that is you!" said Savka, stuffing a scone into his mouth.

"Ye-es . . . I," she muttered, dropping on the ground a bundle of some sort and looking sideways at me. "Yakov sent his greetings to you and told me to give you . . . something here. . . ."

"Come, why tell stories? Yakov!" laughed Savka. "There is no need for lying; the gentleman knows why you have come! Sit down; you shall have supper with us."

Agafya looked sideways at me and sat down irresolutely.

"I thought you weren't coming this evening," Savka said, after a prolonged silence. "Why sit like that? Eat! Or shall I give you a drop of vodka?"

"What an idea!" laughed Agafya; "do you think you have got hold of a drunkard? . . ."

"Oh, drink it up. . . . Your heart will feel warmer. . . . There!"

Savka gave Agafya the crooked glass. She slowly drank the vodka, ate nothing with it, but drew a deep breath when she had finished.

"You've brought something," said Savka, untying the bundle and throwing a condescending, jesting shade into his voice. "Women can never come without bringing something. Ah, pie and potatoes. . . . They live well," he sighed, turning to me. "They are the only ones in the whole village who have got potatoes left from the winter!"

In the darkness I did not see Agafya's face, but
from the movement of her shoulders and head it
seemed to me that she could not take her eyes off
Savka's face. To avoid being the third person
at this tryst, I decided to go for a walk and got
up. But at that moment a nightingale in the wood
suddenly uttered two low contralto notes. Half a
minute later it gave a tiny high trill and then, having
thus tried its voice, began singing. Savka jumped
up and listened.

"It's the same one as yesterday," he said.
" Wait a minute."

And, getting up, he went noiselessly to the wood.

" Why, what do you want with it? " I shouted
out after him, " Stop! "

Savka shook his hand as much as to say, " Don't
shout," and vanished into the darkness. Savka was
an excellent sportsman and fisherman when he liked,
but his talents in this direction were as completely
thrown away as his strength. He was too slothful
to do things in the routine way, and vented his passion for sport in useless tricks. For instance, he
would catch nightingales only with his hands, would
shoot pike with a fowling piece, he would spend
whole hours by the river trying to catch little fish
with a big hook.

Left alone with me, Agafya coughed and passed
her hand several times over her forehead. . . . She
began to feel a little drunk from the vodka.

" How are you getting on, Agasha? " I asked
her, after a long silence, when it began to be awk-
ward to remain mute any longer.

" Very well, thank God. . . . Don't tell anyone, sir, will you? " she added suddenly in a whisper.

" That's all right," I reassured her. " But how reckless you are, Agasha ! . . . What if Yakov finds out? "

" He won't find out."

" But what if he does? "

" No . . . I shall be at home before he is. He is on the line now, and he will come back when the mail train brings him, and from here I can hear when the train's coming. . . ."

Agafya once more passed her hand over her forehead and looked away in the direction in which Savka had vanished. The nightingale was singing. Some night bird flew low down close to the ground and, noticing us, was startled, fluttered its wings and flew across to the other side of the river.

Soon the nightingale was silent, but Savka did not come back. Agafya got up, took a few steps uneasily, and sat down again.

" What is he doing? " she could not refrain from saying. " The train's not coming in to-morrow! I shall have to go away directly."

" Savka," I shouted. " Savka."

I was not answered even by an echo. Agafya moved uneasily and sat down again.

" It's time I was going," she said in an agitated voice. " The train will be here directly! I know when the trains come in."

The poor woman was not mistaken. Before a quarter of an hour had passed a sound was heard in the distance.

Agafya kept her eyes fixed on the copse for a long time and moved her hands impatiently.

" Why, where can he be? " she said, laughing nervously. " Where has the devil carried him? I am going! I really must be going."

Meanwhile the noise was growing more and more distinct. By now one could distinguish the rumble of the wheels from the heavy gasps of the engine. Then we heard the whistle, the train crossed the bridge with a hollow rumble . . . another minute and all was still.

" I'll wait one minute more," said Agafya, sitting down resolutely. " So be it, I'll wait."

At last Savka appeared in the darkness. He walked noiselessly on the crumbling earth of the kitchen gardens and hummed something softly to himself.

" Here's a bit of luck; what do you say to that now? " he said gaily. " As soon as I got up to the bush and began taking aim with my hand it left off singing! Ah, the bald dog! I waited and waited to see when it would begin again, but I had to give it up."

Savka flopped clumsily down to the ground beside Agafya and, to keep his balance, clutched at her waist with both hands.

" Why do you look cross, as though your aunt were your mother? " he asked.

With all his soft-heartedness and good-nature, Savka despised women. He behaved carelessly, condescendingly with them, and even stooped to scornful laughter of their feelings for himself. God knows, perhaps this careless, contemptuous manner was one of the causes of his irresistible attraction for the village Dulcineas. He was handsome and well-built; in his eyes there was always a soft friendliness, even when he was looking at the women he so despised, but the fascination was not to be explained by merely external qualities. Apart from his happy exterior and original manner, one must suppose that the touching position of Savka as an acknowledged failure and an unhappy exile from his own hut to the kitchen gardens also had an influence upon the women.

"Tell the gentleman what you have come here for!" Savka went on, still holding Agafya by the waist. "Come, tell him, you good married woman! Ho-ho! Shall we have another drop of vodka, friend Agasha?"

I got up and, threading my way between the plots, I walked the length of the kitchen garden. The dark beds looked like flattened-out graves. They smelt of dug earth and the tender dampness of plants beginning to be covered with dew. . . . A red light was still gleaming on the left. It winked genially and seemed to smile.

I heard a happy laugh. It was Agafya laughing.

"And the train?" I thought. "The train has come in long ago."

Waiting a little longer, I went back to the shanty. Savka was sitting motionless, his legs crossed like a Turk, and was softly, scarcely audibly humming a song consisting of words of one syllable something like: "Out on you, fie on you . . . I and you."

Agafya, intoxicated by the vodka, by Savka's scornful caresses, and by the stifling warmth of the night, was lying on the earth beside him, pressing her face convulsively to his knees. She was so carried away by her feelings that she did not even notice my arrival.

"Agasha, the train has been in a long time," I said.

"It's time — it's time you were gone," Savka, tossing his head, took up my thought. "What are you sprawling here for? You shameless hussy!"

Agafya started, took her head from his knees, glanced at me, and sank down beside him again.

"You ought to have gone long ago," I said.

Agafya turned round and got up on one knee. . . . She was unhappy. . . . For half a minute her whole figure, as far as I could distinguish it through the darkness, expressed conflict and hesitation. There was an instant when, seeming to come to herself, she drew herself up to get upon her feet, but then some invincible and implacable force seemed to push her whole body, and she sank down beside Savka again.

"Bother him!" she said, with a wild, guttural laugh, and reckless determination, impotence, and pain could be heard in that laugh.

I strolled quietly away to the copse, and from there down to the river, where our fishing lines were set. The river slept. Some soft, fluffy-petalled flower on a tall stalk touched my cheek tenderly like a child who wants to let one know it's awake. To pass the time I felt for one of the lines and pulled

at it. It yielded easily and hung limply — nothing
had been caught. . . . The further bank and the
village could not be seen. A light gleamed in one
hut, but soon went out. I felt my way along the
bank, found a hollow place which I had noticed in
the daylight, and sat down in it as in an arm-chair.
I sat there a long time. . . . I saw the stars begin
to grow misty and lose their brightness; a cool breath
passed over the earth like a faint sigh and touched
the leaves of the slumbering osiers. . . .

"A-ga-fya!" a hollow voice called from the village. "Agafya!"

It was the husband, who had returned home, and
in alarm was looking for his wife in the village.
At that moment there came the sound of unre-
strained laughter: the wife, forgetful of everything,
sought in her intoxication to make up by a few
hours of happiness for the misery awaiting her
next day.

I dropped asleep.

When I woke up Savka was sitting beside me and
lightly shaking my shoulder. The river, the copse,
both banks, green and washed, trees and fields — all
were bathed in bright morning light. Through the
slim trunks of the trees the rays of the newly risen
sun beat upon my back.

"So that's how you catch fish?" laughed Savka.
"Get up!"

I got up, gave a luxurious stretch, and began
greedily drinking in the damp and fragrant air.

"Has Agasha gone?" I asked.

" There she is," said Savka, pointing in the direction of the ford.

I glanced and saw Agafya. Dishevelled, with her kerchief dropping off her head, she was crossing the river, holding up her skirt. Her legs were scarcely moving. . . .

" The cat knows whose meat it has eaten," muttered Savka, screwing up his eyes as he looked at her. " She goes with her tail hanging down. . . . They are sly as cats, these women, and timid as hares. . . . She didn't go, silly thing, in the evening when we told her to! Now she will catch it, and they'll flog me again at the peasant court . . . all on account of the women. . . ."

Agafya stepped upon the bank and went across the fields to the village. At first she walked fairly boldly, but soon terror and excitement got the upper hand; she turned round fearfully, stopped and took breath.

" Yes, you are frightened! " Savka laughed mournfully, looking at the bright green streak left by Agafya in the dewy grass. " She doesn't want to go! Her husband's been standing waiting for her for a good hour. . . . Did you see him? "

Savka said the last words with a smile, but they sent a chill to my heart. In the village, near the furthest hut, Yakov was standing in the road, gazing fixedly at his returning wife. He stood without stirring, and was as motionless as a post. What was he thinking as he looked at her? What words was he preparing to greet her with? Agafya stood still a little while, looked round once more as though expecting help from us, and went on.   I have never seen anyone, drunk or sober, move as she did. Agafya seemed to be shrivelled up by her husband's eyes.   At one time she moved in zigzags, then she moved her feet up and down without going forward, bending her knees and stretching out her hands, then she staggered back.   When she had gone another hundred paces she looked round once more and sat down.

"You ought at least to hide behind a bush . . ." I said to Savka.   "If the husband sees you . . ."

"He knows, anyway, who it is Agafya has come from. . . . The women don't go to the kitchen garden at night for cabbages — we all know that."

I glanced at Savka's face.   It was pale and puckered up with a look of fastidious pity such as one sees in the faces of people watching tortured animals.

"What's fun for the cat is tears for the mouse . . ." he muttered.

Agafya suddenly jumped up, shook her head, and with a bold step went towards her husband.   She had evidently plucked up her courage and made up her mind.

1886

AT CHRISTMAS TIME

AT CHRISTMAS TIME

I

" WHAT shall I write? " said Yegor, and he dipped his pen in the ink.

Vasilisa had not seen her daughter for four years. Her daughter Yefimya had gone after her wedding to Petersburg, had sent them two letters, and since then seemed to vanish out of their lives; there had been no sight nor sound of her. And whether the old woman were milking her cow at dawn, or heating her stove, or dozing at night, she was always thinking of one and the same thing — what was happening to Yefimya, whether she were alive out yonder. She ought to have sent a letter, but the old father could not write, and there was no one to write.

But now Christmas had come, and Vasilisa could not bear it any longer, and went to the tavern to Yegor, the brother of the innkeeper's wife, who had sat in the tavern doing nothing ever since he came back from the army; people said that he could write letters very well if he were properly paid. Vasilisa talked to the cook at the tavern, ·then to the mistress of the house, then to Yegor himself. They agreed upon fifteen kopecks.

And now — it happened on the second day of the holidays, in the tavern kitchen — Yegor was sitting at the table, holding the pen in his hand. Vasilisa was standing before him, pondering with an expression of anxiety and woe on her face. Pyotr, her husband, a very thin old man with a brownish bald patch, had come with her; he stood looking straight before him like a blind man. On the stove a piece of pork was being braised in a saucepan; it was spurting and hissing, and seemed to be actually saying: " Flu-flu-flu." It was stifling.

"What am I to write? " Yegor asked again.

"What? " asked Vasilisa, looking at him angrily and suspiciously. " Don't worry me! You are not writing for nothing; no fear, you'll be paid for it. Come, write: ' To our dear son-in-law, Andrey Hrisanfitch, and to our only beloved daughter, Yefimya Petrovna, with our love we send a low bow and our parental blessing abiding for ever.' "

" Written; fire away."

" ' And we wish them a happy Christmas; we are alive and well, and I wish you the same, please the Lord . . . the Heavenly King.' "

Vasilisa pondered and exchanged glances with the old man.

" ' And I wish you the same, please the Lord . . . the Heavenly King,' " she repeated, beginning to cry.

She could say nothing more. And yet before, when she lay awake thinking at night, it had seemed to her that she could not get all she had to say into a dozen letters. Since the time when her daughter had gone away with her husband much water had flowed into the sea, the old people had lived feeling bereaved, and sighed heavily at night as though they had buried their daughter. And how many events had occurred in the village since then, how many marriages and deaths! How long the winters had been! How long the nights!

"It's hot," said Yegor, unbuttoning his waistcoat. "It must be seventy degrees. What more?" he asked.

The old people were silent.

"What does your son-in-law do in Petersburg?" asked Yegor.

"He was a soldier, my good friend," the old man answered in a weak voice. "He left the service at the same time as you did. He was a soldier, and now, to be sure, he is at Petersburg at a hydropathic establishment. The doctor treats the sick with water. So he, to be sure, is house-porter at the doctor's."

"Here it is written down," said the old woman, taking a letter out of her pocket. "We got it from Yefimya, goodness knows when. Maybe they are no longer in this world."

Yegor thought a little and began writing rapidly:

"At the present time"— he wrote —" since your destiny through your own doing allotted you to the Military Career, we counsel you to look into the Code of Disciplinary Offences and Fundamental Laws of the War Office, and you will see in that law the Civilization of the Officials of the War Office."

He wrote and kept reading aloud what was written, while Vasilisa considered what she ought to write: how great had been their want the year before, how their corn had not lasted even till Christmas, how they had to sell their cow. She ought to ask for money, ought to write that the old father was often ailing and would soon no doubt give up his soul to God . . . but how to express this in words? What must be said first and what afterwards?

"Take note," Yegor went on writing, "in volume five of the Army Regulations soldier is a common noun and a proper one, a soldier of the first rank is called a general, and of the last a private. . . ."

The old man stirred his lips and said softly:

"It would be all right to have a look at the grandchildren."

"What grandchildren?" asked the old woman, and she looked angrily at him; "perhaps there are none."

"Well, but perhaps there are. Who knows?"

"And thereby you can judge," Yegor hurried on, "what is the enemy without and what is the enemy within. The foremost of our enemies within is Bacchus." The pen squeaked, executing upon the paper flourishes like fish-hooks. Yegor hastened and read over every line several times. He sat on a stool sprawling his broad feet under the table, well-fed, bursting with health, with a coarse animal face and a red bull neck. He was vulgarity itself: coarse, conceited, invincible, proud of having been born and bred in a pot-house; and Vasilisa quite understood the vulgarity, but could not express it in words, and could only look angrily and suspiciously at Yegor. Her head was beginning to ache, and her thoughts were in confusion from the sound of his voice and his unintelligible words, from the heat and the stuffiness, and she said nothing and thought nothing, but simply waited for him to finish scribbling. But the old man looked with full confidence. He believed in his old woman who had brought him there, and in Yegor; and when he had mentioned the hydropathic establishment it could be seen that he believed in the establishment and the healing efficacy of water.

Having finished the letter, Yegor got up and read the whole of it through from the beginning. The old man did not understand, but he nodded his head trustfully.

"That's all right; it is smooth . . ." he said. "God give you health. That's all right. . . ."

They laid on the table three five-kopeck pieces and went out of the tavern; the old man looked immovably straight before him as though he were blind, and perfect trustfulness was written on his face; but as Vasilisa came out of the tavern she waved angrily at the dog, and said angrily:

"Ugh, the plague."

The old woman did not sleep all night; she was disturbed by thoughts, and at daybreak she got up, said her prayers, and went to the station to send off the letter.

It was between eight and nine miles to the station.

II

Dr. B. O. Mozelweiser's hydropathic establishment worked on New Year's Day exactly as on
ordinary days; the only difference was that the porter, Andrey Hrisanfitch, had on a uniform with new
braiding, his boots had an extra polish, and he
greeted every visitor with "A Happy New Year
to you!"

It was the morning; Andrey Hrisanfitch was
standing at the door, reading the newspaper.   Just
at ten o'clock there arrived a general, one of the
habitual visitors, and directly after him the postman; Andrey Hrisanfitch helped the general off with
his great-coat, and said:

"A Happy New Year to your Excellency!"

"Thank you, my good fellow; the same to you."

And at the top of the stairs the general asked,
nodding towards the door (he asked the same question every day and always forgot the answer):

"And what is there in that room?"

"The massage room, your Excellency."

When the general's steps had died away Andrey
Hrisanfitch looked at the post that had come, and
found one addressed to himself. He tore it open,
read several lines, then, looking at the newspaper,
he walked without haste to his own room, which
was downstairs close by at the end of the passage.
His wife Yefimya was sitting on the bed, feeding
her baby; another child, the eldest, was standing

by, laying its curly head on her knee; a third was
asleep on the bed.

Going into the room, Andrey gave his wife the
letter and said:

" From the country, I suppose."

Then he walked out again without taking his
eyes from the paper. He could hear Yefimya with
a shaking voice reading the first lines. She read
them and could read no more; these lines were
enough for her. She burst into tears, and hugging
her eldest child, kissing him, she began saying —
and it was hard to say whether she were laughing
or crying:

" It's from granny, from grandfather," she said.
" From the country. . . . The Heavenly Mother,
Saints and Martyrs! The snow lies heaped up under the roofs now . . . the trees are as white as
white. The boys slide on little sledges . . . and
dear old bald grandfather is on the stove . . . and
there is a little yellow dog. . . . My own darlings! "

Andrey Hrisanfitch, hearing this, recalled that his
wife had on three or four occasions given him letters
and asked him to send them to the country, but some
important business had always prevented him; he
had not sent them, and the letters somehow got lost.

" And little hares run about in the fields," Yefimya
went on chanting, kissing her boy and shedding tears.
" Grandfather is kind and gentle; granny is good,
too — kind-hearted. They are warm-hearted in the
country, they are God-fearing . . . and there is a
little church in the village; the peasants sing in the

choir.   Queen of Heaven, Holy Mother and Defender, take us away from here ! "

Andrey Hrisanfitch returned to his room to smoke
a little till there was another ring at the door, and
Yefimya ceased speaking, subsided, and wiped her
eyes, though her lips were still quivering.   She was
very much frightened of him — oh, how frightened
of him !   She trembled and was reduced to terror by
the sound of his steps, by the look in his eyes, and
dared not utter a word in his presence.

Andrey Hrisanfitch lighted a cigarette, but at
that very moment there was a ring from upstairs.
He put out his cigarette, and, assuming a very grave
face, hastened to his front door.

The general was coming downstairs, fresh and
rosy from his bath.

" And what is there in that room ? " he asked,
pointing to a door.

Andrey Hrisanfitch put his hands down swiftly
to the seams of his trousers, and pronounced loudly:

" Charcot douche, your Excellency ! "

1900

GUSEV

GUSEV

I

IT was getting dark; it would soon be night.

Gusev, a discharged soldier, sat up in his hammock and said in an undertone:

" I say, Pavel Ivanitch. A soldier at Sutchan told me: while they were sailing a big fish came into collision with their ship and stove a hole in it."

The nondescript individual whom he was addressing, and whom everyone in the ship's hospital called Pavel Ivanitch, was silent, as though he had not heard.

And again a stillness followed. . . . The wind frolicked with the rigging, the screw throbbed, the waves lashed, the hammocks creaked, but the ear had long ago become accustomed to these sounds, and it seemed that everything around was asleep and silent. It was dreary. The three invalids — two soldiers and a sailor — who had been playing cards all the day were asleep and talking in their dreams.

It seemed as though the ship were beginning to rock. The hammock slowly rose and fell under Gusev, as though it were heaving a sigh, and this was repeated once, twice, three times. . . . Something crashed on to the floor with a clang: it must have been a jug falling down.

"The wind has broken loose from its chain . . ." said Gusev, listening.

This time Pavel Ivanitch cleared his throat and answered irritably:

"One minute a vessel's running into a fish, the next, the wind's breaking loose from its chain. . . . Is the wind a beast that it can break loose from its chain?"

"That's how christened folk talk."

"They are as ignorant as you are then. . . . They say all sorts of things. One must keep a head on one's shoulders and use one's reason. You are a senseless creature."

Pavel Ivanitch was subject to sea-sickness. When the sea was rough he was usually ill-humoured, and the merest trifle would make him irritable. And in Gusev's opinion there was absolutely nothing to be vexed about. What was there strange or wonderful, for instance, in the fish or in the wind's breaking loose from its chain? Suppose the fish were as big as a mountain and its back were as hard as a sturgeon: and in the same way, supposing that away yonder at the end of the world there stood great stone walls and the fierce winds were chained up to the walls . . . if they had not broken loose, why did they tear about all over the sea like maniacs, and struggle to escape like dogs? If they were not chained up, what did become of them when it was calm?

Gusev pondered for a long time about fishes as big as a mountain and stout, rusty chains, then he began to feel dull and thought of his native place to which he was returning after five years' service in the East. He pictured an immense pond covered with snow. . . . On one side of the pond the red-brick building of the potteries with a tall chimney and clouds of black smoke; on the other side — a village. . . . His brother Alexey comes out in a sledge from the fifth yard from the end; behind him sits his little son Vanka in big felt over-boots, and his little girl Akulka, also in big felt boots. Alexey has been drinking, Vanka is laughing, Akulka's face he could not see, she had muffled herself up.

" You never know, he'll get the children frozen . . ." thought Gusev. " Lord send them sense and judgment that they may honour their father and mother and not be wiser than their parents."

" They want re-soleing," a delirious sailor says in a bass voice. " Yes, yes ! "

Gusev's thoughts break off, and instead of a pond there suddenly appears apropos of nothing a huge bull's head without eyes, and the horse and sledge are not driving along, but are whirling round and round in a cloud of smoke. But still he was glad he had seen his own folks. He held his breath from delight, shudders ran all over him, and his fingers twitched.

" The Lord let us meet again," he muttered feverishly, but he at once opened his eyes and sought in the darkness for water.

He drank and lay back, and again the sledge was moving, then again the bull's head without eyes, smoke, clouds. . . . And so on till daybreak.

II

The first outline visible in the darkness was a blue circle — the little round window; then little by little Gusev could distinguish his neighbour in the next hammock, Pavel Ivanitch. The man slept sitting up, as he could not breathe lying down. His face was grey, his nose was long and sharp, his eyes looked huge from the terrible thinness of his face, his temples were sunken, his beard was skimpy, his hair was long. . . . Looking at him you could not make out of what class he was, whether he were a gentleman, a merchant, or a peasant. Judging from his expression and his long hair he might have been a hermit or a lay brother in a monastery — but if one listened to what he said it seemed that he could not be a monk. He was worn out by his cough and his illness and by the stifling heat, and breathed with difficulty, moving his parched lips. Noticing that Gusev was looking at him he turned his face towards him and said:

"I begin to guess. . . . Yes. . . . I understand it all perfectly now."

"What do you understand, Pavel Ivanitch?"

"I'll tell you. . . . It has always seemed to me strange that terribly ill as you are you should be here in a steamer where it is so hot and stifling and we are always being tossed up and down, where, in fact, everything threatens you with death; now it is all clear to me. . . . Yes. . . . Your doctors put you on the steamer to get rid of you. They

get sick of looking after poor brutes like you. . . .
You don't pay them anything, they have a bother
with you, and you damage their records with your
deaths — so, of course, you are brutes! It's not
difficult to get rid of you. . . . All that is necessary
is, in the first place, to have no conscience or hu-
manity, and, secondly, to deceive the steamer authorities. The first condition need hardly be considered,
in that respect we are artists; and one can always
succeed in the second with a little practice. In a
crowd of four hundred healthy soldiers and sailors
half a dozen sick ones are not conspicuous; well,
they drove you all on to the steamer, mixed you with
the healthy ones, hurriedly counted you over, and in
the confusion nothing amiss was noticed, and when
the steamer had started they saw that there were
paralytics and consumptives in the last stage lying
about on the deck. . . ."

Gusev did not understand Pavel Ivanitch; but supposing he was being blamed, he said in self-defence:

" I lay on the deck because I had not the strength
to stand; when we were unloaded from the barge
on to the ship I caught a fearful chill."

" It's revolting," Pavel Ivanitch went on. " The
worst of it is they know perfectly well that you can't
last out the long journey, and yet they put you here.
Supposing you get as far as the Indian Ocean, what
then? It's horrible to think of it. . . . And that's
their gratitude for your faithful, irreproachable
service ! "

Pavel Ivanitch's eyes looked angry; he frowned
contemptuously and said, gasping:

"Those are the people who ought to be plucked in the newspapers till the feathers fly in all directions."

The two sick soldiers and the sailor were awake and already playing cards. The sailor was half reclining in his hammock, the soldiers were sitting near him on the floor in the most uncomfortable attitudes. One of the soldiers had his right arm in a sling, and the hand was swathed up in a regular bundle so that he held his cards under his right arm or in the crook of his elbow while he played with the left. The ship was rolling heavily. They could not stand up, nor drink tea, nor take their medicines.

"Were you an officer's servant?" Pavel Ivanitch asked Gusev.

"Yes, an officer's servant."

"My God, my God!" said Pavel Ivanitch, and he shook his head mournfully. "To tear a man out of his home, drag him twelve thousand miles away, then to drive him into consumption and . . . and what is it all for, one wonders? To turn him into a servant for some Captain Kopeikin or midshipman Dirka! How logical!"

"It's not hard work, Pavel Ivanitch. You get up in the morning and clean the boots, get the samovar, sweep the rooms, and then you have nothing more to do. The lieutenant is all the day drawing plans, and if you like you can say your prayers, if you like you can read a book or go out into the street. God grant everyone such a life."

"Yes, very nice, the lieutenant draws plans all

the day and you sit in the kitchen and pine for home. . . . Plans indeed! . . . It is not plans that matter, but a human life. Life is not given twice, it must be treated mercifully."

"Of course, Pavel Ivanitch, a bad man gets no mercy anywhere, neither at home nor in the army, but if you live as you ought and obey orders, who has any need to insult you? The officers are educated gentlemen, they understand. . . . In five years I was never once in prison, and I was never struck a blow, so help me God, but once."

"What for?"

"For fighting. I have a heavy hand, Pavel Ivanitch. Four Chinamen came into our yard; they were bringing firewood or something, I don't remember. Well, I was bored and I knocked them about a bit, one's nose began bleeding, damn the fellow. . . . The lieutenant saw it through the little window, he was angry and gave me a box on the ear."

"Foolish, pitiful man . . ." whispered Pavel Ivanitch. "You don't understand anything."

He was utterly exhausted by the tossing of the ship and closed his eyes; his head alternately fell back and dropped forward on his breast. Several times he tried to lie down but nothing came of it; his difficulty in breathing prevented it.

"And what did you hit the four Chinamen for?" he asked a little while afterwards.

"Oh, nothing. They came into the yard and I hit them."

And a stillness followed. . . . The card-players

had been playing for two hours with enthusiasm and loud abuse of one another, but the motion of the ship overcame them, too; they threw aside the cards and lay down. Again Gusev saw the big pond, the brick building, the village. . . . Again the sledge was coming along, again Vanka was laughing and Akulka, silly little thing, threw open her fur coat and stuck her feet out, as much as to say: "Look, good people, my snowboots are not like Vanka's, they are new ones."

"Five years old, and she has no sense yet," Gusev muttered in delirium. "Instead of kicking your legs you had better come and get your soldier uncle a drink. I will give you something nice."

Then Andron with a flintlock gun on his shoulder was carrying a hare he had killed, and he was followed by the decrepit old Jew Isaitchik, who offers to barter the hare for a piece of soap; then the black calf in the shed, then Domna sewing at a shirt and crying about something, and then again the bull's head without eyes, black smoke. . . .

Overhead someone gave a loud shout, several sailors ran by, they seemed to be dragging something bulky over the deck, something fell with a crash. Again they ran by. . . . Had something gone wrong? Gusev raised his head, listened, and saw that the two soldiers and the sailor were playing cards again; Pavel Ivanitch was sitting up moving his lips. It was stifling, one hadn't strength to breathe, one was thirsty, the water was warm, disgusting. The ship heaved as much as ever.

Suddenly something strange happened to one of

the soldiers playing cards. . . . He called hearts diamonds, got muddled in his score, and dropped his cards, then with a frightened, foolish smile looked round at all of them.

" I shan't be a minute, mates, I'll . . ." he said, and lay down on the floor.

Everybody was amazed. They called to him, he did not answer.

" Stephan, maybe you are feeling bad, eh? " the soldier with his arm in a sling asked him. " Perhaps we had better bring the priest, eh? "

" Have a drink of water, Stepan . . ." said the sailor. " Here, lad, drink."

" Why are you knocking the jug against his teeth? " said Gusev angrily. " Don't you see, turnip head? '

" What? "

" What? " Gusev repeated, mimicking him. " There is no breath in him, he is dead! That's what! What nonsensical people, Lord have mercy on us . . . ! "

III

The ship was not rocking and Pavel Ivanitch was more cheerful. He was no longer ill-humoured. His face had a boastful, defiant, mocking expression. He looked as though he wanted to say: " Yes, in a minute I will tell you something that will make you split your sides with laughing." The little round window was open and a soft breeze was blowing on Pavel Ivanitch. There was a sound of

voices, of the plash of oars in the water. . . . Just
under the little window someone began droning in
a high, unpleasant voice: no doubt it was a China-
man singing.

"Here we are in the harbour," said Pavel Ivanitch, smiling ironically. "Only another month and
we shall be in Russia. Well, worthy gentlemen and
warriors! I shall arrive at Odessa and from there
go straight to Harkov. In Harkov I have a friend,
a literary man. I shall go to him and say, ' Come,
old man, put aside your horrid subjects, ladies'
amours and the beauties of nature, and show up
human depravity.' "

For a minute he pondered, then said:

"Gusev, do you know how I took them in?"

"Took in whom, Pavel Ivanitch?"

"Why, these fellows. . . . You know that on
this steamer there is only a first-class and a third-
class, and they only allow peasants — that is the
riff-raff — to go in the third. If you have got on
a reefer jacket and have the faintest resemblance
to a gentleman or a bourgeois you must go first-
class, if you please. You must fork out five hundred roubles if you die for it. Why, I ask, have
you made such a rule? Do you want to raise the
prestige of educated Russians thereby? Not a bit
of it. We don't let you go third-class simply because a decent person can't go third-class; it is·very
horrible and disgusting. Yes, indeed. I am very
grateful for such solicitude for decent people's wel-
fare. But in any case, whether it is nasty there or
nice, five hundred roubles I haven't got. I haven't

pilfered government money. I haven't exploited the natives, I haven't trafficked in contraband, I have flogged no one to death, so judge whether I have the right to travel first-class and even less to reckon myself of the educated class? But you won't catch them with logic. . . . One has to resort to deception. I put on a workman's coat and high boots, I assumed a drunken, servile mug and went to the agents: 'Give us a little ticket, your honour,' said I. . . ."

"Why, what class do you belong to?" asked a sailor.

"Clerical. My father was an honest priest, he always told the great ones of the world the truth to their faces; and he had a great deal to put up with in consequence."

Pavel Ivanitch was exhausted with talking and gasped for breath, but still went on:

"Yes, I always tell people the truth to their faces. I am not afraid of anyone or anything. There is a vast difference between me and all of you in that respect. You are in darkness, you are blind, crushed; you see nothing and what you do see you don't understand. . . . You are told the wind breaks loose from its chain, that you are beasts, Petchenyegs, and you believe it; they punch you in the neck, you kiss their hands; some animal in a sable-lined coat robs you and then tips you fifteen kopecks and you: 'Let me kiss your hand, sir.' You are pariahs, pitiful people. . . . I am a different sort. My eyes are open, I see it all as clearly as a hawk or an eagle when it floats over the earth,

and I understand it all. I am a living protest. I
see irresponsible tyranny — I protest. I see cant
and hypocrisy — I protest. I see swine triumphant
— I protest. And I cannot be suppressed, no Span-
ish Inquisition can make me hold my tongue. No.
. . . Cut out my tongue and I would protest in
dumb show; shut me up in a cellar — I will shout
from it to be heard half a mile away, or I will starve
myself to death that they may have another weight
on their black consciences. Kill me and I will
haunt them with my ghost. All my acquaintances
say to me: 'You are a most insufferable person,
Pavel Ivanitch.' I am proud of such a reputation.
I have served three years in the far East, and I
shall be remembered there for a hundred years:
I had rows with everyone. My friends write to me
from Russia, ' Don't come back,' but here I am
going back to spite them . . . yes. . . . That is
life as I understand it. That is what one can call
life."

Gusev was looking at the little window and was
not listening. A boat was swaying on the transparent, soft, turquoise water all bathed in hot, dazzling sunshine. In it there were naked Chinamen
holding up cages with canaries and calling out:

" It sings, it sings! "

Another boat knocked against the first; the steam
cutter darted by. And then there came another boat
with a fat Chinaman sitting in it, eating rice with
little sticks.

Languidly the water heaved, languidly the white
seagulls floated over it.

" I should like to give that fat fellow one in the neck," thought Gusev, gazing at the stout China-man, with a yawn.

He dozed off, and it seemed to him that all nature was dozing, too. Time flew swiftly by; imperceptibly the day passed, imperceptibly the darkness came on. . . . The steamer was no longer standing still, but moving on further.

IV

Two days passed, Pavel Ivanitch lay down instead of sitting up; his eyes were closed, his nose seemed to have grown sharper.

" Pavel Ivanitch," Gusev called to him. " Hey, Pavel Ivanitch."

Pavel Ivanitch opened his eyes and moved his lips.

" Are you feeling bad? "

" No . . . it's nothing . . ." answered Pavel Ivanitch, gasping. " Nothing; on the contrary . . . I am rather better. . . . You see I can lie down. . . . I am a little easier. . . ."

" Well, thank God for that, Pavel Ivanitch."

" When I compare myself with you I am sorry for you . . . poor fellow. My lungs are all right, it is only a stomach cough. . . . I can stand hell, let alone the Red Sea. Besides I take a critical attitude to my illness and to the medicines they give me for it. While you . . . you are in darkness. . . . It's hard for you, very, very hard! "

The ship was not rolling, it was calm, but as hot

and stifling as a bath-house; it was not only hard to speak but even hard to listen. Gusev hugged his knees, laid his head on them and thought of his home. Good heavens, what a relief it was to think of snow and cold in that stifling heat! You drive in a sledge, all at once the horses take fright at something and bolt. . . . Regardless of the road, the ditches, the ravines, they dash like mad things, right through the village, over the pond by the pottery works, out across the open fields. " Hold on," the pottery hands and the peasants shout, meeting them. " Hold on." But why? Let the keen, cold wind beat in one's face and bite one's hands; let the lumps of snow, kicked up by the horses' hoofs, fall on one's cap, on one's back, down one's collar, on one's chest; let the runners ring on the snow, and the traces and the sledge be smashed, deuce take them one and all! And how delightful when the sledge upsets and you go flying full tilt into a drift, face downwards in the snow, and then you get up white all over with icicles on your moustaches; no cap, no gloves, your belt undone. . . . People laugh, the dogs bark. . . .

Pavel Ivanitch half opened one eye, looked at Gusev with it, and asked softly:

" Gusev, did your commanding officer steal? "

" Who can tell, Pavel Ivanitch! We can't say, it didn't reach us."

And after that a long time passed in silence. Gusev brooded, muttered something in delirium, and kept drinking water; it was hard for him to talk and hard to listen, and he was afraid of being talked

to. An hour passed, a second, a third; evening came
on, then night, but he did not notice it. He still
sat dreaming of the frost.

There was a sound as though someone came into
the hospital, and voices were audible, but a few minutes passed and all was still again.

" The Kingdom of Heaven and eternal peace,"
said the soldier with his arm in a sling. " He was
an uncomfortable man."

" What? " asked Gusev. " Who? "

" He is dead, they have just carried him up."

" Oh, well," muttered Gusev, yawning, " the Kingdom of Heaven be his."

" What do you think? " the soldier with his arm
in a sling asked Gusev. " Will he be in the Kingdom of Heaven or not? "

" Who is it you are talking about? "

" Pavel Ivanitch."

" He will be . . . he suffered so long. And there
is another thing, he belonged to the clergy, and the
priests always have a lot of relations. Their prayers will save him."

The soldier with the sling sat down on a hammock near Gusev and said in an undertone:

" And you, Gusev, are not long for this world.
You will never get to Russia."

" Did the doctor or his assistant say so? " asked
Gusev.

" It isn't that they said so, but one can see it. . . .
One can see directly when a man's going to die.
You don't eat, you don't drink; it's dreadful to see
how thin you've got. It's consumption, in fact. I

say it, not to upset you, but because maybe you
would like to have the sacrament and extreme unc-
tion.   And if you have any money you had better
give it to the senior officer."

"I haven't written home . . ." Gusev sighed.
"I shall die and they won't know."

"They'll hear of it," the sick sailor brought out
in a bass voice.   "When you die they will put it
down in the *Gazette,* at Odessa they will send in a
report to the commanding officer there and he will
send it to the parish or somewhere. . . ."

Gusev began to be uneasy after such a conversation and to feel a vague yearning.   He drank water — it was not that; he dragged himself to the
window and breathed the hot, moist air — it was
not that; he tried to think of home, of the frost —
it was not that. . . . At last it seemed to him one
minute longer in the ward and he would certainly
expire.

"It's stifling, mates . . ." he said.   "I'll go on
deck.   Help me up, for Christ's sake."

"All right," assented the soldier with the sling.
"I'll carry you, you can't walk, hold on to my neck."

Gusev put his arm round the soldier's neck, the
latter put his unhurt arm round him and carried
him up.   On the deck sailors and time-expired soldiers were lying asleep side by side; there were so
many of them it was difficult to pass.

"Stand down," the soldier with the sling said
softly.   "Follow me quietly, hold on to my
shirt. . . ."

It was dark.   There was no light on deck, nor

on the masts, nor anywhere on the sea around. At the furthest end of the ship the man on watch was standing perfectly still like a statue, and it looked as though he were asleep. It seemed as though the steamer were abandoned to itself and were going at its own will.

"Now they will throw Pavel Ivanitch into the sea," said the soldier with the sling. "In a sack and then into the water."

"Yes, that's the rule."

"But it's better to lie at home in the earth. Anyway, your mother comes to the grave and weeps."

"Of course."

There was a smell of hay and of dung. There were oxen standing with drooping heads by the ship's rail. One, two, three; eight of them! And there was a little horse. Gusev put out his hand to stroke it, but it shook its head, showed its teeth, and tried to bite his sleeve.

"Damned brute . . ." said Gusev angrily.

The two of them, he and the soldier, threaded their way to the head of the ship, then stood at the rail and looked up and down. Overhead deep sky, bright stars, peace and stillness, exactly as at home in the village, below darkness and disorder. The tall waves were resounding, no one could tell why. Whichever wave you looked at each one was trying to rise higher than all the rest and to chase and crush the next one; after it a third as fierce and hideous flew noisily, with a glint of light on its white crest.

The sea has no sense and no pity. If the steamer

had been smaller and not made of thick iron, the waves would have crushed it to pieces without the slightest compunction, and would have devoured all the people in it with no distinction of saints or sinners. The steamer had the same cruel and meaningless expression. This monster with its huge beak was dashing onwards, cutting millions of waves in its path; it had no fear of the darkness nor the wind, nor of space, nor of solitude, caring for nothing, and if the ocean had its people, this monster would have crushed them, too, without distinction of saints or sinners.

" Where are we now? " asked Gusev.

" I don't know. We must be in the ocean."

" There is no sight of land. . . ."

" No indeed! They say we shan't see it for seven days."

The two soldiers watched the white foam with the phosphorus light on it and were silent, thinking. Gusev was the first to break the silence.

" There is nothing to be afraid of," he said, " only one is full of dread as though one were sitting in a dark forest; but if, for instance, they let a boat down on to the water this minute and an officer ordered me to go a hundred miles over the sea to catch fish, I'd go. Or, let's say, if a Christian were to fall into the water this minute, I'd go in after him. A German or a Chinaman I wouldn't save, but I'd go in after a Christian."

" And are you afraid to die? "

" Yes. I am sorry for the folks at home. My brother at home, you know, isn't steady; he drinks, he beats his wife for nothing, he does not honour his parents. Everything will go to ruin without me, and father and my old mother will be begging their bread, I shouldn't wonder. But my legs won't bear me, brother, and it's hot here. Let's go to sleep."

V

Gusev went back to the ward and got into his hammock. He was again tormented by a vague craving, and he could not make out what he wanted. There was an oppression on his chest, a throbbing in his head, his mouth was so dry that it was difficult for him to move his tongue. He dozed, and murmured in his sleep, and, worn out with nightmares, his cough, and the stifling heat, towards morning he fell into a sound sleep. He dreamed that they were just taking the bread out of the oven in the barracks and he climbed into the stove and had a steam bath in it, lashing himself with a bunch of birch twigs. He slept for two days, and at midday on the third two sailors came down and carried him out.

He was sewn up in sailcloth and to make him heavier they put with him two iron weights. Sewn up in the sailcloth he looked like a carrot or a radish: broad at the head and narrow at the feet. . . . Before sunset they brought him up to the deck and put him on a plank; one end of the plank lay on the side of the ship, the other on a box, placed on a stool. Round him stood the soldiers and the officers with their caps off.

" Blessed be the Name of the Lord . . ." the priest began. " As it was in the beginning, is now, and ever shall be."

" Amen," chanted three sailors.

The soldiers and the officers crossed themselves and looked away at the waves. It was strange that a man should be sewn up in sailcloth and should soon be flying into the sea. Was it possible that such a thing might happen to anyone?

The priest strewed earth upon Gusev and bowed down. They sang " Eternal Memory."

The man on watch duty tilted up the end of the plank, Gusev slid off and flew head foremost, turned a somersault in the air and splashed into the sea. He was covered with foam and for a moment looked as though he were wrapped in lace, but the minute passed and he disappeared in the waves.

He went rapidly towards the bottom. Did he reach it? It was said to be three miles to the bottom. After sinking sixty or seventy feet, he began moving more and more slowly, swaying rhythmically, as though he were hesitating and, carried along by the current, moved more rapidly sideways than downwards.

Then he was met by a shoal of the fish called harbour pilots. Seeing the dark body the fish stopped as though petrified, and suddenly turned round and disappeared. In less than a minute they flew back swift as an arrow to Gusev, and began zig-zagging round him in the water.

After that another dark body appeared. It was a shark. It swam under Gusev with dignity and no show of interest, as though it did not notice him, and sank down upon its back, then it turned belly upwards, basking in the warm, transparent water and languidly opened its jaws with two rows of teeth. The harbour pilots are delighted, they stop to see what will come next. After playing a little with the body the shark nonchalantly puts its jaws under it, cautiously touches it with its teeth, and the sail-cloth is rent its full length from head to foot; one of the weights falls out and frightens the harbour pilots, and striking the shark on the ribs goes rapidly to the bottom.

Overhead at this time the clouds are massed together on the side where the sun is setting; one cloud like a triumphal arch, another like a lion, a third like a pair of scissors. . . . From behind the clouds a broad, green shaft of light pierces through and stretches to the middle of the sky; a little later another, violet-coloured, lies beside it; next that, one of gold, then one rose-coloured. . . . The sky turns a soft lilac. Looking at this gorgeous, enchanted sky, at first the ocean scowls, but soon it, too, takes tender, joyous, passionate colours for which it is hard to find a name in human speech.

1890

THE STUDENT

THE STUDENT

AT first the weather was fine and still. The thrushes were calling, and in the swamps close by something alive droned pitifully with a sound like blowing into an empty bottle. A snipe flew by, and the shot aimed at it rang out with a gay, resounding note in the spring air. But when it began to get dark in the forest a cold, penetrating wind blew inappropriately from the east, and everything sank into silence. Needles of ice stretched across the pools, and it felt cheerless, remote, and lonely in the forest. There was a whiff of winter.

Ivan Velikopolsky, the son of a sacristan, and a student of the clerical academy, returning home from shooting, walked all the time by the path in the water-side meadow. His fingers were numb and his face was burning with the wind. It seemed to him that the cold that had suddenly come on had destroyed the order and harmony of things, that nature itself felt ill at ease, and that was why the evening darkness was falling more rapidly than usual. All around it was deserted and peculiarly gloomy. The only light was one gleaming in the widows' gardens near the river; the village, over three miles away, and everything in the distance all round was plunged in the cold evening mist. The student remembered that, as he went out from the house, his mother was sitting barefoot on the floor in the entry, cleaning the samovar, while his father lay on the stove coughing; as it was Good Friday nothing had been cooked, and the student was terribly hungry. And now, shrinking from the cold, he thought that just such a wind had blown in the days of Rurik and in the time of Ivan the Terrible and Peter, and in their time there had been just the same desperate poverty and hunger, the same thatched roofs with holes in them, ignorance, misery, the same desolation around, the same darkness, the same feeling of oppression — all these had existed, did exist, and would exist, and the lapse of a thousand years would make life no better. And he did not want to go home.

The gardens were called the widows' because they were kept by two widows, mother and daughter. A camp fire was burning brightly with a crackling sound, throwing out light far around on the ploughed earth. The widow Vasilisa, a tall, fat old woman in a man's coat, was standing by and looking thoughtfully into the fire; her daughter Lukerya, a little pock-marked woman with a stupid-looking face, was sitting on the ground, washing a caldron and spoons. Apparently they had just had supper. There was a sound of men's voices; it was the labourers watering their horses at the river.

" Here you have winter back again," said the student, going up to the camp fire. " Good evening."

Vasilisa started, but at once recognized him and smiled cordially.

" I did not know you; God bless you," she said. " You'll be rich."

They talked. Vasilisa, a woman of experience, who had been in service with the gentry, first as a wet-nurse, afterwards as a children's nurse, expressed herself with refinement, and a soft, sedate smile never left her face; her daughter Lukerya, a village peasant woman, who had been crushed by her husband, simply screwed up her eyes at the student and said nothing, and she had a strange expression like that of a deaf mute.

" At just such a fire the Apostle Peter warmed himself," said the student, stretching out his hands to the fire, " so it must have been cold then, too. Ah, what a terrible night it must have been, granny! An utterly dismal long night! "

He looked round at the darkness, shook his head abruptly and asked:

" No doubt you have been at the reading of the Twelve Gospels? "

" Yes, I have," answered Vasilisa.

" If you remember at the Last Supper Peter said to Jesus, ' I am ready to go with Thee into darkness and unto death.' And our Lord answered him thus: ' I say unto thee, Peter, before the cock croweth thou wilt have denied Me thrice.' After the supper Jesus went through the agony of death in the garden and prayed, and poor Peter was weary in spirit and faint, his eyelids were heavy and he could not struggle against sleep. He fell asleep. Then you heard how Judas the same night kissed Jesus and betrayed Him to His tormentors. They took Him bound to the high priest and beat Him, while Peter, exhausted, worn out with misery and alarm, hardly awake, you know, feeling that something awful was just going to happen on earth, followed behind. . . . He loved Jesus passionately, intensely, and now he saw from far off how He was beaten. . . ."

Lukerya left the spoons and fixed an immovable stare upon the student.

" They came to the high priest's," he went on; " they began to question Jesus, and meantime the labourers made a fire in the yard as it was cold, and warmed themselves. Peter, too, stood with them near the fire and warmed himself as I am doing. A woman, seeing him, said: ' He was with Jesus, too '— that is as much as to say that he, too, should be taken to be questioned. And all the labourers that were standing near the fire must have looked sourly and suspiciously at him, because he was confused and said: ' I don't know Him.' A little while after again someone recognized him as one of Jesus' disciples and said: ' Thou, too, art one of them,' but again he denied it. And for the third time someone turned to him: ' Why, did I not see thee with Him in the garden to-day? ' For the third time he denied it. And immediately after that time the cock crowed, and Peter, looking from afar off at Jesus, remembered the words He had said to him in the evening. . . . He remembered, he came to himself, went out of the yard and wept bitterly — bitterly. In the Gospel it is written: ' He went out and wept bitterly.' I imagine it: the still, still, dark, dark garden, and in the stillness, faintly audible, smothered sobbing. . . ."

The student sighed and sank into thought. Still

smiling, Vasilisa suddenly gave a gulp, big tears flowed freely down her cheeks, and she screened her face from the fire with her sleeve as though ashamed of her tears, and Lukerya, staring immovably at the student, flushed crimson, and her expression became strained and heavy like that of someone enduring intense pain.

The labourers came back from the river, and one of them riding a horse was quite near, and the light from the fire quivered upon him. The student said good-night to the widows and went on. And again the darkness was about him and his fingers began to be numb. A cruel wind was blowing, winter really had come back and it did not feel as though Easter would be the day after to-morrow.

Now the student was thinking about Vasilisa: since she had shed tears all that had happened to Peter the night before the Crucifixion must have some relation to her. . . .

He looked round. The solitary light was still gleaming in the darkness and no figures could be seen near it now. The student thought again that if Vasilisa had shed tears, and her daughter had been troubled, it was evident that what he had just been telling them about, which had happened nineteen centuries ago, had a relation to the present — to both women, to the desolate village, to himself, to all people. The old woman had wept, not because he could tell the story touchingly, but because Peter was near to her, because her whole being was interested in what was passing in Peter's soul.

And joy suddenly stirred in his soul, and he even

stopped for a minute to take breath. "The past," he thought, "is linked with the present by an unbroken chain of events flowing one out of another." And it seemed to him that he had just seen both ends of that chain; that when he touched one end the other quivered.

When he crossed the river by the ferry boat and afterwards, mounting the hill, looked at his village and towards the west where the cold purple sunset lay a narrow streak of light, he thought that truth and beauty which had guided human life there in the garden and in the yard of the high priest had continued without interruption to this day, and had evidently always been the chief thing in human life and in all earthly life, indeed; and the feeling of youth, health, vigour — he was only twenty-two — and the inexpressible sweet expectation of happiness, of unknown mysterious happiness, took possession of him little by little, and life seemed to him enchanting, marvellous, and full of lofty meaning.

1894

IN THE RAVINE

IN THE RAVINE

I

THE village of Ukleevo lay in a ravine so that only the belfry and the chimneys of the printed cottons factories could be seen from the high road and the railway-station.   When visitors asked what village this was, they were told:

" That's the village where the deacon ate all the caviare at the funeral."

It had happened at the dinner at the funeral of Kostukov that the old deacon saw among the savouries some large-grained caviare and began eating it greedily; people nudged him, tugged at his arm, but he seemed petrified with enjoyment: felt nothing, and only went on eating.   He ate up all the caviare, and there were four pounds in the jar.   And years had passed since then, the deacon had long been dead, but the caviare was still remembered. Whether life was so poor here or people had not been clever enough to notice anything but that unimportant incident that had occurred ten years before, anyway the people had nothing else to tell about the village Ukleevo.

The village was never free from fever, and there was boggy mud there even in the summer, especially under the fences over which hung old willow-trees that gave deep shade. Here there was always a smell from the factory refuse and the acetic acid which was used in the finishing of the cotton print.

The three cotton factories and the tanyard were not in the village itself, but a little way off. They were small factories, and not more than four hundred workmen were employed in all of them. The tanyard often made the water in the little river stink; the refuse contaminated the meadows, the peasants' cattle suffered from Siberian plague, and orders were given that the factory should be closed. It was considered to be closed, but went on working in secret with the connivance of the local police officer and the district doctor, who was paid ten roubles a month by the owner. In the whole village there were only two decent houses built of brick with iron roofs; one of them was the local court, in the other, a two-storied house just opposite the church, there lived a shopkeeper from Epifan called Grigory Petrovitch Tsybukin.

Grigory kept a grocer's shop, but that was only for appearance' sake: in reality he sold vodka, cattle, hides, grain, and pigs; he traded in anything that came to hand, and when, for instance, magpies were wanted abroad for ladies' hats, he made some thirty kopecks on every pair of birds; he bought timber for felling, lent money at interest, and altogether was a sharp old man, full of resources.

He had two sons. The elder, Anisim, was in the police in the detective department and was rarely at home. The younger, Stepan, had gone in for trade and helped his father: but no great help was expected from him as he was weak in health and deaf; his wife Aksinya, a handsome woman with a good figure, who wore a hat and carried a parasol on holidays, got up early and went to bed late, and ran about all day long, picking up her skirts and jingling her keys, going from the granary to the cellar and from there to the shop, and old Tsybukin looked at her good-humouredly while his eyes glowed, and at such moments he regretted she had not been married to his elder son instead of to the younger one, who was deaf, and who evidently knew very little about female beauty.

The old man had always an inclination for family life, and he loved his family more than anything on earth, especially his elder son, the detective, and his daughter-in-law. Aksinya had no sooner married the deaf son than she began to display an extraordinary gift for business, and knew who could be allowed to run up a bill and who could not: she kept the keys and would not trust them even to her husband; she kept the accounts by means of the reckoning beads, looked at the horses' teeth like a peasant, and was always laughing or shouting; and whatever she did or said the old man was simply delighted and muttered:

" Well done, daughter-in-law! You are a smart wench! "

He was a widower, but a year after his son's marriage he could not resist getting married himself. A girl was found for him, living twenty miles from Ukleevo, called Varvara Nikolaevna, no longer quite young, but good-looking, comely, and belonging to a decent family. As soon as she was installed into the upper-storey room everything in the house seemed to brighten up as though new glass had been put into all the windows. The lamps gleamed before the ikons, the tables were covered with snow-white cloths, flowers with red buds made their appearance in the windows and in the front garden, and at dinner, instead of eating from a single bowl, each person had a separate plate set for him. Varvara Nikolaevna had a pleasant, friendly smile, and it seemed as though the whole house were smiling, too. Beggars and pilgrims, male and female, began to come into the yard, a thing which had never happened in the past; the plaintive sing-song voices of the Ukleevo peasant women and the apologetic coughs of weak, seedy-looking men, who had been dismissed from the factory for drunkenness were heard under the windows. Varvara helped them with money, with bread, with old clothes, and afterwards, when she felt more at home, began taking things out of the shop. One day the deaf man saw her take four ounces of tea and that disturbed him.

"Here, mother's taken four ounces of tea," he informed his father afterwards; "where is that to be entered?"

The old man made no reply but stood still and thought a moment, moving his eyebrows, and then went upstairs to his wife.

"Varvarushka, if you want anything out of the shop," he said affectionately, "take it, my dear. Take it and welcome; don't hesitate."

And the next day the deaf man, running across the yard, called to her:

"If there is anything you want, mother, take it."

There was something new, something gay and light-hearted in her giving of alms, just as there was in the lamps before the ikons and in the red flowers. When at Carnival or at the church festival, which lasted for three days, they sold the peasants tainted salt meat, smelling so strong it was hard to stand near the tub of it, and took scythes, caps, and their wives' kerchiefs in pledge from the drunken men; when the factory hands stupefied with bad vodka lay rolling in the mud, and sin seemed to hover thick like a fog in the air, then it was a relief to think that up there in the house there was a gentle, neatly dressed woman who had nothing to do with salt meat or vodka; her charity had in those burdensome, murky days the effect of a safety valve in a machine.

The days in Tsybukin's house were spent in business cares. Before the sun had risen in the morning Aksinya was panting and puffing as she washed in the outer room, and the samovar was boiling in the kitchen with a hum that boded no good. Old Grigory Petrovitch, dressed in a long black coat, cotton breeches and shiny top boots, looking a dapper little figure, walked about the rooms, tapping with his little heels like the father-in-law in a well-known song. The shop was opened. When it was daylight a racing droshky was brought up to the front door and the old man got jauntily on to it, pulling his big cap down to his ears; and, looking at him, no one would have said he was fifty-six. His wife and daughter-in-law saw him off, and at such times when he had on a good, clean coat, and had in the droshky a huge black horse that had cost three hundred roubles, the old man did not like the peasants to come up to him with their complaints and petitions; he hated the peasants and disdained them, and if he saw some peasants waiting at the gate, he would shout angrily:

"Why are you standing there?   Go further off."

Or if it were a beggar, he would say:

"God will provide!"

He used to drive off on business; his wife, in a dark dress and a black apron, tidied the rooms or helped in the kitchen. Aksinya attended to the shop, and from the yard could be heard the clink of bottles and of money, her laughter and loud talk, and the anger of customers whom she had offended; and at the same time it could be seen that the secret sale of vodka was already going on in the shop. The deaf man sat in the shop, too, or walked about the street bare-headed, with his hands in his pockets looking absent-mindedly now at the huts, now at the sky overhead.   Six times a day they had tea; four times a day they sat down to meals; and in the evening they counted over their takings, put them down, went to bed, and slept soundly.

All the three cotton factories in Ukleevo and the houses of the factory owners — Hrymin Seniors, Hrymin Juniors, and Kostukov — were on a telephone. The telephone was laid on in the local court, too, but it soon ceased to work as bugs and beetles bred there. The elder of the rural district had had little education and wrote every word in the official documents in capitals. But when the telephone was spoiled he said:

" Yes, now we shall be badly off without a telephone."

The Hrymin Seniors were continually at law with the Juniors, and sometimes the Juniors quarrelled among themselves and began going to law, and their factory did not work for a month or two till they were reconciled again, and this was an entertainment for the people of Ukleevo, as there was a great deal of talk and gossip on the occasion of each quarrel. On holidays Kostukov and the Juniors used to get up races, used to dash about Ukleevo and run over calves. Aksinya, rustling her starched petticoats, used to promenade in a low-necked dress up and down the street near her shop; the Juniors used to snatch her up and carry her off as though by force. Then old Tsybukin would drive out to show his new horse and take Varvara with him.

In the evening, after the races, when people were going to bed, an expensive concertina was played in the Juniors' yard and, if it were a moonlight night, those sounds sent a thrill of delight to the heart, and Ukleevo no longer seemed a wretched hole.

II

The elder son Anisim came home very rarely, only on great holidays, but he often sent by a returning villager presents and letters written in very good writing by some other hand, always on a sheet of foolscap in the form of a petition. The letters were full of expressions that Anisim never made use of in conversation: " Dear papa and mamma, I send you a pound of flower tea for the satisfaction of your physical needs."

At the bottom of every letter was scratched, as though with a broken pen: " Anisim Tsybukin," and again in the same excellent hand: " Agent."

The letters were read aloud several times, and the old father, touched, red with emotion, would say:

" Here he did not care to stay at home, he has gone in for an intellectual line. Well, let him! Every man to his own job! "

It happened just before Carnival there was a heavy storm of rain mixed with hail; the old man and Varvara went to the window to look at it, and lo and behold! Anisim drove up in a sledge from the station. He was quite unexpected. He came indoors, looking anxious and troubled about something, and he remained the same all the time; there was something free and easy in his manner. He was in no haste to go away, it seemed, as though he had been dismissed from the service. Varvara was pleased at his arrival; she looked at him with a sly expression, sighed, and shook her head.

" How is this, my friends? " she said. " Tut, tut, the lad's in his twenty-eighth year, and he is still leading a gay bachelor life; tut, tut, tut. . . ."

From the other room her soft, even speech sounded like tut, tut, tut. She began whispering with her husband and Aksinya, and their faces wore

the same sly and mysterious expression as though
they were conspirators.

It was decided to marry Anisim.

" Oh, tut, tut . . . the younger brother has been
married long ago," said Varvara, " and you are still
without a helpmate like a cock at a fair. What is
the meaning of it? Tut, tut, you will be married,
please God, then as you choose — you will go into
the service and your wife will remain here at home
to help us. There is no order in your life, young
man, and I see you have forgotten how to live properly. Tut, tut, it's the same trouble with all you
townspeople."

When the Tsybukins married, the most handsome
girls were chosen as brides for them as rich men.
For Anisim, too, they found a handsome one. He
was himself of an uninteresting and inconspicuous
appearance; of a feeble, sickly build and short stature; he had full, puffy cheeks which looked as though
he were blowing them out; his eyes looked with a
keen, unblinking stare; his beard was red and scanty,
and when he was thinking he always put it into his
mouth and bit it; moreover he often drank too much,
and that was noticeable from his face and his walk.
But when he was informed that they had found a
very beautiful bride for him, he said:

" Oh well, I am not a fright myself. All of us
Tsybukins are handsome, I may say."

The village of Torguevo was near the town.
Half of it had lately been incorporated into the
town, the other half remained a village. In the
first — the town half — there was a widow living in

her own little house; she had a sister living with her who was quite poor and went out to work by the day, and this sister had a daughter called Lipa, a girl who went out to work, too. People in Torguevo were already talking about Lipa's good looks, but her terrible poverty put everyone off; people opined that some widower or elderly man would marry her regardless of her poverty, or would perhaps take her to himself without marriage, and that her mother would get enough to eat living with her. Varvara heard about Lipa from the matchmakers, and she drove over to Torguevo.

Then a visit of inspection was arranged at the aunt's, with lunch and wine all in due order, and Lipa wore a new pink dress made on purpose for this occasion, and a crimson ribbon like a flame gleamed in her hair. She was pale-faced, thin, and frail, with soft, delicate features sunburnt from working in the open air; a shy, mournful smile always hovered about her face, and there was a childlike look in her eyes, trustful and curious.

She was young, quite a little girl, her bosom still scarcely perceptible, but she could be married because she had reached the legal age. She really was beautiful, and the only thing that might be thought unattractive was her big masculine hands which hung idle now like two big claws.

"There is no dowry — and we don't think much of that," said Tsybukin to the aunt. "We took a wife from a poor family for our son Stepan, too, and now we can't say too much for her. In house and in business alike she has hands of gold."

Lipa stood in the doorway and looked as though she would say: " Do with me as you will, I trust you," while her mother Praskovya the work-woman hid herself in the kitchen numb with shyness. At one time in her youth a merchant whose floors she was scrubbing stamped at her in a rage; she went chill with terror and there always was a feeling of fear at the bottom of her heart. When she was frightened her arms and legs trembled and her cheeks twitched. Sitting in the kitchen she tried to hear what the visitors were saying, and she kept crossing herself, pressing her fingers to her forehead, and gazing at the ikons. Anisim, slightly drunk, opened the door into the kitchen and said in a free-and-easy way:

" Why are you sitting in here, precious mamma? We are dull without you."

And Praskovya, overcome with timidity, pressing her hands to her lean, wasted bosom, said:

" Oh, not at all. . . . It's very kind of you."

After the visit of inspection the wedding day was fixed. Then Anisim walked about the rooms at home whistling, or suddenly thinking of something, would fall to brooding and would look at the floor fixedly, silently, as though he would probe to the depths of the earth. He expressed neither pleasure that he was to be married, married so soon, on Low Sunday, nor a desire to see his bride, but simply went on whistling. And it was evident he was only getting married because his father and stepmother wished him to, and because it was the custom in the village to marry the son in order to have a woman to help in the house. When he went away he seemed in no haste, and behaved altogether not as he had done on previous visits — was particularly free and easy, and talked inappropriately.

III

In the village Shikalovo lived two dressmakers, sisters, belonging to the Flagellant sect. The new clothes for the wedding were ordered from them, and they often came to try them on, and stayed a long while drinking tea. They were making Varvara a brown dress with black lace and bugles on it, and Aksinya a light green dress with a yellow front, with a train. When the dressmakers had finished their work Tsybukin paid them not in money but in goods from the shop, and they went away depressed, carrying parcels of tallow candles and tins of sardines which they did not in the least need, and when they got out of the village into the open country they sat down on a hillock and cried.

Anisim arrived three days before the wedding, rigged out in new clothes from top to toe. He had dazzling india-rubber goloshes, and instead of a cravat wore a red cord with little balls on it, and over his shoulder he had hung an overcoat, also new, without putting his arms into the sleeves.

After crossing himself sedately before the ikon, he greeted his father and gave him ten silver roubles and ten half-roubles; to Varvara he gave as much, and to Aksinya twenty quarter-roubles. The chief charm of the present lay in the fact that all the coins, as though carefully matched, were new and glittered in the sun. Trying to seem grave and sedate he pursed up his face and puffed out his cheeks, and he smelt of spirits. Probably he had visited the refreshment bar at every station. And again there was a free-and-easiness about the man — something superfluous and out of place. Then Anisim had lunch and drank tea with the old man, and Varvara turned the new coins over in her hand and inquired about villagers who had gone to live in the town.

" They are all right, thank God, they get on quite well," said Anisim. " Only something has happened to Ivan Yegorov: his old wife Sofya Nikiforovna is dead. From consumption. They ordered the memorial dinner for the peace of her soul at the confectioner's at two and a half roubles a head. And there was real wine. Those who were peasants from our village — they paid two and a half roubles for them, too. They ate nothing, as though a peasant would understand sauce ! "

" Two and a half," said his father, shaking his head.

" Well, it's not like the country there, you go into a restaurant to have a snack of something, you ask for one thing and another, others join till there is a party of us, one has a drink — and before you know where you are it is daylight and you've three or four roubles each to pay. And when one is with Samorodov he likes to have coffee with brandy in it after everything, and brandy is sixty kopecks for a little glass."

" And he is making it all up," said the old man enthusiastically; " he is making it all up, lying ! "

" I am always with Samorodov now. It is Samorodov who writes my letters to you. He writes splendidly. And if I were to tell you, mamma," Anisim went on gaily, addressing Varvara, " the sort of fellow that Samorodov is, you would not believe me. We call him Muhtar, because he is black like an Armenian. I can see through him, I know all his affairs like the five fingers of my hand, and he feels that, and he always follows me about, we are regular inseparables. He seems not to like it in a way, but he can't get on without me. Where I go he goes. I have a correct, trustworthy eye, mamma. One sees a peasant selling a shirt in the market place. ' Stay, that shirt's stolen.' And really it turns out it is so : the shirt was a stolen one."

" What do you tell from ? " asked Varvara.

" Not from anything, I have just an eye for it. I know nothing about the shirt, only for some reason I seem drawn to it : it's stolen, and that's all I can say. Among us detectives it's come to their saying, ' Oh, Anisim has gone to shoot snipe ! ' That means looking for stolen goods. Yes. . . . Anybody can steal, but it is another thing to keep ! The earth is wide, but there is nowhere to hide stolen goods."

" In our village a ram and two ewes were carried off last week," said Varvara, and she heaved a sigh, " and there is no one to try and find them. . . . Oh, tut, tut. . . ."

" Well, I might have a try. I don't mind."

The day of the wedding arrived. It was a cool but bright, cheerful April day. People were driving about Ukleevo from early morning with pairs or teams of three horses decked with many-coloured ribbons on their yokes and manes, with a jingle of bells. The rooks, disturbed by this activity, were cawing noisily in the willows, and the starlings sang their loudest unceasingly as though rejoicing that there was a wedding at the Tsybukins'.

Indoors the tables were already covered with long fish, smoked hams, stuffed fowls, boxes of sprats, pickled savouries of various sorts, and a number of bottles of vodka and wine; there was a smell of smoked sausage and of sour tinned lobster. Old Tsybukin walked about near the tables, tapping with his heels and sharpening the knives against each other. They kept calling Varvara and asking for things, and she was constantly with a distracted face running breathlessly into the kitchen, where the man cook from Kostukov's and the woman cook from Hrymin Juniors' had been at work since early morning. Aksinya, with her hair curled, in her stays without her dress on, in new creaky boots, flew about the yard like a whirlwind showing glimpses of her bare knees and bosom.

It was noisy, there was a sound of scolding and oaths; passers-by stopped at the wide-open gates, and in everything there was a feeling that something extraordinary was happening.

" They have gone for the bride! "

The bells began jingling and died away far beyond the village. . . . Between two and three o'clock people ran up: again there was a jingling of bells: they were bringing the bride! The church was full, the candelabra were lighted, the choir were singing from music books as old Tsybukin had wished it. The glare of the lights and the bright coloured dresses dazzled Lipa; she felt as though the singers with their loud voices were hitting her on the head with a hammer. Her boots and the stays, which she had put on for the first time in her life, pinched her, and her face looked as though she had only just come to herself after fainting; she gazed about without understanding. Anisim, in his black coat with a red cord instead of a tie, stared at the same spot lost in thought, and when the singers shouted loudly he hurriedly crossed himself. He felt touched and disposed to weep. This church was familiar to him from earliest childhood; at one time his dead mother used to bring him here to take the sacrament; at one time he used to sing in the choir; every ikon he remembered so well, every corner. Here he was being married, he had to take a wife for the sake of doing the proper thing, but he was not thinking of that now, he had forgotten his wedding completely. Tears dimmed his eyes so that he could not see the ikons, he felt heavy at heart; he prayed and besought God that the misfortunes that threatened him, that were ready to burst upon him to-morrow, if not to-day, might somehow pass him by as storm-clouds in time of drought pass over the village without yielding one drop of rain. And so many sins were heaped up in the past, so many sins, all getting away

from them or setting them right was so beyond hope
that it seemed incongruous even to ask forgiveness.
But he did ask forgiveness, and even gave a loud sob,
but no one took any notice of that, since they all
supposed he had had a drop too much.

There was a sound of a fretful childish wail:

" Take me away, mamma darling! "

" Quiet there! " cried the priest.

When they returned from the church people ran
after them; there were crowds, too, round the shop,
round the gates, and in the yard under the windows.
The peasant women came in to sing songs of con-
gratulation to them. The young couple had scarcely
crossed the threshold when the singers, who were already standing in the outer room with their music
books, broke into a loud chant at the top of their
voices; a band ordered expressly from the town
began playing. Foaming Don wine was brought in
tall wine-glasses, and Elizarov, a carpenter who did
jobs by contract, a tall, gaunt old man with eyebrows
so bushy that his eyes could scarcely be seen, said,
addressing the happy pair:

" Anisim and you, my child, love one another,
live in God's way, little children, and the Heavenly
Mother will not abandon you."

He leaned his face on the old father's shoulder
and gave a sob.

" Grigory Petrovitch, let us weep, let us weep with
joy! " he said in a thin voice, and then at once burst
out laughing in a loud bass guffaw. " Ho-ho-ho!
This is a fine daughter-in-law for you too! Every-

thing is in its place in her; all runs smoothly, no creaking, the mechanism works well, lots of screws in it."

He was a native of the Yegoryevsky district, but had worked in the factories in Ukleevo and the neighborhood from his youth up, and had made it his home. He had been a familiar figure for years as old and gaunt and lanky as now, and for years he had been nicknamed " Crutch." Perhaps because he had been for forty years occupied in repairing the factory machinery he judged everybody and everything by its soundness or its need of repair. And before sitting down to the table he tried several chairs to see whether they were solid, and he touched the smoked fish also.

After the Don wine, they all sat down to the table. The visitors talked, moving their chairs. The singers were singing in the outer room. The band was playing, and at the same time the peasant women in the yard were singing their songs all in chorus — and there was an awful, wild medley of sounds which made one giddy.

Crutch turned round in his chair and prodded his neighbours with his elbows, prevented people from talking, and laughed and cried alternately.

" Little children, little children, little children," he muttered rapidly. " Aksinya my dear, Varvara darling, we will live all in peace and harmony, my dear little axes. . . ."

He drank little and was now only drunk from one glass of English bitters. The revolting bitters, made from nobody knows what, intoxicated every-

one who drank it as though it had stunned them.
Their tongues began to falter.

The local clergy, the clerks from the factories
with their wives, the tradesmen and tavern-keepers
from the other villages were present. The clerk and
the elder of the rural district who had served together for fourteen years, and who had during all
that time never signed a single document for anybody nor let a single person out of the local court
without deceiving or insulting him, were sitting now
side by side, both fat and well-fed, and it seemed as
though they were so saturated in injustice and false-
hood that even the skin of their faces was somehow
peculiar, fraudulent. The clerk's wife, a thin
woman with a squint, had brought all her children
with her, and like a bird of prey looked aslant at
the plates and snatched anything she could get hold
of to put in her own or her children's pockets.

Lipa sat as though turned to stone, still with the
same expression as in church. Anisim had not said
a single word to her since he had made her acquaint-
ance, so that he did not yet know the sound of her
voice; and now, sitting beside her, he remained mute
and went on drinking bitters, and when he got
drunk he began talking to the aunt who was sitting
opposite:

" I have a friend called Samorodov. A peculiar
man. He is by rank an honorary citizen, and he
can talk. But I know him through and through,
auntie, and he feels it. Pray join me in drinking to
the health of Samorodov, auntie! "

Varvara, worn out and distracted, walked round

the table pressing the guests to eat, and was evidently
pleased that there were so many dishes and that
everything was so lavish — no one could disparage
them now.   The sun set, but the dinner went on:
the guests were beyond knowing what they were
eating or drinking, it was impossible to distinguish
what was said, and only from time to time when the
band subsided some peasant woman could be heard
shouting:

"They have sucked the blood out of us, the
Herods; a pest on them!"

In the evening they danced to the band.   The
Hrymin Juniors came, bringing their wine, and one
of them, when dancing a quadrille, held a bottle in
each hand and a wineglass in his mouth, and that
made everyone laugh.   In the middle of the quadrille they suddenly crooked their knees and danced
in a squatting position; Aksinya in green flew by like
a flash, stirring up a wind with her train.   Someone
trod on her flounce and Crutch shouted:

"Aie, they have torn off the panel!   Children!"

Aksinya had naïve grey eyes which rarely blinked,
and a naïve smile played continually on her face.
And in those unblinking eyes, and in that little head
on the long neck, and in her slenderness there was
something snake-like; all in green but for the yellow
on her bosom, she looked with a smile on her face
as a viper looks out of the young rye in the spring at
the passers-by, stretching itself and lifting its head.
The Hrymins were free in their behaviour to her,
and it was very noticeable that she was on intimate
terms with the elder of them.   But her deaf husband

saw nothing, he did not look at her; he sat with his legs crossed and ate nuts, cracking them so loudly that it sounded like pistol shots.

But, behold, old Tsybukin himself walked into the middle of the room and waved his handkerchief as a sign that he, too, wanted to dance the Russian dance, and all over the house and from the crowd in the yard rose a roar of approbation:

"*He's* going to dance!   *He* himself!"

Varvara danced, but the old man only waved his handkerchief and kicked up his heels, but the people in the yard, propped against one another, peeping in at the windows, were in raptures, and for the moment forgave him everything — his wealth and the wrongs he had done them.

"Well done, Grigory Petrovitch!" was heard in the crowd.   "That's right, do your best!   You can still play your part!   Ha-ha!"

It was kept up till late, till two o'clock in the morning.   Anisim, staggering, went to take leave of the singers and bandsmen, and gave each of them a new half-rouble.   His father, who was not staggering but still seemed to be standing on one leg, saw his guests off, and said to each of them:

"The wedding has cost two thousand."

As the party was breaking up, someone took the Shikalovo innkeeper's good coat instead of his own old one, and Anisim suddenly flew into a rage and began shouting:

"Stop, I'll find it at once; I know who stole it, stop."

He ran out into the street and pursued someone.

He was caught, brought back home and shoved, drunken, red with anger, and wet, into the room where the aunt was undressing Lipa, and was locked in.

IV

Five days had passed. Anisim, who was preparing to go, went upstairs to say good-bye to Varvara. All the lamps were burning before the ikons, there was a smell of incense, while she sat at the window knitting a stocking of red wool.

" You have not stayed with us long," she said. " You've been dull, I dare say. Oh, tut, tut. . . . We live comfortably; we have plenty of everything. We celebrated your wedding properly, in good style; your father says it came to two thousand. In fact we live like merchants, only it's dreary. We treat the people very badly. My heart aches, my dear; how we treat them, my goodness! Whether we exchange a horse or buy something or hire a labourer — it's cheating in everything. Cheating and cheating. The Lenten oil in the shop is bitter, rancid, the people have pitch that is better. But surely, tell me pray, couldn't we sell good oil ? "

" Every man to his job, mamma."

" But you know we all have to die? Oy, oy, really you ought to talk to your father . . . ! "

" Why, you should talk to him yourself."

" Well, well, I did put in my word, but he said just what you do: ' Every man to his own job.'

Do you suppose in the next world they'll consider what job you have been put to? God's judgment is just."

"Of course no one will consider," said Anisim, and he heaved a sigh. "There is no God, anyway, you know, mamma, so what considering can there be?"

Varvara looked at him with surprise, burst out laughing, and clasped her hands. Perhaps because she was so genuinely surprised at his words and looked at him as though he were a queer person, he was confused.

"Perhaps there is a God, only there is no faith. When I was being married I was not myself. Just as you may take an egg from under a hen and there is a chicken chirping in it, so my conscience was beginning to chirp in me, and while I was being married I thought all the time there was a God! But when I left the church it was nothing. And indeed, how can I tell whether there is a God or not? We are not taught right from childhood, and while the babe is still at his mother's breast he is only taught 'every man to his own job.' Father does not believe in God, either. You were saying that Guntorev had some sheep stolen. . . . I have found them; it was a peasant at Shikalovo stole them; he stole them, but father's got the fleeces . . . so that's all his faith amounts to."

Anisim winked and wagged his head.

"The elder does not believe in God, either," he went on. "And the clerk and the deacon, too. And as for their going to church and keeping the fasts, that is simply to prevent people talking ill of them, and in case it really may be true that there will be a Day of Judgment. Nowadays people say that the end of the world has come because people have grown weaker, do not honour their parents, and so on. All that is nonsense. My idea, mamma, is that all our trouble is because there is so little conscience in people. I see through things, mamma, and I understand. If a man has a stolen shirt I see it. A man sits in a tavern and you fancy he is drinking tea and no more, but to me the tea is neither here nor there; I see further, he has no conscience. You can go about the whole day and not meet one man with a conscience. And the whole reason is that they don't know whether there is a God or not. . . . Well, good-bye, mamma, keep alive and well, don't remember evil against me."

Anisim bowed down at Varvara's feet.

" I thank you for everything, mamma," he said. " You are a great gain to our family. You are a very ladylike woman, and I am very pleased with you."

Much moved, Anisim went out, but returned again and said:

" Samorodov has got me mixed up in something: I shall either make my fortune or come to grief. If anything happens, then you must comfort my father, mamma."

" Oh, nonsense, don't you worry, tut, tut, tut . . . God is merciful. And, Anisim, you should be affectionate to your wife, instead of giving each other sulky looks as you do; you might smile at least."

" Yes, she is rather a queer one," said Anisim,
and he gave a sigh. " She does not understand anything, she never speaks. She is very young, let her
grow up."

A tall, sleek white stallion was already standing
at the front door, harnessed to the chaise.

Old Tsybukin jumped in jauntily with a run and
took the reins. Anisim kissed Varvara, Aksinya,
and his brother. On the steps Lipa, too, was standing; she was standing motionless, looking away, and
it seemed as though she had not come to see him off
but just by chance for some unknown reason. Anisim went up to her and just touched her cheek with
his lips.

" Good-bye," he said.

And without looking at him she gave a strange
smile; her face began to quiver, and everyone for
some reason felt sorry for her. Anisim, too, leaped
into the chaise with a bound and put his arms jauntily akimbo, for he considered himself a good-looking
fellow.

When they drove up out of the ravine Anisim kept
looking back towards the village. It was a warm,
bright day. The cattle were being driven out for
the first time, and the peasant girls and women were
walking by the herd in their holiday dresses. The
dun-coloured bull bellowed, glad to be free, and
pawed the ground with his forefeet. On all sides,
above and below, the larks were singing. Anisim
looked round at the elegant white church — it had
only lately been whitewashed — and he thought how
he had been praying in it five days before; he looked

round at the school with its green roof, at the little
river in which he used once to bathe and catch fish,
and there was a stir of joy in his heart, and he
wished that walls might rise up from the ground
and prevent him from going further, and that he
might be left with nothing but the past.

At the station they went to the refreshment room
and drank a glass of sherry each.   His father felt
in his pocket for his purse to pay.

" I will stand treat," said Anisim.   The old man,
touched and delighted, slapped him on the shoulder,
and winked to the waiter as much as to say, " See
what a fine son I have got."

" You ought to stay at home in the business,
Anisim," he said; " you would be worth any price to
me!   I would shower gold on you from head to
foot, my son."

" It can't be done, papa."

The sherry was sour and smelt of sealing-wax, but
they had another glass.

When old Tsybukin returned home from the station, for the first moment he did not recognize his
younger daughter-in-law.   As soon as her husband
had driven out of the yard, Lipa was transformed
and suddenly brightened up.   Wearing a thread-
bare old petticoat, with her feet bare and her sleeves
tucked up to the shoulders, she was scrubbing
the stairs in the entry and singing in a silvery little
voice, and when she brought out a big tub of
dirty water and looked up at the sun with her
childlike smile it seemed as though she, too, were a
lark.

An old labourer who was passing by the door shook his head and cleared his throat.

"Yes, indeed, your daughters-in-law, Grigory Petrovitch, are a blessing from God," he said. "Not women, but treasures!"

V

On Friday the 8th of July, Elizarov, nicknamed Crutch, and Lipa were returning from the village of Kazanskoe, where they had been to a service on the occasion of a church holiday in the honour of the Holy Mother of Kazan. A good distance after them walked Lipa's mother Praskovya, who always fell behind, as she was ill and short of breath. It was drawing towards evening.

"A-a-a . . ." said Crutch, wondering as he listened to Lipa. "A-a! . . . We-ell!"

"I am very fond of jam, Ilya Makaritch," said Lipa. "I sit down in my little corner and drink tea and eat jam. Or I drink it with Varvara Nikolaevna, and she tells some story full of feeling. We have a lot of jam — four jars. 'Have some, Lipa; eat as much as you like.'"

"A-a-a, four jars!"

"They live very well. We have white bread with our tea; and meat, too, as much as one wants. They live very well, only I am frightened with them, Ilya Makaritch. Oh, oh, how frightened I am!"

"Why are you frightened, child?" asked Crutch, and he looked back to see how far Praskovya was behind.

" To begin with, when the wedding had been celebrated I was afraid of Anisim Grigoritch.　Anisim
Grigoritch did nothing, he didn't ill-treat me, only
when he comes near me a cold shiver runs all over
me, through all my bones.　And I did not sleep one
night, I trembled all over and kept praying to God.
And now I am afraid of Aksinya, Ilya Makaritch.
It's not that she does anything, she is always laughing, but sometimes she glances at the window, and
her eyes are so fierce and there is a gleam of green
in them — like the eyes of the sheep in the shed.
The Hrymin Juniors are leading her astray: ' Your
old man,' they tell her, ' has a bit of land at Butyokino, a hundred and twenty acres,' they say, ' and
there is sand and water there, so you, Aksinya,' they
say, ' build a brickyard there and we will go shares
in it.'　Bricks now are twenty roubles the thousand,
it's a profitable business.　Yesterday at dinner Aksinya said to my father-in-law:　' I want to build a
brickyard at Butyokino; I'm going into business on
my own account.'　She laughed as she said it.　And
Grigory Petrovitch's face darkened, one could see he
did not like it.　' As long as I live,' he said, ' the
family must not break up, we must go on altogether.'
She gave a look and gritted her teeth. . . .　Frit-
ters were served, she would not eat them."

" A-a-a! . . ."　Crutch was surprised.

" And tell me, if you please, when does she
sleep? " said Lipa.　" She sleeps for half an hour,
then jumps up and keeps walking and walking about
to see whether the peasants have not set fire to something, have not stolen something. . . .　I am fright-

ened with her, Ilya Makaritch. And the Hrymin Juniors did not go to bed after the wedding, but drove to the town to go to law with each other; and folks do say it is all on account of Aksinya. Two of the brothers have promised to build her a brickyard, but the third is offended, and the factory has been at a standstill for a month, and my uncle Prohor is without work and goes about from house to house getting crusts. ' Hadn't you better go working on the land or sawing up wood, meanwhile, uncle?' I tell him; ' why disgrace yourself?' ' I've got out of the way of it,' he says; ' I don't know how to do any sort of peasant's work now, Lipinka.' . . ."

They stopped to rest and wait for Praskovya near a copse of young aspen-trees. Elizarov had long been a contractor in a small way, but he kept no horses, going on foot all over the district with nothing but a little bag in which there was bread and onions, and stalking along with big strides, swinging his arms. And it was difficult to walk with him.

At the entrance to the copse stood a milestone. Elizarov touched it; read it. Praskovya reached them out of breath. Her wrinkled and always scared-looking face was beaming with happiness; she had been at church to-day like anyone else, then she had been to the fair and there had drunk pear cider. For her this was unusual, and it even seemed to her now that she had lived for her own pleasure that day for the first time in her life. After resting they all three walked on side by side. The sun had already set, and its beams filtered through the copse,

casting a light on the trunks of the trees. There
was a faint sound of voices ahead. The Ukleevo
girls had long before pushed on ahead but had lingered in the copse, probably gathering mushrooms.

"Hey, wenches!" cried Elizarov. "Hey, my
beauties!"

There was a sound of laughter in response.

"Crutch is coming! Crutch! The old horse-
radish."

And the echo laughed, too. And then the copse
was left behind. The tops of the factory chimneys
came into view. The cross on the belfry glittered:
this was the village: "the one at which the deacon
ate all the caviare at the funeral." Now they were
almost home; they only had to go down into the big
ravine. Lipa and Praskovya, who had been walking barefooted, sat down on the grass to put on their
boots; Elizar sat down with them. If they looked
down from above Ukleevo looked beautiful and
peaceful with its willow-trees, its white church, and
its little river, and the only blot on the picture was
the roof of the factories, painted for the sake of
cheapness a gloomy ashen grey. On the slope on
the further side they could see the rye — some in
stacks and sheaves here and there as though strewn
about by the storm, and some freshly cut lying in
swathes; the oats, too, were ripe and glistened now
in the sun like mother-of-pearl. It was harvest-time.
To-day was a holiday, to-morrow they would harvest
the rye and carry the hay, and then Sunday a holiday
again; every day there were mutterings of distant
thunder. It was misty and looked like rain, and,

gazing now at the fields, everyone thought, God grant we get the harvest in in time; and everyone felt gay and joyful and anxious at heart.

"Mowers ask a high price nowadays," said Praskovya. "One rouble and forty kopecks a day."

People kept coming and coming from the fair at Kazanskoe: peasant women, factory workers in new caps, beggars, children. . . . Here a cart would drive by stirring up the dust and behind it would run an unsold horse, and it seemed glad it had not been sold; then a cow was led along by the horns, resisting stubbornly; then a cart again, and in it drunken peasants swinging their legs. An old woman led a little boy in a big cap and big boots; the boy was tired out with the heat and the heavy boots which prevented his bending his legs at the knees, but yet blew unceasingly with all his might at a tin trumpet. They had gone down the slope and turned into the street, but the trumpet could still be heard.

"Our factory owners don't seem quite themselves . . ." said Elizarov. "There's trouble. Kostukov is angry with me. 'Too many boards have gone on the cornices.' 'Too many? As many have gone on it as were needed, Vassily Danilitch; I don't eat them with my porridge.' 'How can you speak to me like that?' said he, 'you good-for-nothing blockhead! Don't forget yourself! It was I made you a contractor.' 'That's nothing so wonderful,' said I. 'Even before I was a contractor I used to have tea every day.' 'You are a rascal . . .' he said. I said nothing. 'We are rascals in this world,' thought I, ' and you will be rascals in the next. . . .' Ha-ha-ha! The next day he was softer. ' Don't you bear malice against me for my words, Makaritch,' he said. ' If I said too much,' says he, ' what of it? I am a merchant of the first guild, your superior — you ought to hold your tongue.' ' You,' said I, ' are a merchant of the first guild and I am a carpenter, that's correct. And Saint Joseph was a carpenter, too. Ours is a righteous calling and pleasing to God, and if you are pleased to be my superior you are very welcome to it, Vassily Danilitch.' And later on, after that conversation I mean, I thought: ' Which was the superior? A merchant of the first guild or a carpenter?' The carpenter must be, my child! "

Crutch thought a minute and added:

" Yes, that's how it is, child. He who works, he who is patient is the superior."

By now the sun had set and a thick mist as white as milk was rising over the river, in the church enclosure, and in the open spaces round the factories. Now when the darkness was coming on rapidly, when lights were twinkling below, and when it seemed as though the mists were hiding a fathomless abyss, Lipa and her mother who were born in poverty and prepared to live so till the end, giving up to others everything except their frightened, gentle souls, may have fancied for a minute perhaps that in the vast, mysterious world, among the endless series of lives, they, too, counted for something, and they, too, were superior to someone; they liked sitting here at the top, they smiled happily and forgot that they must go down below again all the same.

In the Ravine 209

At last they went home again. The mowers were sitting on the ground at the gates near the shop. As a rule the Ukleevo peasants did not go to Tsybukin's to work, and they had to hire strangers, and now in the darkness it seemed as though there were men sitting there with long black beards. The shop was open, and through the doorway they could see the deaf man playing draughts with a boy. The mowers were singing softly, scarcely audibly, or loudly demanding their wages for the previous day, but they were not paid for fear they should go away before to-morrow. Old Tsybukin, with his coat off, was sitting in his waistcoat with Aksinya under the birch-tree, drinking tea; a lamp was burning on the table.

" I say, grandfather," a mower called from outside the gates, as though taunting him, " pay us half anyway! Hey, grandfather."

And at once there was the sound of laughter, and then again they sang hardly audibly. . . . Crutch, too, sat down to have some tea.

" We have been at the fair, you know," he began telling them. " We have had a walk, a very nice walk, my children, praise the Lord. But an unfortunate thing happened: Sashka the blacksmith bought some tobacco and gave the shopman half a rouble to be sure. And the half rouble was a false one "— Crutch went on, and he meant to speak in a whisper, but he spoke in a smothered husky voice which was audible to everyone. " The half-rouble turned out to be a bad one. He was asked where he got it. ' Anisim Tsybukin gave it me,' he said. ' When I

went to his wedding,' he said. They called the
police inspector, took the man away. . . . Look
out, Grigory Petrovitch, that nothing comes of it,
no talk. . . ."

" Gra-ndfather! " the same voice called taunt-
ingly outside the gates. " Gra-andfather! "

A silence followed.

" Ah, little children, little children, little children . . ." Crutch muttered rapidly, and he got up.
He was overcome with drowsiness. " Well, thank
you for the tea, for the sugar, little children. It is
time to sleep. I am like a bit of rotten timber nowadays, my beams are crumbling under me. Ho-ho-
ho! I suppose it's time I was dead."

And he gave a gulp. Old Tsybukin did not finish
his tea but sat on a little, pondering; and his face
looked as though he were listening to the footsteps
of Crutch, who was far away down the street.

" Sashka the blacksmith told a lie, I expect," said
Aksinya, guessing his thoughts.

He went into the house and came back a little
later with a parcel; he opened it, and there was the
gleam of roubles — perfectly new coins. He took
one, tried it with his teeth, flung it on the tray; then
flung down another.

" The roubles really are false . . ." he said, looking at Aksinya and seeming perplexed. " These are
those Anisim brought, his present. Take them,
daughter," he whispered, and thrust the parcel into
her hands. " Take them and throw them into the
well . . . confound them! And mind there is no

talk about it. Harm might come of it. . . . Take
away the samovar, put out the light."

Lipa and her mother sitting in the barn saw the
lights go out one after the other; only overhead in
Varvara's room there were blue and red lamps
gleaming, and a feeling of peace, content, and happy
ignorance seemed to float down from there. Praskovya could never get used to her daughter's being
married to a rich man, and when she came she huddled timidly in the outer room with a deprecating
smile on her face, and tea and sugar were sent out
to her. And Lipa, too, could not get used to it
either, and after her husband had gone away she
did not sleep in her bed, but lay down anywhere to
sleep, in the kitchen or the barn, and every day she
scrubbed the floor or washed the clothes, and felt as
though she were hired by the day. And now, on
coming back from the service, they drank tea in the
kitchen with the cook, then they went into the barn
and lay down on the ground between the sledge and
the wall. It was dark here and smelt of harness.
The lights went out about the house, then they could
hear the deaf man shutting up the shop, the mowers
settling themselves about the yard to sleep. In the
distance at the Hrymin Juniors' they were playing
on the expensive concertina. . . . Praskovya and
Lipa began to go to sleep.

And when they were awakened by somebody's
steps it was bright moonlight; at the entrance of the
barn stood Aksinya with her bedding in her arms.

" Maybe it's a bit cooler here," she said; then she

came in and lay down almost in the doorway so that the moonlight fell full upon her.

She did not sleep, but breathed heavily, tossing from side to side with the heat, throwing off almost all the bedclothes. And in the magic moonlight what a beautiful, what a proud animal she was! A little time passed, and then steps were heard again: the old father, white all over, appeared in the doorway.

"Aksinya," he called, "are you here?"

"Well?" she responded angrily.

"I told you just now to throw the money into the well, have you done so?"

"What next, throwing property into the water! I gave them to the mowers. . . ."

"Oh my God!" cried the old man, dumbfounded and alarmed. "Oh my God! you wicked woman. . . ."

He flung up his hands and went out, and he kept saying something as he went away. And a little later Aksinya sat up and sighed heavily with annoyance, then got up and, gathering up her bedclothes in her arms, went out.

"Why did you marry me into this family, mother?" said Lipa.

"One has to be married, daughter. It was not us who ordained it."

And a feeling of inconsolable woe was ready to take possession of them. But it seemed to them that someone was looking down from the height of the heavens, out of the blue from where the stars were seeing everything that was going on in Ukleevo,

watching over them. And however great was wick-
edness, still the night was calm and beautiful, and
still in God's world there is and will be truth and
justice as calm and beautiful, and everything on
earth is only waiting to be made one with truth
and justice, even as the moonlight is blended with
the night.

And both, huddling close to one another, fell
asleep comforted.

VI

News had come long before that Anisim had been
put in prison for coining and passing bad money.
Months passed, more than half a year passed, the
long winter was over, spring had begun, and everyone in the house and the village had grown used to
the fact that Anisim was in prison. And when anyone passed by the house or the shop at night he
would remember that Anisim was in prison; and
when they rang at the churchyard for some reason,
that, too, reminded them that he was in prison awaiting trial.

It seemed as though a shadow had fallen upon the
house. The house looked darker, the roof was
rustier, the heavy, iron-bound door into the shop,
which was painted green, was covered with cracks,
or, as the deaf man expressed it, " blisters "; and old
Tsybukin seemed to have grown dingy, too. He
had given up cutting his hair and beard, and looked
shaggy. He no longer sprang jauntily into his
chaise, nor shouted to beggars: " God will pro-

vide!" His strength was on the wane, and that was evident in everything. People were less afraid of him now, and the police officer drew up a formal charge against him in the shop though he received his regular bribe as before; and three times the old man was called up to the town to be tried for illicit dealing in spirits, and the case was continually adjourned owing to the non-appearance of witnesses, and old Tsybukin was worn out with worry.

He often went to see his son, hired somebody, handed in a petition to somebody else, presented a holy banner to some church. He presented the governor of the prison in which Anisim was confined with a silver glass stand with a long spoon and the inscription: "The soul knows its right measure."

"There is no one to look after things for us," said Varvara. "Tut, tut. . . . You ought to ask someone of the gentlefolks, they would write to the head officials. . . . At least they might let him out on bail! Why wear the poor fellow out?"

She, too, was grieved, but had grown stouter and whiter; she lighted the lamps before the ikons as before, and saw that everything in the house was clean, and regaled the guests with jam and apple cheese. The deaf man and Aksinya looked after the shop. A new project was in progress — a brick-yard in Butyokino — and Aksinya went there almost every day in the chaise. She drove herself, and when she met acquaintances she stretched out her neck like a snake out of the young rye, and smiled naïvely and enigmatically. Lipa spent her time playing with the baby which had been born to her before Lent. It was a tiny, thin, pitiful little baby, and it was strange that it should cry and gaze about and be considered a human being, and even be called Nikifor. He lay in his swinging cradle, and Lipa would walk away towards the door and say, bowing to him:

"Good-day, Nikifor Anisimitch!"

And she would rush at him and kiss him. Then she would walk away to the door, bow again, and say:

'Good-day, Nikifor Anisimitch!"

And he kicked up his little red legs, and his crying was mixed with laughter like the carpenter Elizarov's.

At last the day of the trial was fixed. Tsybukin went away five days before. Then they heard that the peasants called as witnesses had been fetched; their old workman who had received a notice to appear went too.

The trial was on a Thursday. But Sunday had passed, and Tsybukin was still not back, and there was no news. Towards the evening on Tuesday Varvara was sitting at the open window, listening for her husband to come. In the next room Lipa was playing with her baby. She was tossing him up in her arms and saying enthusiastically:

"You will grow up ever so big, ever so big. You will be a peasant, we shall go out to work together! We shall go out to work together!"

"Come, come," said Varvara, offended. "Go out to work, what an idea, you silly girl! He will be a merchant . . .!"

Lipa sang softly, but a minute later she forgot and again:

"You will grow ever so big, ever so big. You will be a peasant, we'll go out to work together."

"There she is at it again!"

Lipa, with Nikifor in her arms, stood still in the doorway and asked:

"Why do I love him so much, mamma? Why do I feel so sorry for him?" she went on in a quivering voice, and her eyes glistened with tears. "Who is he? What is he like? As light as a little feather, as a little crumb, but I love him; I love him like a real person. Here he can do nothing, he can't talk, and yet I know what he wants with his little eyes."

Varvara was listening; the sound of the evening train coming in to the station reached her. Had her husband come? She did not hear and she did not heed what Lipa was saying, she had no idea how the time passed, but only trembled all over — not from dread, but intense curiosity. She saw a cart full of peasants roll quickly by with a rattle. It was the witnesses coming back from the station. When the cart passed the shop the old workman jumped out and walked into the yard. She could hear him being greeted in the yard and being asked some questions. . . .

"Deprivation of rights and all his property," he said loudly, "and six years' penal servitude in Siberia."

She could see Aksinya come out of the shop by the back way; she had just been selling kerosene, and in one hand held a bottle and in the other a can, and in her mouth she had some silver coins.

" Where is father? " she asked, lisping.

" At the station," answered the labourer. " ' When it gets a little darker,' he said, ' then I shall come.' "

And when it became known all through the household that Anisim was sentenced to penal servitude, the cook in the kitchen suddenly broke into a wail as though at a funeral, imagining that this was demanded by the proprieties:

" There is no one to care for us now you have gone, Anisim Grigoritch, our bright falcon. . . ."

The dogs began barking in alarm. Varvara ran to the window, and rushing about in distress, shouted to the cook with all her might, straining her voice:

" Sto-op, Stepanida, sto-op! Don't harrow us, for Christ's sake! "

They forgot to set the samovar, they could think of nothing. Only Lipa could not make out what it was all about and went on playing with her baby.

When the old father arrived from the station they asked him no questions. He greeted them and walked through all the rooms in silence; he had no supper.

" There was no one to see about things . . ." Varvara began when they were alone. " I said you should have asked some of the gentry, you would not heed me at the time. . . . A petition would . . ."

" I saw to things," said her husband with a wave of his hand. " When Anisim was condemned I

went to the gentleman who was defending him.
' It's no use now,' he said, ' it's too late '; and Anisim said the same; it's too late.   But all the same
as I came out of the court I made an agreement
with a lawyer, I paid him something in advance.
I'll wait a week and then I will go again.   It is as
God wills."

Again the old man walked through all the rooms,
and when he went back to Varvara he said:
" I must be ill.   My head's in a sort of . . . fog.
My thoughts are in a maze."

He closed the door that Lipa might not hear, and
went on softly:
" I am unhappy about my money.   Do you remember on Low Sunday before his wedding Anisim's
bringing me some new roubles and half-roubles?
One parcel I put away at the time, but the others I
mixed with my own money.   When my uncle Dmitri
Filatitch — the kingdom of heaven be his — was
alive, he used constantly to go journeys to Moscow
and to the Crimea to buy goods.   He had a wife,
and this same wife, when he was away buying goods,
used to take up with other men.   She had half a
dozen children.   And when uncle was in his cups he
would laugh and say: ' I never can make out,' he
used to say, ' which are my children and which are
other people's.'   An easy-going disposition, to be
sure; and so I now can't distinguish which are genuine roubles and which are false ones.   And it
seems to me that they are all false."

" Nonsense, God bless you."

" I take a ticket at the station, I give the man

three roubles, and I keep fancying they are false.
And I am frightened. I must be ill."

" There's no denying it, we are all in God's hands.
. . . Oh dear, dear . . ." said Varvara, and she
shook her head. " You ought to think about this,
Grigory Petrovitch: you never know, anything may
happen, you are not a young man. See they don't
wrong your grandchild when you are dead and gone.
Oy, I am afraid they will be unfair to Nikifor! He
has as good as no father, his mother's young and
foolish . . . you ought to secure something for him,
poor little boy, at least the land, Butyokino, Grigory Petrovitch, really! Think it over!" Varvara
went on persuading him. " The pretty boy, one is
sorry for him! You go to-morrow and make out a
deed; why put it off? "

" I'd forgotten about my grandson," said Tsybukin. " I must go and have a look at him. So
you say the boy is all right? Well, let him grow up,
please God."

He opened the door and, crooking his finger,
beckoned to Lipa. She went up to him with the
baby in her arms.

" If there is anything you want, Lipinka, you ask
for it," he said. " And eat anything you like, we
don't grudge it, so long as it does you good. . . ."
He made the sign of the cross over the baby.
" And take care of my grandchild. My son is gone,
but my grandson is left."

Tears rolled down his cheeks; he gave a sob and
went away. Soon afterwards he went to bed and
slept soundly after seven sleepless nights.

VII

Old Tsybukin went to the town for a short time.
Someone told Aksinya that he had gone to the notary
to make his will and that he was leaving Butyokino,
the very place where she had set up a brickyard, to
Nikifor, his grandson. She was informed of this in
the morning when old Tsybukin and Varvara were
sitting near the steps under the birch-tree, drinking
their tea. She closed the shop in the front and at
the back, gathered together all the keys she had, and
flung them at her father-in-law's feet.

"I am not going on working for you," she began
in a loud voice, and suddenly broke into sobs. "It
seems I am not your daughter-in-law, but a servant!
Everybody's jeering and saying, ' See what a servant
the Tsybukins have got hold of!' I did not come
to you for wages! I am not a beggar, I am not a
slave, I have a father and mother."

She did not wipe away her tears, she fixed upon
her father-in-law eyes full of tears, vindictive,
squinting with wrath; her face and neck were red
and tense, and she was shouting at the top of her
voice.

"I don't mean to go on being a slave!" she went
on. "I am worn out. When it is work, when it is
sitting in the shop day in and day out, scurrying out
at night for vodka — then it is my share, but when
it is giving away the land then it is for that convict's
wife and her imp. She is mistress here, and I am

her servant. Give her everything, the convict's wife, and may it choke her! I am going home! Find yourselves some other fool, you damned Herods!"

Tsybukin had never in his life scolded or punished his children, and had never dreamed that one of his family could speak to him rudely or behave disrespectfully; and now he was very much frightened; he ran into the house and there hid behind the cupboard. And Varvara was so much flustered that she could not get up from her seat, and only waved her hands before her as though she were warding off a bee.

"Oh, Holy Saints! what's the meaning of it?" she muttered in horror. "What is she shouting? Oh, dear, dear! . . . People will hear! Hush. Oh, hush!"

"He has given Butyokino to the convict's wife," Aksinya went on bawling. "Give her everything now, I don't want anything from you! Let me alone! You are all a gang of thieves here! I have seen my fill of it, I have had enough! You have robbed folks coming in and going out; you have robbed old and young alike, you brigands! And who has been selling vodka without a licence? And false money? You've filled boxes full of false coins, and now I am no more use!"

A crowd had by now collected at the open gate and was staring into the yard.

"Let the people look," bawled Aksinya. "I will shame you all! You shall burn with shame! You shall grovel at my feet. Hey! Stepan," she

called to the deaf man, " let us go home this minute! Let us go to my father and mother; I don't
want to live with convicts.   Get ready! "

Clothes were hanging on lines stretched across
the yard; she snatched off her petticoats and blouses
still wet and flung them into the deaf man's arms.
Then in her fury she dashed about the yard by the
linen, tore down all of it, and what was not hers
she threw on the ground and trampled upon.

" Holy Saints, take her away," moaned Varvara.
" What a woman! Give her Butyokino! Give it
her, for the Lord's sake! "

" Well! Wha-at a woman! " people were saying at the gate. " She's a wo-oman! She's going
it — something like! "

Aksinya ran into the kitchen where washing was
going on. Lipa was washing alone, the cook had
gone to the river to rinse the clothes. Steam was
rising from the trough and from the caldron on the
side of the stove, and the kitchen was thick and
stifling from the steam. On the floor was a heap
of unwashed clothes, and Nikifor, kicking up his
little red legs, had been put down on a bench near
them, so that if he fell he should not hurt himself.
Just as Aksinya went in Lipa took the former's
chemise out of the heap and put it in the trough,
and was just stretching out her hand to a big
ladle of boiling water which was standing on the
table.

" Give it here," said Aksinya, looking at her with
hatred, and snatching the chemise out of the trough;
" it is not your business to touch my linen! You

are a convict's wife, and ought to know your place
and who you are."

Lipa gazed at her, taken aback, and did not understand, but suddenly she caught the look Aksinya
turned upon the child, and at once she understood
and went numb all over.

" You've taken my land, so here you are ! " Saying this Aksinya snatched up the ladle with the boiling water and flung it over Nikifor.

After this there was heard a scream such as had
never been heard before in Ukleevo, and no one
would have believed that a little weak creature like
Lipa could scream like that. And it was suddenly
silent in the yard.

Aksinya walked into the house with her old naïve
smile. . . . The deaf man kept moving about the
yard with his arms full of linen, then he began hanging it up again, in silence, without haste. And until
the cook came back from the river no one ventured
to go into the kitchen and see what was there.

VIII

Nikifor was taken to the district hospital, and
towards evening he died there. Lipa did not wait
for them to come for her, but wrapped the dead
baby in its little quilt and carried it home.

The hospital, a new one recently built, with big
windows, stood high up on a hill; it was glittering
from the setting sun and looked as though it were
on fire from inside. There was a little village below. Lipa went down along the road, and before

reaching the village sat down by a pond. A woman brought a horse down to drink and the horse did not drink.

"What more do you want?" said the woman to it softly. "What do you want?"

A boy in a red shirt, sitting at the water's edge, was washing his father's boots. And not another soul was in sight either in the village or on the hill.

"It's not drinking," said Lipa, looking at the horse.

Then the woman with the horse and the boy with the boots walked away, and there was no one left at all. The sun went to bed wrapped in cloth of gold and purple, and long clouds, red and lilac, stretched across the sky, guarded its slumbers. Somewhere far away a bittern cried, a hollow, melancholy sound like a cow shut up in a barn. The cry of that mysterious bird was heard every spring, but no one knew what it was like or where it lived. At the top of the hill by the hospital, in the bushes close to the pond, and in the fields the nightingales were trilling. The cuckoo kept reckoning someone's years and losing count and beginning again. In the pond the frogs called angrily to one another, straining themselves to bursting, and one could even make out the words: "That's what you are! That's what you are!" What a noise there was! It seemed as though all these creatures were singing and shouting so that no one might sleep on that spring night, so that all, even the angry frogs, might appreciate and enjoy every minute: life is given only once.

A silver half-moon was shining in the sky; there were many stars. Lipa had no idea how long she sat by the pond, but when she got up and walked on everybody was asleep in the little village, and there was not a single light. It was probably about nine miles' walk home, but she had not the strength, she had not the power to think how to go: the moon gleamed now in front, now on the right, and the same cuckoo kept calling in a voice grown husky, with a chuckle as though gibing at her: " Oy, look out, you'll lose your way! " Lipa walked rapidly; she lost the kerchief from her head . . . she looked at the sky and wondered where her baby's soul was now: was it following her, or floating aloft yonder among the stars and thinking nothing now of his mother? Oh, how lonely it was in the open country at night, in the midst of that singing when one cannot sing oneself; in the midst of the incessant cries of joy when one cannot oneself be joyful, when the moon, which cares not whether it is spring or winter, whether men are alive or dead, looks down as lonely, too. . . . When there is grief in the heart it is hard to be without people. If only her mother, Praskovya, had been with her, or Crutch, or the cook, or some peasant!

" Boo-oo! " cried the bittern. " Boo-oo! "

And suddenly she heard clearly the sound of human speech:

" Put the horses in, Vavila! "

By the wayside a camp fire was burning ahead of her: the flames had died down, there were only red embers. She could hear the horses munching.

In the darkness she could see the outlines of two carts, one with a barrel, the other, a lower one with sacks in it, and the figures of two men; one was leading a horse to put it into the shafts, the other was standing motionless by the fire with his hands behind his back. A dog growled by the carts. The one who was leading the horse stopped and said:

" It seems as though someone were coming along the road."

" Sharik, be quiet! " the other called to the dog.

And from the voice one could tell that the second was an old man. Lipa stopped and said:

" God help you."

The old man went up to her and answered not immediately:

" Good-evening! "

" Your dog does not bite, grandfather? "

" No, come along, he won't touch you."

" I have been at the hospital," said Lipa after a pause. " My little son died there. Here I am carrying him home."

It must have been unpleasant for the old man to hear this, for he moved away and said hurriedly:

" Never mind, my dear. It's God's will. You are very slow, lad," he added, addressing his companion; " look alive! "

" Your yoke's nowhere," said the young man; " it is not to be seen."

" You are a regular Vavila."

The old man picked up an ember, blew on it — only his eyes and nose were lighted up — then, when they had found the yoke, he went with the light to

Lipa and looked at her, and his look expressed compassion and tenderness.

" You are a mother," he said; " every mother grieves for her child."

And he sighed and shook his head as he said it. Vavila threw something on the fire, stamped on it — and at once it was very dark; the vision vanished, and as before there were only the fields, the sky with the stars, and the noise of the birds hindering each other from sleep. And the landrail called, it seemed, in the very place where the fire had been.

But a minute passed, and again she could see the two carts and the old man and lanky Vavila. The carts creaked as they went out on the road.

" Are you holy men? " Lipa asked the old man.

" No. We are from Firsanovo."

" You looked at me just now and my heart was softened. And the young man is so gentle. I thought you must be holy men."

" Are you going far? "

" To Ukleevo."

" Get in, we will give you a lift as far as Kuzmenki, then you go straight on and we turn off to the left."

Vavila got into the cart with the barrel and the old man and Lipa got into the other. They moved at a walking pace, Vavila in front.

" My baby was in torment all day," said Lipa. " He looked at me with his little eyes and said nothing; he wanted to speak and could not. Holy Father, Queen of Heaven! In my grief I kept fall-

ing down on the floor. I stood up and fell down
by the bedside. And tell me, grandfather, why a
little thing should be tormented before his death?
When a grown-up person, a man or woman, are in
torment their sins are forgiven, but why a little
thing, when he has no sins? Why?"

" Who can tell? " answered the old man.

They drove on for half an hour in silence.

" We can't know everything, how and wherefore,"
said the old man. " It is ordained for the bird to
have not four wings but two because it is able to
fly with two; and so it is ordained for man not to
know everything but only a half or a quarter. As
much as he needs to know so as to live, so much he
knows."

" It is better for me to go on foot, grandfather.
Now my heart is all of a tremble."

" Never mind, sit still."

The old man yawned and made the sign of the
cross over his mouth.

" Never mind," he repeated. " Yours is not the
worst of sorrows. Life is long, there will be good
and bad to come, there will be everything. Great
is mother Russia," he said, and looked round on each
side of him. " I have been all over Russia, and I
have seen everything in her, and you may believe
my words, my dear. There will be good and there
will be bad. I went as a delegate from my village
to Siberia, and I have been to the Amur River and
the Altai Mountains and I settled in Siberia; I
worked the land there, then I was homesick for
mother Russia and I came back to my native village.

We came back to Russia on foot; and I remember we went on a steamer, and I was thin as thin, all in rags, barefoot, freezing with cold, and gnawing a crust, and a gentleman who was on the steamer — the kingdom of heaven be his if he is dead — looked at me pitifully, and the tears came into his eyes. ' Ah,' he said, ' your bread is black, your days are black. . . .' And when I got home, as the saying is, there was neither stick nor stall; I had a wife, but I left her behind in Siberia, she was buried there. So I am living as a day labourer. And yet I tell you: since then I have had good as well as bad. Here I do not want to die, my dear, I would be glad to live another twenty years; so there has been more of the good. And great is our mother Russia! " and again he gazed to each side and looked round.

" Grandfather," Lipa asked, " when anyone dies, how many days does his soul walk the earth? "

" Who can tell! Ask Vavila here, he has been to school. Now they teach them everything. Vavila! " the old man called to him.

" Yes! "

" Vavila, when anyone dies how long does his soul walk the earth? "

Vavila stopped the horse and only then answered:

" Nine days. My uncle Kirilla died and his soul lived in our hut thirteen days after."

" How do you know? "

" For thirteen days there was a knocking in the stove."

" Well, that's all right. Go on," said the old

man, and it could be seen that he did not believe a word of all that.

Near Kuzmenki the cart turned into the high road while Lipa went straight on. It was by now getting light. As she went down into the ravine the Ukleevo huts and the church were hidden in fog. It was cold, and it seemed to her that the same cuckoo was calling still.

When Lipa reached home the cattle had not yet been driven out; everyone was asleep. She sat down on the steps and waited. The old man was the first to come out; he understood all that had happened from the first glance at her, and for a long time he could not articulate a word, but only moved his lips without a sound.

"Ech, Lipa," he said, "you did not take care of my grandchild. . . ."

Varvara was awakened. She clasped her hands and broke into sobs, and immediately began laying out the baby.

"And he was a pretty child . . ." she said. "Oh, dear, dear. . . . You only had the one child, and you did not take care enough of him, you silly girl. . . ."

There was a requiem service in the morning and the evening. The funeral took place the next day, and after it the guests and the priests ate a great deal, and with such greed that one might have thought that they had not tasted food for a long time. Lipa waited at table, and the priest, lifting his fork on which there was a salted mushroom, said to her:

" Don't grieve for the babe.   For of such is the kingdom of heaven."

And only when they had all separated Lipa realized fully that there was no Nikifor and never would be, she realized it and broke into sobs.   And she did not know what room to go into to sob, for she felt that now that her child was dead there was no place for her in the house, that she had no reason to be here, that she was in the way; and the others felt it, too.

" Now what are you bellowing for? " Aksinya shouted, suddenly appearing in the doorway; in honour of the funeral she was dressed all in new clothes and had powdered her face.   " Shut up! "

Lipa tried to stop but could not, and sobbed louder than ever.

" Do you hear? " shouted Aksinya, and she stamped her foot in violent anger.   " Who is it I am speaking to? Go out of the yard and don't set foot here again, you convict's wife.   Get away."

" There, there, there," the old man put in fussily. " Aksinya, don't make such an outcry, my girl. . . . She is crying, it is only natural . . . her child is dead. . . ."

" ' It's only natural,' " Aksinya mimicked him. " Let her stay the night here, and don't let me see a trace of her here to-morrow!   ' It's only natural! ' . . ." she mimicked him again, and, laughing, she went into the shop.

Early the next morning Lipa went off to her mother at Torguevo.

IX

At the present time the steps and the front door of the shop have been repainted and are as bright as though they were new, there are gay geraniums in the windows as of old, and what happened in Tsybukin's house and yard three years ago is almost forgotten.

Grigory Petrovitch is looked upon as the master as he was in old days, but in reality everything has passed into Aksinya's hands; she buys and sells, and nothing can be done without her consent. The brickyard is working well; and as bricks are wanted for the railway the price has gone up to twenty-four roubles a thousand; peasant women and girls cart the bricks to the station and load them up in the trucks and earn a quarter-rouble a day for the work.

Aksinya has gone into partnership with the Hrymin Juniors, and their factory is now called Hrymin Juniors and Co. They have opened a tavern near the station, and now the expensive concertina is played not at the factory but at the tavern, and the head of the post office often goes there, and he, too, is engaged in some sort of traffic, and the stationmaster, too. Hrymin Juniors have presented the deaf man Stepan with a gold watch, and he is constantly taking it out of his pocket and putting it to his ear.

People say of Aksinya that she has become a person of power; and it is true that when she drives

in the morning to her brickyard, handsome and
happy, with the naïve smile on her face, and afterwards when she is giving orders there, one is aware
of great power in her. Everyone is afraid of her
in the house and in the village and in the brickyard.
When she goes to the post the head of the postal
department jumps up and says to her:

"I humbly beg you to be seated, Aksinya Abramovna!"

A certain landowner, middle-aged but foppish, in
a tunic of fine cloth and patent leather high boots,
sold her a horse, and was so carried away by talking to her that he knocked down the price to meet
her wishes. He held her hand a long time and,
looking into her merry, sly, naïve eyes, said:

"For a woman like you, Aksinya Abramovna, I
should be ready to do anything you please. Only
say when we can meet where no one will interfere
with us?"

"Why, when you please."

And since then the elderly fop drives up to the
shop almost every day to drink beer. And the beer
is horrid, bitter as wormwood. The landowner
shakes his head, but he drinks it.

Old Tsybukin does not have anything to do with
the business now at all. He does not keep any
money because he cannot distinguish between the
good and the false, but he is silent, he says nothing
of this weakness. He has become forgetful, and
if they don't give him food he does not ask for it.
They have grown used to having dinner without
him, and Varvara often says:

" He went to bed again yesterday without any supper."

And she says it unconcernedly because she is used to it. For some reason, summer and winter alike, he wears a fur coat, and only in very hot weather he does not go out but sits at home. As a rule putting on his fur coat, wrapping it round him and turning up his collar, he walks about the village, along the road to the station, or sits from morning till night on the seat near the church gates. He sits there without stirring. Passers-by bow to him, but he does not respond, for as of old he dislikes the peasants. If he is asked a question he answers quite rationally and politely, but briefly.

There is a rumour going about in the village that his daughter-in-law turns him out of the house and gives him nothing to eat, and that he is fed by charity; some are glad, others are sorry for him.

Varvara has grown even fatter and whiter, and as before she is active in good works, and Aksinya does not interfere with her.

There is so much jam now that they have not time to eat it before the fresh fruit comes in; it goes sugary, and Varvara almost sheds tears, not knowing what to do with it.

They have begun to forget about Anisim. A letter has come from him written in verse on a big sheet of paper as though it were a petition, all in the same splendid handwriting. Evidently his friend Samorodov was sharing his punishment. Under the verses in an ugly, scarcely legible handwriting there was a single line: " I am ill here all the time; I am wretched, for Christ's sake help me! "

Towards evening — it was a fine autumn day — old Tsybukin was sitting near the church gates, with the collar of his fur coat turned up and nothing of him could be seen but his nose and the peak of his cap. At the other end of the long seat was sitting Elizarov the contractor, and beside him Yakov the school watchman, a toothless old man of seventy. Crutch and the watchman were talking.

" Children ought to give food and drink to the old. . . . Honour thy father and mother . . ." Yakov was saying with irritation, " while she, this daughter-in-law, has turned her father-in-law out of his own house; the old man has neither food nor drink, where is he to go? He has not had a morsel for these three days."

" Three days! " said Crutch, amazed.

" Here he sits and does not say a word. He has grown feeble. And why be silent? He ought to prosecute her, they wouldn't flatter her in the police court."

" Wouldn't flatter whom? " asked Crutch, not hearing.

" What? "

" The woman's all right, she does her best. In their line of business they can't get on without that . . . without sin, I mean. . . ."

" From his own house," Yakov went on with irritation. " Save up and buy your own house, then turn people out of it! She is a nice one, to be sure! A pla-ague! "

Tsybukin listened and did not stir.

"Whether it is your own house or others' it makes no difference so long as it is warm and the women don't scold . . ." said Crutch, and he laughed. "When I was young I was very fond of my Nastasya. She was a quiet woman. And she used to be always at it: ' Buy a house, Makaritch! Buy a house, Makaritch! Buy a house, Makaritch!' She was dying and yet she kept on saying, ' Buy yourself a racing droshky, Makaritch, that you may not have to walk.' And I bought her nothing but gingerbread."

"Her husband's deaf and stupid," Yakov went on, not hearing Crutch; " a regular fool, just like a goose. He can't understand anything. Hit a goose on the head with a stick and even then it does not understand."

Crutch got up to go home to the factory. Yakov also got up, and both of them went off together, still talking. When they had gone fifty paces old Tsybukin got up, too, and walked after them, stepping uncertainly as though on slippery ice.

The village was already plunged in the dusk of evening and the sun only gleamed on the upper part of the road which ran wriggling like a snake up the slope. Old women were coming back from the woods and children with them; they were bringing baskets of mushrooms. Peasant women and girls came in a crowd from the station where they had been loading the trucks with bricks, and their noses and their cheeks under their eyes were covered with red brick-dust. They were singing. Ahead of

them all was Lipa singing in a high voice, with her
eyes turned upwards to the sky, breaking into trills
as though triumphant and ecstatic that at last the
day was over and she could rest. In the crowd
was her mother Praskovya, who was walking with
a bundle in her arms and breathless as usual.

"Good-evening, Makaritch!" cried Lipa, seeing
Crutch. "Good-evening, darling!"

"Good-evening, Lipinka," cried Crutch delighted.
"Dear girls and women, love the rich carpenter!
Ho-ho! My little children, my little children.
(Crutch gave a gulp.) My dear little axes!"

Crutch and Yakov went on further and could still
be heard talking. Then after them the crowd was
met by old Tsybukin and there was a sudden hush.
Lipa and Praskovya had dropped a little behind,
and when the old man was on a level with them
Lipa bowed down low and said:

"Good-evening, Grigory Petrovitch."

Her mother, too, bowed down. The old man
stopped and, saying nothing, looked at the two in
silence; his lips were quivering and his eyes full of
tears. Lipa took out of her mother's bundle a
piece of savoury turnover and gave it him. He
took it and began eating.

The sun had by now set: its glow died away on
the road above. It grew dark and cool. Lipa
and Praskovya walked on and for some time they
kept crossing themselves.

1900

THE HUNTSMAN

THE HUNTSMAN

A SULTRY, stifling midday. Not a cloudlet in the
sky. . . . The sun-baked grass had a disconsolate,
hopeless look: even if there were rain it could never
be green again. . . . The forest stood silent, motionless, as though it were looking at something
with its tree-tops or expecting something.

At the edge of the clearing a tall, narrow-shoul-
dered man of forty in a red shirt, in patched trousers
that had been a gentleman's, and in high boots, was
slouching along with a lazy, shambling step. He
was sauntering along the road. On the right was
the green of the clearing, on the left a golden sea of
ripe rye stretched to the very horizon. He was red
and perspiring, a white cap with a straight jockey
peak, evidently a gift from some open-handed young
gentleman, perched jauntily on his handsome flaxen
head. Across his shoulder hung a game-bag with a
blackcock lying in it. The man held a double-
barrelled gun cocked in his hand, and screwed up his
eyes in the direction of his lean old dog who was
running on ahead sniffing the bushes. There was
stillness all round, not a sound . . . everything living was hiding away from the heat.

" Yegor Vlassitch! " the huntsman suddenly heard
a soft voice.

He started and, looking round, scowled. Beside

him, as though she had sprung out of the earth, stood a pale-faced woman of thirty with a sickle in her hand. She was trying to look into his face, and was smiling diffidently.

" Oh, it is you, Pelagea! " said the huntsman, stopping and deliberately uncocking the gun. " H'm! . . . How have you come here? "

" The women from our village are working here, so I have come with them. . . . As a labourer, Yegor Vlassitch."

" Oh . . ." growled Yegor Vlassitch, and slowly walked on.

Pelagea followed him. They walked in silence for twenty paces.

" I have not seen you for a long time, Yegor Vlassitch . . ." said Pelagea looking tenderly at the huntsman's moving shoulders. " I have not seen you since you came into our hut at Easter for a drink of water . . . you came in at Easter for a minute and then God knows how . . . drunk . . . you scolded and beat me and went away . . . I have been waiting and waiting . . . I've tired my eyes out looking for you. Ah, Yegor Vlassitch, Yegor Vlassitch! you might look in just once! "

" What is there for me to do there? "

" Of course there is nothing for you to do . . . though to be sure . . . there is the place to look after. . . . To see how things are going. . . . You are the master. . . . I say, you have shot a black-cock, Yegor Vlassitch! You ought to sit down and rest! "

As she said all this Pelagea laughed like a silly

girl and looked up at Yegor's face. Her face was simply radiant with happiness.

"Sit down? If you like . . ." said Yegor in a tone of indifference, and he chose a spot between two fir-trees. "Why are you standing? You sit down too."

Pelagea sat a little way off in the sun and, ashamed of her joy, put her hand over her smiling mouth. Two minutes passed in silence.

"You might come for once," said Pelagea.

"What for?" sighed Yegor, taking off his cap and wiping his red forehead with his hand. "There is no object in my coming. To go for an hour or two is only waste of time, it's simply upsetting you, and to live continually in the village my soul could not endure. . . . You know yourself I am a pampered man. . . . I want a bed to sleep in, good tea to drink, and refined conversation. . . . I want all the niceties, while you live in poverty and dirt in the village. . . . I couldn't stand it for a day. Suppose there were an edict that I must live with you, I should either set fire to the hut or lay hands on myself. From a boy I've had this love for ease; there is no help for it."

"Where are you living now?"

"With the gentleman here, Dmitry Ivanitch, as a huntsman. I furnish his table with game, but he keeps me . . . more for his pleasure than anything."

"That's not proper work you're doing, Yegor Vlassitch. . . . For other people it's a pastime, but with you it's like a trade . . . like real work."

" You don't understand, you silly," said Yegor, gazing gloomily at the sky. " You have never understood, and as long as you live you will never understand what sort of man I am. . . . You think of me as a foolish man, gone to the bad, but to anyone who understands I am the best shot there is in the whole district. The gentry feel that, and they have even printed things about me in a magazine. There isn't a man to be compared with me as a sportsman. . . . And it is not because I am pampered and proud that I look down upon your village work. From my childhood, you know, I have never had any calling apart from guns and dogs. If they took away my gun, I used to go out with the fishing-hook, if they took the hook I caught things with my hands. And I went in for horse-dealing too, I used to go to the fairs when I had the money, and you know that if a peasant goes in for being a sportsman, or a horse-dealer, it's good-bye to the plough. Once the spirit of freedom has taken a man you will never root it out of him. In the same way, if a gentleman goes in for being an actor or for any other art, he will never make an official or a landowner. You are a woman, and you do not understand, but one must understand that."

" I understand, Yegor Vlassitch."

" You don't understand if you are going to cry. . . ."

" I . . . I'm not crying," said Pelagea, turning away. " It's a sin, Yegor Vlassitch! You might stay a day with luckless me, anyway. It's twelve years since I was married to you, and . . . and

. . . there has never once been love between us!
. . . I . . . I am not crying."

"Love . . ." muttered Yegor, scratching his hand. "There can't be any love. It's only in name we are husband and wife; we aren't really. In your eyes I am a wild man, and in mine you are a simple peasant woman with no understanding. Are we well matched? I am a free, pampered, profligate man, while you are a working woman, going in bark shoes and never straightening your back. The way I think of myself is that I am the foremost man in every kind of sport, and you look at me with pity. . . . Is that being well matched?"

"But we are married, you know, Yegor Vlassitch," sobbed Pelagea.

"Not married of our free will. . . . Have you forgotten? You have to thank Count Sergey Pavlovitch and yourself. Out of envy, because I shot better than he did, the Count kept giving me wine for a whole month, and when a man's drunk you could make him change his religion, let alone getting married. To pay me out he married me to you when I was drunk. . . . A huntsman to a herd-girl! You saw I was drunk, why did you marry me? You were not a serf, you know; you could have resisted. Of course it was a bit of luck for a herd-girl to marry a huntsman, but you ought to have thought about it. Well, now be miserable, cry. It's a joke for the Count, but a crying matter for you. : . . Beat yourself against the wall."

A silence followed. Three wild ducks flew over the clearing. Yegor followed them with his eyes

till, transformed into three scarcely visible dots, they
sank down far beyond the forest.

" How do you live ? " he asked, moving his eyes
from the ducks to Pelagea.

" Now I am going out to work, and in the winter
I take a child from the Foundling Hospital and
bring it up on the bottle.   They give me a rouble and
a half a month."

" Oh. . . ."

Again a silence.   From the strip that had been
reaped floated a soft song which broke off at the
very beginning.   It was too hot to sing.

" They say you have put up a new hut for Aku-
lina," said Pelagea.

Yegor did not speak.

" So she is dear to you. . . ."

" It's your luck, it's fate ! " said the huntsman,
stretching.   " You must put up with it, poor thing.
But good-bye, I've been chattering long enough.
. . . I must be at Boltovo by the evening."

Yegor rose, stretched himself, and slung his gun
over his shoulder; Pelagea got up.

" And when are you coming to the village ? " she
asked softly.

" I have no reason to, I shall never come sober,
and you have little to gain from me drunk; I am
spiteful when I am drunk.   Good-bye ! "

" Good-bye, Yegor Vlassitch."

Yegor put his cap on the back of his head and,
clicking to his dog, went on his way.   Pelagea stood
still looking after him. . . . She saw his moving
shoulder-blades, his jaunty cap, his lazy, careless

step, and her eyes were full of sadness and tender affection. . . . Her gaze flitted over her husband's tall, lean figure and caressed and fondled it. . . . He, as though he felt that gaze, stopped and looked round. . . . He did not speak, but from his face, from his shrugged shoulders, Pelagea could see that he wanted to say something to her. She went up to him timidly and looked at him with imploring eyes.

" Take it," he said, turning round.

He gave her a crumpled rouble note and walked quickly away.

" Good-bye, Yegor Vlassitch," she said, mechanically taking the rouble.

He walked by a long road, straight as a taut strap. She, pale and motionless as a statue, stood, her eyes seizing every step he took. But the red of his shirt melted into the dark colour of his trousers, his step could not be seen, and the dog could not be distinguished from the boots. Nothing could be seen but the cap, and . . . suddenly Yegor turned off sharply into the clearing and the cap vanished in the greenness.

" Good-bye, Yegor Vlassitch," whispered Pelagea, and she stood on tiptoe to see the white cap once more.

1885

HAPPINESS

HAPPINESS

A FLOCK of sheep was spending the night on the broad steppe road that is called the great highway. Two shepherds were guarding it. One, a toothless old man of eighty, with a tremulous face, was lying on his stomach at the very edge of the road, leaning his elbows on the dusty leaves of a plantain; the other, a young fellow with thick black eyebrows and no moustache, dressed in the coarse canvas of which cheap sacks are made, was lying on his back, with his arms under his head, looking upwards at the sky, where the stars were slumbering and the Milky Way lay stretched exactly above his face.

The shepherds were not alone. A couple of yards from them in the dusk that shrouded the road a horse made a patch of darkness, and, beside it, leaning against the saddle, stood a man in high boots and a short full-skirted jacket who looked like an overseer on some big estate. Judging from his upright and motionless figure, from his manners, and his behaviour to the shepherds and to his horse, he was a serious, reasonable man who knew his own value; even in the darkness signs could be detected in him of military carriage and of the majestically condescending expression gained by frequent intercourse with the gentry and their stewards.

The sheep were asleep. Against the grey background of the dawn, already beginning to cover the eastern part of the sky, the silhouettes of sheep that were not asleep could be seen here and there; they stood with drooping heads, thinking. Their thoughts, tedious and oppressive, called forth by images of nothing but the broad steppe and the sky, the days and the nights, probably weighed upon them themselves, crushing them into apathy; and, standing there as though rooted to the earth, they noticed neither the presence of a stranger nor the uneasiness of the dogs.

The drowsy, stagnant air was full of the monotonous noise inseparable from a summer night on the steppes; the grasshoppers chirruped incessantly; the quails called, and the young nightingales trilled languidly half a mile away in a ravine where a stream flowed and willows grew.

The overseer had halted to ask the shepherds for a light for his pipe. He lighted it in silence and smoked the whole pipe; then, still without uttering a word, stood with his elbow on the saddle, plunged in thought. The young shepherd took no notice of him, he still lay gazing at the sky while the old man slowly looked the overseer up and down and then asked:

" Why, aren't you Panteley from Makarov's estate? "

" That's myself," answered the overseer.

" To be sure, I see it is. I didn't know you — that is a sign you will be rich. Where has God brought you from? "

" From the Kovylyevsky fields."

" That's a good way. Are you letting the land on the part-crop system? "

" Part of it. Some like that, and some we are letting on lease, and some for raising melons and cucumbers. I have just come from the mill."

A big shaggy old sheep-dog of a dirty white colour with woolly tufts about its nose and eyes walked three times quietly round the horse, trying to seem unconcerned in the presence of strangers, then all at once dashed suddenly from behind at the overseer with an angry aged growl; the other dogs could not refrain from leaping up too.

" Lie down, you damned brute," cried the old man, raising himself on his elbow; " blast you, you devil's creature."

When the dogs were quiet again, the old man resumed his former attitude and said quietly:

" It was at Kovyli on Ascension Day that Yefim Zhmenya died. Don't speak of it in the dark, it is a sin to mention such people. He was a wicked old man. I dare say you have heard."

" No, I haven't."

" Yefim Zhmenya, the uncle of Styopka, the black-smith. The whole district round knew him. Aye, he was a cursed old man, he was! I knew him for sixty years, ever since Tsar Alexander who beat the French was brought from Taganrog to Moscow. We went together to meet the dead Tsar, and in those days the great highway did not run to Bahmut, but from Esaulovka to Gorodishtche, and where Kovyli is now, there were bustards' nests — there was a bustard's nest at every step. Even then I had noticed that Yefim had given his soul to damnation, and that the Evil One was in him. I have observed that if any man of the peasant class is apt to be silent, takes up with old women's jobs, and tries to live in solitude, there is no good in it, and Yefim from his youth up was always one to hold his tongue and look at you sideways, he always seemed to be sulky and bristling like a cock before a hen. To go to church or to the tavern or to lark in the street with the lads was not his fashion, he would rather sit alone or be whispering with old women. When he was still young he took jobs to look after the bees and the market gardens. Good folks would come to his market garden sometimes and his melons were whistling. One day he caught a pike, when folks were looking on, and it laughed aloud, ' Ho-ho-ho-ho ! ' "

" It does happen," said Panteley.

The young shepherd turned on his side and, lifting his black eyebrows, stared intently at the old man.

" Did you hear the melons whistling? " he asked.

" Hear them I didn't, the Lord spared me," sighed the old man, " but folks told me so. It is no great wonder . . . the Evil One will begin whistling in a stone if he wants to. Before the Day of Freedom a rock was humming for three days and three nights in our parts. I heard it myself. The pike laughed because Yefim caught a devil instead of a pike."

The old man remembered something. He got up

quickly on to his knees and, shrinking as though
from the cold, nervously thrusting his hands into
his sleeves, he muttered in a rapid womanish gab-
ble:

"Lord save us and have mercy upon us! I was
walking along the river bank one day to Novopavlovka. A storm was gathering, such a tempest it
was, preserve us Holy Mother, Queen of Heaven.
. . . I was hurrying on as best I could, I looked,
and beside the path between the thorn bushes —
the thorn was in flower at the time — there was a
white bullock coming along. I wondered whose
bullock it was, and what the devil had sent it there
for. It was coming along and swinging its tail and
moo-oo-oo! but would you believe it, friends, I over-
take it, I come up close — and it's not a bullock,
but Yefim — holy, holy, holy! I make the sign of
the cross while he stares at me and mutters, showing
the whites of his eyes; wasn't I frightened! We
came alongside, I was afraid to say a word to him —
the thunder was crashing, the sky was streaked with
lightning, the willows were bent right down to the
water — all at once, my friends, God strike me dead
that I die impenitent, a hare ran across the path . . .
it ran and stopped, and said like a man: 'Good-
evening, peasants.' Lie down, you brute!" the old
man cried to the shaggy dog, who was moving
round the horse again. "Plague take you!"

"It does happen," said the overseer, still leaning on the saddle and not stirring; he said this in
the hollow, toneless voice in which men speak when
they are plunged in thought.

" It does happen," he repeated, in a tone of profundity and conviction.

" Ugh, he was a nasty old fellow," the old shepherd went on with somewhat less fervour. " Five years after the Freedom he was flogged by the commune at the office, so to show his spite he took and sent the throat illness upon all Kovyli. Folks died out of number, lots and lots of them, just as in cholera. . . ."

" How did he send the illness? " asked the young shepherd after a brief silence.

" We all know how, there is no great cleverness needed where there is a will to it. Yefim murdered people with viper's fat. That is such a poison that folks will die from the mere smell of it, let alone the fat."

" That's true," Panteley agreed.

" The lads wanted to kill him at the time, but the old people would not let them. It would never have done to kill him; he knew the place where the treasure is hidden, and not another soul did know. The treasures about here are charmed so that you may find them and not see them, but he did see them. At times he would walk along the river bank or in the forest, and under the bushes and under the rocks there would be little flames, little flames . . . little flames as though from brimstone. I have seen them myself. Everyone expected that Yefim would show people the places or dig the treasure up himself, but he — as the saying is, like a dog in the manger — so he died without digging it up himself or showing other people."

The overseer lit a pipe, and for an instant lighted up his big moustaches and his sharp, stern-looking, and dignified nose. Little circles of light danced from his hands to his cap, raced over the saddle along the horse's back, and vanished in its mane near its ears.

"There are lots of hidden treasures in these parts," he said.

And slowly stretching, he looked round him, resting his eyes on the whitening east and added:

"There must be treasures."

"To be sure," sighed the old man, "one can see from every sign there are treasures, only there is no one to dig them, brother. No one knows the real places; besides, nowadays, you must remember, all the treasures are under a charm. To find them and see them you must have a talisman, and without a talisman you can do nothing, lad. Yefim had talismans, but there was no getting anything out of him, the bald devil. He kept them, so that no one could get them."

The young shepherd crept two paces nearer to the old man and, propping his head on his fists, fastened his fixed stare upon him. A childish expression of terror and curiosity gleamed in his dark eyes, and seemed in the twilight to stretch and flatten out the large features of his coarse young face. He was listening intently.

"It is even written in the Scriptures that there are lots of treasures hidden here," the old man went on; "it is so for sure . . . and no mistake about it. An old soldier of Novopavlovka was

shown at Ivanovka a writing, and in this writing it
was printed about the place of the treasure and even
how many pounds of gold was in it and the sort
of vessel it was in; they would have found the treasures long ago by that writing, only the treasure is
under a spell, you can't get at it."

"Why can't you get at it, grandfather?" asked
the young man.

"I suppose there is some reason, the soldier didn't
say. It is under a spell . . . you need a talisman."

The old man spoke with warmth, as though he
were pouring out his soul before the overseer. He
talked through his nose and, being unaccustomed to
talk much and rapidly, stuttered; and, conscious of
his defects, he tried to adorn his speech with gesticu-
lations of the hands and head and thin shoulders,
and at every movement his hempen shirt crumpled
into folds, slipped upwards and displayed his back,
black with age and sunburn. He kept pulling it
down, but it slipped up again at once. At last, as
though driven out of all patience by the rebellious
shirt, the old man leaped up and said bitterly:

"There is fortune, but what is the good of it
if it is buried in the earth? It is just riches wasted
with no profit to anyone, like chaff or sheep's dung,
and yet there are riches there, lad, fortune enough
for all the country round, but not a soul sees it!
It will come to this, that the gentry will dig it up
or the government will take it away. The gentry
have begun digging the barrows. . . . They scented
something! They are envious of the peasants' luck!
The government, too, is looking after itself. It is

written in the law that if any peasant finds the treasure he is to take it to the authorities! I dare say, wait till you get it! There is a brew but not for you!"

The old man laughed contemptuously and sat down on the ground. The overseer listened with attention and agreed, but from his silence and the expression of his figure it was evident that what the old man told him was not new to him, that he had thought it all over long ago, and knew much more than was known to the old shepherd.

"In my day, I must own, I did seek for fortune a dozen times," said the old man, scratching himself nervously. "I looked in the right places, but I must have come on treasures under a charm. My father looked for it, too, and my brother, too — but not a thing did they find, so they died without luck. A monk revealed to my brother Ilya — the Kingdom of Heaven be his — that in one place in the fortress of Taganrog there was a treasure under three stones, and that that treasure was under a charm, and in those days — it was, I remember, in the year '38 — an Armenian used to live at Matvyeev Barrow who sold talismans. Ilya bought a talisman, took two other fellows with him, and went to Taganrog. Only when he got to the place in the fortress, brother, there was a soldier with a gun, standing at the very spot. . . ."

A sound suddenly broke on the still air, and floated in all directions over the steppe. Something in the distance gave a menacing bang, crashed against stone, and raced over the steppe, uttering,

" Tah! tah! tah! tah! " When the sound had died away the old man looked inquiringly at Panteley, who stood motionless and unconcerned.

" It's a bucket broken away at the pits," said the young shepherd after a moment's thought.

It was by now getting light. The Milky Way had turned pale and gradually melted like snow, losing its outlines; the sky was becoming dull and dingy so that you could not make out whether it was clear or covered thickly with clouds, and only from the bright leaden streak in the east and from the stars that lingered here and there could one tell what was coming.

The first noiseless breeze of morning, cautiously stirring the spurges and the brown stalks of last year's grass, fluttered along the road.

The overseer roused himself from his thoughts and tossed his head. With both hands he shook the saddle, touched the girth and, as though he could not make up his mind to mount the horse, stood still again, hesitating.

" Yes," he said, " your elbow is near, but you can't bite it. There is fortune, but there is not the wit to find it."

And he turned facing the shepherds. His stern face looked sad and mocking, as though he were a disappointed man.

" Yes, so one dies without knowing what happiness is like . . ." he said emphatically, lifting his left leg into the stirrup. " A younger man may live to see it, but it is time for us to lay aside all thought of it."

Stroking his long moustaches covered with dew, he seated himself heavily on the horse and screwed up his eyes, looking into the distance, as though he had forgotten something or left something unsaid. In the bluish distance where the furthest visible hillock melted into the mist nothing was stirring; the ancient barrows, once watch-mounds and tombs, which rose here and there above the horizon and the boundless steppe had a sullen and death-like look; there was a feeling of endless time and utter indifference to man in their immobility and silence; another thousand years would pass, myriads of men would die, while they would still stand as they had stood, with no regret for the dead nor interest in the living, and no soul would ever know why they stood there, and what secret of the steppes was hidden under them.

The rooks awakening, flew one after another in silence over the earth. No meaning was to be seen in the languid flight of those long-lived birds, nor in the morning which is repeated punctually every twenty-four hours, nor in the boundless expanse of the steppe.

The overseer smiled and said:

" What space, Lord have mercy upon us! You would have a hunt to find treasure in it! Here," he went on, dropping his voice and making a serious face, " here there are two treasures buried for a certainty. The gentry don't know of them, but the old peasants, particularly the soldiers, know all about them. Here, somewhere on that ridge [the overseer pointed with his whip] robbers one time attacked

a caravan of gold; the gold was being taken from
Petersburg to the Emperor Peter who was building
a fleet at the time at Voronezh. The robbers killed
the men with the caravan and buried the gold, but
did not find it again afterwards. Another treasure
was buried by our Cossacks of the Don. In the year
'12 they carried off lots of plunder of all sorts from
the French, goods and gold and silver. When they
were going homewards they heard on the way that
the government wanted to take away all the gold
and silver from them. Rather than give up their
plunder like that to the government for nothing, the
brave fellows took and buried it, so that their children, anyway, might get it; but where they buried
it no one knows."

"I have heard of those treasures," the old man
muttered grimly.

"Yes . . ." Panteley pondered again. "So it
is. . . ."

A silence followed. The overseer looked dreamily into the distance, gave a laugh and pulled the
rein, still with the same expression as though he had
forgotten something or left something unsaid. The
horse reluctantly started at a walking pace. After
riding a hundred paces Panteley shook his head
resolutely, roused himself from his thoughts and,
lashing his horse, set off at a trot.

The shepherds were left alone.

"That was Panteley from Makarov's estate,"
said the old man. "He gets a hundred and fifty
a year and provisions found, too. He is a man of
education. . . ."

The sheep, waking up — there were about three thousand of them — began without zest to while away the time, nipping at the low, half-trampled grass. The sun had not yet risen, but by now all the barrows could be seen and, like a cloud in the distance, Saur's Grave with its peaked top. If one clambered up on that tomb one could see the plain from it, level and boundless as the sky, one could see villages, manor-houses, the settlements of the Germans and of the Molokani, and a long-sighted Kalmuck could even see the town and the railway-station. Only from there could one see that there was something else in the world besides the silent steppe and the ancient barrows, that there was another life that had nothing to do with buried treasure and the thoughts of sheep.

The old man felt beside him for his crook — a long stick with a hook at the upper end — and got up. He was silent and thoughtful. The young shepherd's face had not lost the look of childish terror and curiosity. He was still under the influence of what he had heard in the night, and impatiently awaiting fresh stories.

"Grandfather," he asked, getting up and taking his crook, "what did your brother Ilya do with the soldier?"

The old man did not hear the question. He looked absent-mindedly at the young man, and answered, mumbling with his lips:

"I keep thinking, Sanka, about that writing that was shown to that soldier at Ivanovka. I didn't tell Panteley — God be with him — but you know

in that writing the place was marked out so that
even a woman could find it. Do you know where
it is? At Bogata Bylotchka at the spot, you know,
where the ravine parts like a goose's foot into three
little ravines; it is the middle one."

"Well, will you dig?"

"I will try my luck . . ."

"And, grandfather, what will you do with the
treasure when you find it?"

"Do with it?" laughed the old man. "H'm!
. . . If only I could find it then. . . . I would show
them all. . . . H'm! . . . I should know what to
do. . . ."

And the old man could not answer what he would
do with the treasure if he found it. That question
had presented itself to him that morning probably
for the first time in his life, and judging from the
expression of his face, indifferent and uncritical, it
did not seem to him important and deserving of
consideration. In Sanka's brain another puzzled
question was stirring: why was it only old men
searched for hidden treasure, and what was the use
of earthly happiness to people who might die any
day of old age? But Sanka could not put this perplexity into words, and the old man could scarcely
have found an answer to it.

An immense crimson sun came into view surrounded by a faint haze. Broad streaks of light,
still cold, bathing in the dewy grass, lengthening out
with a joyous air as though to prove they were not
weary of their task, began spreading over the earth.
The silvery wormwood, the blue flowers of the pig's

onion, the yellow mustard, the corn-flowers — all burst into gay colours, taking the sunlight for their own smile.

The old shepherd and Sanka parted and stood at the further sides of the flock. Both stood like posts, without moving, staring at the ground and thinking. The former was haunted by thoughts of fortune, the latter was pondering on what had been said in the night; what interested him was not the fortune itself, which he did not want and could not imagine, but the fantastic, fairy-tale character of human happiness.

A hundred sheep started and, in some inexplicable panic as at a signal, dashed away from the flock; and as though the thoughts of the sheep — tedious and oppressive — had for a moment infected Sanka also, he, too, dashed aside in the same inexplicable animal panic, but at once he recovered himself and shouted:

" You crazy creatures! You've gone mad, plague take you! "

When the sun, promising long hours of overwhelming heat, began to bake the earth, all living things that in the night had moved and uttered sounds were sunk in drowsiness. The old shepherd and Sanka stood with their crooks on opposite sides of the flock, stood without stirring, like fakirs at their prayers, absorbed in thought. They did not heed each other; each of them was living in his own life. The sheep were pondering, too.

1887

A MALEFACTOR

A MALEFACTOR

AN exceedingly lean little peasant, in a striped hempen shirt and patched drawers, stands facing the investigating magistrate. His face overgrown with hair and pitted with smallpox, and his eyes scarcely visible under thick, overhanging eyebrows have an expression of sullen moroseness. On his head there is a perfect mop of tangled, unkempt hair, which gives him an even more spider-like air of moroseness. He is barefooted.

"Denis Grigoryev!" the magistrate begins. "Come nearer, and answer my questions. On the seventh of this July the railway watchman, Ivan Semyonovitch Akïnfov, going along the line in the morning, found you at the hundred-and-forty-first mile engaged in unscrewing a nut by which the rails are made fast to the sleepers. Here it is, the nut! . . . With the aforesaid nut he detained you. Was that so?"

"Wha-at?"

"Was this all as Akinfov states?"

"To be sure, it was."

"Very good; well, what were you unscrewing the nut for?"

"Wha-at?"

"Drop that 'wha-at' and answer the question; what were you unscrewing the nut for?"

"If I hadn't wanted it I shouldn't have un-screwed it," croaks Denis, looking at the ceiling.

"What did you want that nut for?"

"The nut? We make weights out of those nuts for our lines."

"Who is 'we'?"

"We, people. . . . The Klimovo peasants, that is."

"Listen, my man; don't play the idiot to me, but speak sensibly. It's no use telling lies here about weights!"

"I've never been a liar from a child, and now I'm telling lies . . ." mutters Denis, blinking. "But can you do without a weight, your honour? If you put live bait or maggots on a hook, would it go to the bottom without a weight? . . . I am telling lies," grins Denis. . . . "What the devil is the use of the worm if it swims on the surface! The perch and the pike and the eel-pout always go to the bottom, and a bait on the surface is only taken by a shillisper, not very often then, and there are no shillispers in our river. . . . That fish likes plenty of room."

"Why are you telling me about shillispers?"

"Wha-at? Why, you asked me yourself! The gentry catch fish that way too in our parts. The silliest little boy would not try to catch a fish with-out a weight. Of course anyone who did not under-stand might go to fish without a weight. There is no rule for a fool."

"So you say you unscrewed this nut to make a weight for your fishing line out of it?"

" What else for?   It wasn't to play knuckle-bones with! "

" But you might have taken lead, a bullet . . . a nail of some sort. . . ."

" You don't pick up lead in the road, you have to buy it, and a nail's no good.   You can't find anything better than a nut. . . . It's heavy, and there's a hole in it."

" He keeps pretending to be a fool! as though he'd been born yesterday or dropped from heaven! Don't you understand, you blockhead, what un- screwing these nuts leads to?   If the watchman had not noticed it the train might have run off the rails, people would have been killed — you would have killed people."

" God forbid, your honour!   What should I kill them for?   Are we heathens or wicked people? Thank God, good gentlemen, we have lived all our lives without ever dreaming of such a thing. . . . Save, and have mercy on us, Queen of Heaven! . . . What are you saying? "

" And what do you suppose railway accidents do come from?   Unscrew two or three nuts and you have an accident."

Denis grins, and screws up his eye at the magis- trate incredulously.

" Why! how many years have we all in the vil- lage been unscrewing nuts, and the Lord has been merciful; and you talk of accidents, killing people. If I had carried away a rail or put a log across the line, say, then maybe it might have upset the train, but . . . pouf! a nut! "

" But you must understand that the nut holds the rail fast to the sleepers ! "

" We understand that. . . . We don't unscrew them all . . . we leave some. . . . We don't do it thoughtlessly . . . we understand. . . ."

Denis yawns and makes the sign of the cross over his mouth.

" Last year the train went off the rails here," says the magistrate. " Now I see why ! "

" What do you say, your honour? "

" I am telling you that now I see why the train went off the rails last year. . . . I understand ! "

" That's what you are educated people for, to understand, you kind gentlemen. The Lord knows to whom to give understanding. . . . Here you have reasoned how and what, but the watchman, a peasant like ourselves, with no understanding at all, catches one by the collar and hauls one along. . . . You should reason first and then haul me off. It's a saying that a peasant has a peasant's wit. . . . Write down, too, your honour, that he hit me twice — in the jaw and in the chest."

" When your hut was searched they found another nut. . . . At what spot did you unscrew that, and when? "

" You mean the nut which lay under the red box? "

" I don't know where it was lying, only it was found. When did you unscrew it? "

" I didn't unscrew it; Ignashka, the son of one-eyed Semyon, gave it me. I mean the one which was under the box, but the one which was in the sledge in the yard Mitrofan and I unscrewed together."

" What Mitrofan? "

" Mitrofan Petrov. . . . Haven't you heard of him? He makes nets in our village and sells them to the gentry. He needs a lot of those nuts. Reckon a matter of ten for each net."

" Listen. Article 1081 of the Penal Code lays down that every wilful damage of the railway line committed when it can expose the traffic on that line to danger, and the guilty party knows that an accident must be caused by it . . . (Do you understand? Knows! And you could not help knowing what this unscrewing would lead to . . .) is liable to penal servitude."

" Of course, you know best. . . . We are ignorant people. . . . What do we understand? "

" You understand all about it! You are lying, shamming! "

" What should I lie for? Ask in the village if you don't believe me. Only a bleak is caught without a weight, and there is no fish worse than a gudgeon, yet even that won't bite without a weight."

" You'd better tell me about the shillisper next," said the magistrate, smiling.

" There are no shillispers in our parts. . . . We cast our line without a weight on the top of the water with a butterfly; a mullet may be caught that way, though that is not often."

" Come, hold your tongue."

A silence follows. Denis shifts from one foot to the other, looks at the table with the green cloth on it, and blinks his eyes violently as though what was before him was not the cloth but the sun. The magistrate writes rapidly.

" Can I go? " asks Denis after a long silence.

" No. I must take you under guard and send you to prison."

Denis leaves off blinking and, raising his thick eyebrows, looks inquiringly at the magistrate.

" How do you mean, to prison? Your honour! I have no time to spare, I must go to the fair; I must get three roubles from Yegor for some tallow! . . ."

" Hold your tongue; don't interrupt."

" To prison. . . . If there was something to go for, I'd go; but just to go for nothing! What for? I haven't stolen anything, I believe, and I've not been fighting. . . . If you are in doubt about the arrears, your honour, don't believe the elder. . . . You ask the agent . . . he's a regular heathen, the elder, you know."

" Hold your tongue."

" I am holding my tongue, as it is," mutters Denis; " but that the elder has lied over the account, I'll take my oath for it. . . . There are three of us brothers: Kuzma Grigoryev, then Yegor Grigoryev, and me, Denis Grigoryev."

" You are hindering me. . . . Hey, Semyon," cries the magistrate, " take him away! "

" There are three of us brothers," mutters Denis, as two stalwart soldiers take him and lead him out of the room. " A brother is not responsible for a brother. Kuzma does not pay, so you, Denis, must

answer for it. . . . Judges indeed! Our master
the general is dead — the Kingdom of Heaven be
his — or he would have shown you judges. . . .
You ought to judge sensibly, not at random. . . .
Flog if you like, but flog someone who deserves it,
flog with conscience."

1885

PEASANTS

PEASANTS

I

NIKOLAY TCHIKILDYEEV, a waiter in the Moscow hotel, Slavyansky Bazaar, was taken ill. His legs went numb and his gait was affected, so that on one occasion, as he was going along the corridor, he tumbled and fell down with a tray full of ham and peas. He had to leave his job. All his own savings and his wife's were spent on doctors and medicines; they had nothing left to live upon. He felt dull with no work to do, and he made up his mind he must go home to the village. It is better to be ill at home, and living there is cheaper; and it is a true saying that the walls of home are a help.

He reached Zhukovo towards evening. In his memories of childhood he had pictured his home as bright, snug, comfortable. Now, going into the hut, he was positively frightened; it was so dark, so crowded, so unclean. His wife Olga and his daughter Sasha, who had come with him, kept looking in bewilderment at the big untidy stove, which filled up almost half the hut and was black with soot and flies. What lots of flies! The stove was on one side, the beams lay slanting on the walls, and it looked as though the hut were just going to fall to pieces. In the corner, facing the door, under the

279

holy images, bottle labels and newspaper cuttings were stuck on the walls instead of pictures. The poverty, the poverty! Of the grown-up people there were none at home; all were at work at the harvest. On the stove was sitting a white-headed girl of eight, unwashed and apathetic; she did not even glance at them as they came in. On the floor a white cat was rubbing itself against the oven fork.

" Puss, puss! " Sasha called to her. " Puss! "

" She can't hear," said the little girl; " she has gone deaf."

" How is that? "

" Oh, she was beaten."

Nikolay and Olga realized from the first glance what life was like here, but said nothing to one another; in silence they put down their bundles, and went out into the village street. Their hut was the third from the end, and seemed the very poorest and oldest-looking; the second was not much better; but the last one had an iron roof, and curtains in the windows. That hut stood apart, not enclosed; it was a tavern. The huts were in a single row, and the whole of the little village — quiet and dreamy, with willows, elders, and mountain-ash trees peeping out from the yards — had an attractive look.

Beyond the peasants' homesteads there was a slope down to the river, so steep and precipitous that huge stones jutted out bare here and there through the clay. Down the slope, among the stones and holes dug by the potters, ran winding paths; bits of broken pottery, some brown, some red, lay piled up in heaps, and below there stretched a broad, level, bright green meadow, from which the hay had been already carried, and in which the peasants' cattle were wandering. The river, three-quarters of a mile from the village, ran twisting and turning, with beautiful leafy banks; beyond it was again a broad meadow, a herd of cattle, long strings of white geese; then, just as on the near side, a steep ascent uphill, and on the top of the hill a hamlet, and a church with five domes, and at a little distance the manor-house.

"It's lovely here in your parts!" said Olga, crossing herself at the sight of the church. "What space, oh Lord!"

Just at that moment the bell began ringing for service (it was Saturday evening). Two little girls, down below, who were dragging up a pail of water, looked round at the church to listen to the bell.

"At this time they are serving the dinners at the Slavyansky Bazaar," said Nikolay dreamily.

Sitting on the edge of the slope, Nikolay and Olga watched the sun setting, watched the gold and crimson sky reflected in the river, in the church windows, and in the whole air — which was soft and still and unutterably pure as it never was in Moscow. And when the sun had set the flocks and herds passed, bleating and lowing; geese flew across from the further side of the river, and all sank into silence; the soft light died away in the air, and the dusk of evening began quickly moving down upon them.

Meanwhile Nikolay's father and mother, two gaunt, bent, toothless old people, just of the same height, came back. The women — the sisters-in-law Marya and Fyokla — who had been working on the landowner's estate beyond the river, arrived home, too. Marya, the wife of Nikolay's brother Kiryak, had six children, and Fyokla, the wife of Nikolay's brother Denis — who had gone for a soldier — had two; and when Nikolay, going into the hut, saw all the family, all those bodies big and little moving about on the lockers, in the hanging cradles and in all the corners, and when he saw the greed with which the old father and the women ate the black bread, dipping it in water, he realized he had made a mistake in coming here, sick, penniless, and with a family, too — a great mistake!

"And where is Kiryak?" he asked after they had exchanged greetings.

"He is in service at the merchant's," answered his father; "a keeper in the woods. He is not a bad peasant, but too fond of his glass."

"He is no great help!" said the old woman tearfully. "Our men are a grievous lot; they bring nothing into the house, but take plenty out. Kiryak drinks, and so does the old man; it is no use hiding a sin; he knows his way to the tavern. The Heavenly Mother is wroth."

In honour of the visitors they brought out the samovar. The tea smelt of fish; the sugar was grey and looked as though it had been nibbled; cockroaches ran to and fro over the bread and among the crockery. It was disgusting to drink, and the conversation was disgusting, too — about nothing but poverty and illnesses. But before they had time

to empty their first cups there came a loud, prolonged, drunken shout from the yard:

" Ma-arya! "

" It looks as though Kiryak were coming," said
the old man. " Speak of the devil."

All were hushed. And again, soon afterwards,
the same shout, coarse and drawn-out as though it
came out of the earth:

" Ma-arya! "

Marya, the elder sister-in-law, turned pale and
huddled against the stove, and it was strange to
see the look of terror on the face of the strong,
broad-shouldered, ugly woman. Her daughter, the
child who had been sitting on the stove and looked so
apathetic, suddenly broke into loud weeping.

" What are you howling for, you plague? "
Fyokla, a handsome woman, also strong and broad-
shouldered, shouted to her. " He won't kill you,
no fear! "

From his old father Nikolay learned that Marya
was afraid to live in the forest with Kiryak, and
that when he was drunk he always came for her,
made a row, and beat her mercilessly.

" Ma-arya! " the shout sounded close to the door.

" Protect me, for Christ's sake, good people! "
faltered Marya, breathing as though she had been
plunged into very cold water. " Protect me, kind
people. . . ."

All the children in the hut began crying, and
looking at them, Sasha, too, began to cry. They
heard a drunken cough, and a tall, black-bearded
peasant wearing a winter cap came into the hut,

and was the more terrible because his face could
not be seen in the dim light of the little lamp. It
was Kiryak. Going up to his wife, he swung his
arm and punched her in the face with his fist.
Stunned by the blow, she did not utter a sound,
but sat down, and her nose instantly began bleeding.

"What a disgrace! What a disgrace!" muttered the old man, clambering up on to the stove.
"Before visitors, too! It's a sin!"

The old mother sat silent, bowed, lost in thought;
Fyokla rocked the cradle.

Evidently conscious of inspiring fear, and pleased
at doing so, Kiryak seized Marya by the arm,
dragged her towards the door, and bellowed like
an animal in order to seem still more terrible; but
at that moment he suddenly caught sight of the visitors and stopped.

"Oh, they have come, . . ." he said, letting his
wife go; "my own brother and his family. . . ."

Staggering and opening wide his red, drunken eyes,
he said his prayer before the image and went on:

"My brother and his family have come to the
parental home . . . from Moscow, I suppose.
The great capital Moscow, to be sure, the mother
of cities. . . . Excuse me."

He sank down on the bench near the samovar
and began drinking tea, sipping it loudly from the
saucer in the midst of general silence. . . . He
drank off a dozen cups, then reclined on the bench
and began snoring.

They began going to bed. Nikolay, as an in-
valid, was put on the stove with his old father;

Sasha lay down on the floor, while Olga went with the other women into the barn.

"Aye, aye, dearie," she said, lying down on the hay beside Marya; "you won't mend your trouble with tears. Bear it in patience, that is all. It is written in the Scriptures: 'If anyone smite thee on the right cheek, offer him the left one also.' . . . Aye, aye, dearie."

Then in a low singsong murmur she told them about Moscow, about her own life, how she had been a servant in furnished lodgings.

"And in Moscow the houses are big, built of brick," she said; "and there are ever so many churches, forty times forty, dearie; and they are all gentry in the houses, so handsome and so proper!"

Marya told her that she had not only never been in Moscow, but had not even been in their own district town; she could not read or write, and knew no prayers, not even "Our Father." Both she and Fyokla, the other sister-in-law, who was sitting a little way off listening, were extremely ignorant and could understand nothing. They both disliked their husbands; Marya was afraid of Kiryak, and whenever he stayed with her she was shaking with fear, and always got a headache from the fumes of vodka and tobacco with which he reeked. And in answer to the question whether she did not miss her husband, Fyokla answered with vexation:

"Miss him!"

They talked a little and sank into silence.

It was cool, and a cock crowed at the top of his

voice near the barn, preventing them from sleeping. When the bluish morning light was already peeping through all the crevices, Fyokla got up stealthily and went out, and then they heard the sound of her bare feet running off somewhere.

II

Olga went to church, and took Marya with her. As they went down the path towards the meadow both were in good spirits. Olga liked the wide view, and Marya felt that in her sister-in-law she had someone near and akin to her. The sun was rising. Low down over the meadow floated a drowsy hawk. The river looked gloomy; there was a haze hovering over it here and there, but on the further bank a streak of light already stretched across the hill. The church was gleaming, and in the manor garden the rooks were cawing furiously.

"The old man is all right," Marya told her, "but Granny is strict; she is continually nagging. Our own grain lasted till Carnival. We buy flour now at the tavern. She is angry about it; she says we eat too much."

"Aye, aye, dearie! Bear it in patience, that is all. It is written: 'Come unto Me, all ye that labour and are heavy laden.'"

Olga spoke sedately, rhythmically, and she walked like a pilgrim woman, with a rapid, anxious step. Every day she read the gospel, read it aloud like a deacon; a great deal of it she did not understand, but the words of the gospel moved her to tears, and words like "forasmuch as" and "verily" she pronounced with a sweet flutter at her heart. She believed in God, in the Holy Mother, in the Saints; she believed one must not offend anyone in the world — not simple folks, nor Germans, nor gypsies, nor Jews — and woe even to those who have no compassion on the beasts. She believed this was written in the Holy Scriptures; and so, when she pronounced phrases from Holy Writ, even though she did not understand them, her face grew softened, compassionate, and radiant.

"What part do you come from?" Marya asked her.

"I am from Vladimir. Only I was taken to Moscow long ago, when I was eight years old."

They reached the river. On the further side a woman was standing at the water's edge, undressing.

"It's our Fyokla," said Marya, recognizing her. "She has been over the river to the manor yard. To the stewards. She is a shameless hussy and foul-mouthed — fearfully!"

Fyokla, young and vigorous as a girl, with her black eyebrows and her loose hair, jumped off the bank and began splashing the water with her feet, and waves ran in all directions from her.

"Shameless — dreadfully!" repeated Marya.

The river was crossed by a rickety little bridge of logs, and exactly below it in the clear, limpid water was a shoal of broad-headed mullets. The dew was glistening on the green bushes that looked into the water. There was a feeling of warmth; it was comforting! What a lovely morning! And how lovely life would have been in this world, in all likelihood, if it were not for poverty, horrible, hopeless poverty, from which one can find no refuge! One had only to look round at the village to remember vividly all that had happened the day before, and the illusion of happiness which seemed to surround them vanished instantly.

They reached the church. Marya stood at the entrance, and did not dare to go farther. She did not dare to sit down either. Though they only began ringing for mass between eight and nine, she remained standing the whole time.

While the gospel was being read the crowd suddenly parted to make way for the family from the great house. Two young girls in white frocks and wide-brimmed hats walked in; with them a chubby, rosy boy in a sailor suit. Their appearance touched Olga; she made up her mind from the first glance that they were refined, well-educated, handsome people. Marya looked at them from under her brows, sullenly, dejectedly, as though they were not human beings coming in, but monsters who might crush her if she did not make way for them.

And every time the deacon boomed out something in his bass voice she fancied she heard " Ma-arya! " and she shuddered.

III

The arrival of the visitors was already known in the village, and directly after mass a number of people gathered together in the hut. The Leonyt-

chevs and Matvyeitchevs and the Ilyitchovs came to
inquire about their relations who were in service in
Moscow. All the lads of Zhukovo who could read
and write were packed off to Moscow and hired out
as butlers or waiters (while from the village on the
other side of the river the boys all became bakers),
and that had been the custom from the days of serf-
dom long ago when a certain Luka Ivanitch, a peasant from Zhukovo, now a legendary figure, who had
been a waiter in one of the Moscow clubs, would
take none but his fellow-villagers into his service,
and found jobs for them in taverns and restaurants;
and from that time the village of Zhukovo was
always called among the inhabitants of the surround-
ing districts Slaveytown. Nikolay had been taken
to Moscow when he was eleven, and Ivan Makaritch, one of the Matvyeitchevs, at that time a head-
waiter in the "Hermitage" garden, had put him
into a situation. And now, addressing the
Matvyeitchevs, Nikolay said emphatically:

"Ivan Makaritch was my benefactor, and I am
bound to pray for him day and night, as it is owing
to him I have become a good man."

"My good soul!" a tall old woman, the sister
of Ivan Makaritch, said tearfully, "and not a word
have we heard about him, poor dear."

"In the winter he was in service at Omon's, and
this season there was a rumour he was somewhere
out of town, in gardens. . . . He has aged! In
old days he would bring home as much as ten roubles
a day in the summer-time, but now things are very
quiet everywhere. The old man frets."

The women looked at Nikolay's feet, shod in felt boots, and at his pale face, and said mournfully:

" You are not one to get on, Nikolay Osipitch; you are not one to get on! No, indeed! "

And they all made much of Sasha. She was ten years old, but she was little and very thin, and might have been taken for no more than seven. Among the other little girls, with their sunburnt faces and roughly cropped hair, dressed in long faded smocks, she with her white little face, with her big dark eyes, with a red ribbon in her hair, looked funny, as though she were some little wild creature that had been caught and brought into the hut.

" She can read, too," Olga said in her praise, looking tenderly at her daughter. " Read a little, child! " she said, taking the gospel from the corner. " You read, and the good Christian people will listen."

The testament was an old and heavy one in leather binding, with dog's-eared edges, and it exhaled a smell as though monks had come into the hut. Sasha raised her eyebrows and began in a loud rhythmic chant:

" ' And the angel of the Lord . . . appeared unto Joseph, saying unto him: Rise up, and take the Babe and His mother.' "

" The Babe and His mother," Olga repeated, and flushed all over with emotion.

" ' And flee into Egypt, . . . and tarry there until such time as . . .' "

At the word " tarry " Olga could not refrain from tears. Looking at her, Marya began to whimper,

and after her Ivan Makaritch's sister. The old
father cleared his throat, and bustled about to find
something to give his grand-daughter, but, finding
nothing, gave it up with a wave of his hand. And
when the reading was over the neighbours dispersed
to their homes, feeling touched and very much
pleased with Olga and Sasha.

As it was a holiday, the family spent the whole
day at home. The old woman, whom her husband,
her daughters-in-law, her grandchildren all alike
called Granny, tried to do everything herself; she
heated the stove and set the samovar with her own
hands, even waited at the midday meal, and then
complained that she was worn out with work. And
all the time she was uneasy for fear someone should
eat a piece too much, or that her husband and
daughters-in-law would sit idle. At one time she
would hear the tavern-keeper's geese going at the
back of the huts to her kitchen-garden, and she
would run out of the hut with a long stick and spend
half an hour screaming shrilly by her cabbages, which
were as gaunt and scraggy as herself; at another
time she fancied that a crow had designs on her
chickens, and she rushed to attack it with loud words
of abuse. She was cross and grumbling from
morning till night. And often she raised such an
outcry that passers-by stopped in the street.

She was not affectionate towards the old man, re-
viling him as a lazy-bones and a plague. He was
not a responsible, reliable peasant, and perhaps if
she had not been continually nagging at him he would
not have worked at all, but would have simply sat

on the stove and talked. He talked to his son at
great length about certain enemies of his, complained of the insults he said he had to put up with
every day from the neighbours, and it was tedious
to listen to him.

"Yes," he would say, standing with his arms
akimbo, "yes. . . . A week after the Exaltation of
the Cross I sold my hay willingly at thirty kopecks a
pood. . . . Well and good. . . . So you see I was
taking the hay in the morning with a good will; I
was interfering with no one. In an unlucky hour
I see the village elder, Antip Syedelnikov, coming
out of the tavern. 'Where are you taking it, you
ruffian?' says he, and takes me by the ear."

Kiryak had a fearful headache after his drinking
bout, and was ashamed to face his brother.

"What vodka does! Ah, my God!" he muttered, shaking his aching head. "For Christ's sake,
forgive me, brother and sister; I'm not happy myself."

As it was a holiday, they bought a herring at the
tavern and made a soup of the herring's head. At
midday they all sat down to drink tea, and went on
drinking it for a long time, till they were all perspiring; they looked positively swollen from the tea-
drinking, and after it began sipping the broth from
the herring's head, all helping themselves out of one
bowl. But the herring itself Granny had hidden.

In the evening a potter began firing pots on the
ravine. In the meadow below the girls got up a
choral dance and sang songs. They played the concertina. And on the other side of the river a kiln

for baking pots was lighted, too, and the girls sang songs, and in the distance the singing sounded soft and musical. The peasants were noisy in and about the tavern. They were singing with drunken voices, each on his own account, and swearing at one another, so that Olga could only shudder and say:

"Oh, holy Saints!"

She was amazed that the abuse was incessant, and those who were loudest and most persistent in this foul language were the old men who were so near their end. And the girls and children heard the swearing, and were not in the least disturbed by it, and it was evident that they were used to it from their cradles.

It was past midnight, the kilns on both sides of the river were put out, but in the meadow below and in the tavern the merrymaking still went on. The old father and Kiryak, both drunk, walking arm-in-arm and jostling against each other's shoulders, went to the barn where Olga and Marya were lying.

"Let her alone," the old man persuaded him; "let her alone. . . . She is a harmless woman. . . . It's a sin. . . ."

"Ma-arya!" shouted Kiryak.

"Let her be. . . . It's a sin. . . . She is not a bad woman."

Both stopped by the barn and went on.

"I lo-ove the flowers of the fi-ield," the old man began singing suddenly in a high, piercing tenor. "I lo-ove to gather them in the meadows!"

Then he spat, and with a filthy oath went into the hut.

IV

Granny put Sasha by her kitchen-garden and told her to keep watch that the geese did not go in.   It was a hot August day.   The tavernkeeper's geese could make their way into the kitchen-garden by the backs of the huts, but now they were busily engaged picking up oats by the tavern, peacefully conversing together, and only the gander craned his head high as though trying to see whether the old woman were coming with her stick.   The other geese might come up from below, but they were now grazing far away the other side of the river, stretched out in a long white garland about the meadow.   Sasha stood about a little, grew weary, and, seeing that the geese were not coming, went away to the ravine.

There she saw Marya's eldest daughter Motka, who was standing motionless on a big stone, staring at the church.   Marya had given birth to thirteen children, but she only had six living, all girls, not one boy, and the eldest was eight.   Motka in a long smock was standing barefooted in the full sunshine; the sun was blazing down right on her head, but she did not notice that, and seemed as though turned to stone.   Sasha stood beside her and said, looking at the church:

" God lives in the church.   Men have lamps and candles, but God has little green and red and blue lamps like little eyes.   At night God walks about the church, and with Him the Holy Mother of God and Saint Nikolay, thud, thud, thud! . . . And the

watchman is terrified, terrified! Aye, aye, dearie,"
she added, imitating her mother. "And when the
end of the world comes all the churches will be carried up to heaven."

"With the-ir be-ells?" Motka asked in her deep
voice, drawling every syllable.

"With their bells. And when the end of the
world comes the good will go to Paradise, but the
angry will burn in fire eternal and unquenchable,
dearie. To my mother as well as to Marya God
will say: 'You never offended anyone, and for that
go to the right to Paradise'; but to Kiryak and
Granny He will say: 'You go to the left into the
fire.' And anyone who has eaten meat in Lent will
go into the fire, too."

She looked upwards at the sky, opening wide her
eyes, and said:

"Look at the sky without winking, you will see
angels."

Motka began looking at the sky, too, and a minute
passed in silence.

"Do you see them?" asked Sasha.

"I don't," said Motka in her deep voice.

"But I do. Little angels are flying about the sky
and flap, flap with their little wings as though they
were gnats."

Motka thought for a little, with her eyes on the
ground, and asked:

"Will Granny burn?"

"She will, dearie."

From the stone an even gentle slope ran down to
the bottom, covered with soft green grass, which one

longed to lie down on or to touch with one's hands.
. . . Sasha lay down and rolled to the bottom.
Motka with a grave, severe face, taking a deep
breath, lay down, too, and rolled to the bottom, and
in doing so tore her smock from the hem to the
shoulder.

"What fun it is!" said Sasha, delighted.

They walked up to the top to roll down again, but
at that moment they heard a shrill, familiar voice.
Oh, how awful it was! Granny, a toothless, bony,
hunchbacked figure, with short grey hair which was
fluttering in the wind, was driving the geese out of
the kitchen-garden with a long stick, shouting.

"They have trampled all the cabbages, the
damned brutes! I'd cut your throats, thrice accursed
plagues! Bad luck to you!"

She saw the little girls, flung down the stick and
picked up a switch, and, seizing Sasha by the neck
with her fingers, thin and hard as the gnarled
branches of a tree, began whipping her. Sasha cried
with pain and terror, while the gander, waddling and
stretching his neck, went up to the old woman and
hissed at her, and when he went back to his flock
all the geese greeted him approvingly with "Ga-
ga-ga!" Then Granny proceeded to whip Motka,
and in this Motka's smock was torn again. Feeling in despair, and crying loudly, Sasha went to the
hut to complain. Motka followed her; she, too,
was crying on a deeper note, without wiping her
tears, and her face was as wet as though it had been
dipped in water.

"Holy Saints!" cried Olga, aghast, as the two came into the hut. "Queen of Heaven!"

Sasha began telling her story, while at the same time Granny walked in with a storm of shrill cries and abuse; then Fyokla flew into a rage, and there was an uproar in the hut.

"Never mind, never mind!" Olga, pale and upset, tried to comfort them, stroking Sasha's head. "She is your grandmother; it's a sin to be angry with her. Never mind, my child."

Nikolay, who was worn out already by the everlasting hubbub, hunger, stifling fumes, filth, who hated and despised the poverty, who was ashamed for his wife and daughter to see his father and mother, swung his legs off the stove and said in an irritable, tearful voice, addressing his mother:

"You must not beat her! You have no right to beat her!"

"You lie rotting on the stove, you wretched creature!" Fyokla shouted at him spitefully. "The devil brought you all on us, eating us out of house and home."

Sasha and Motka and all the little girls in the hut huddled on the stove in the corner behind Nikolay's back, and from that refuge listened in silent terror, and the beating of their little hearts could be distinctly heard. Whenever there is someone in a family who has long been ill, and hopelessly ill, there come painful moments when all timidly, secretly, at the bottom of their hearts long for his death; and only the children fear the death of someone near them, and always feel horrified at the thought of it. And now the children, with bated breath, with a mournful look on their faces, gazed at Nikolay and thought that he was soon to die; and they wanted to cry and to say something friendly and compassionate to him.

He pressed close to Olga, as though seeking protection, and said to her softly in a quavering voice:

" Olya darling, I can't stay here longer.   It's more than I can bear.   For God's sake, for Christ's sake, write to your sister Klavdia Abramovna.   Let her sell and pawn everything she has; let her send us the money.   We will go away from here.   Oh, Lord," he went on miserably, " to have one peep at Moscow!   If I could see it in my dreams, the dear place ! "

And when the evening came on, and it was dark in the hut, it was so dismal that it was hard to utter a word.   Granny, very ill-tempered, soaked some crusts of rye bread in a cup, and was a long time, a whole hour, sucking at them.   Marya, after milking the cow, brought in a pail of milk and set it on a bench; then Granny poured it from the pail into a jug just as slowly and deliberately, evidently pleased that it was now the Fast of the Assumption, so that no one would drink milk and it would be left untouched. And she only poured out a very little in a saucer for Fyokla's baby.   When Marya and she carried the jug down to the cellar Motka suddenly stirred, clambered down from the stove, and going to the bench where stood the wooden cup full of crusts, sprinkled into it some milk from the saucer.

Granny, coming back into the hut, sat down to her soaked crusts again, while Sasha and Motka, sitting on the stove, gazed at her, and they were glad that she had broken her fast and now would go to hell. They were comforted and lay down to sleep, and Sasha as she dozed off to sleep imagined the Day of Judgment: a huge fire was burning, somewhat like a potter's kiln, and the Evil One, with horns like a cow's, and black all over, was driving Granny into the fire with a long stick, just as Granny herself had been driving the geese.

V

On the day of the Feast of the Assumption, between ten and eleven in the evening, the girls and lads who were merrymaking in the meadow suddenly raised a clamour and outcry, and ran in the direction of the village; and those who were above on the edge of the ravine could not for the first moment make out what was the matter.

" Fire! Fire! " they heard desperate shouts from below. " The village is on fire! "

Those who were sitting above looked round, and a terrible and extraordinary spectacle met their eyes. On the thatched roof of one of the end cottages stood a column of flame, seven feet high, which curled round and scattered sparks in all directions as though it were a fountain. And all at once the whole roof burst into bright flame, and the crackling of the fire was audible.

The light of the moon was dimmed, and the whole village was by now bathed in a red quivering glow: black shadows moved over the ground, there was a smell of burning, and those who ran up from below were all gasping and could not speak for trembling; they jostled against each other, fell down, and they could hardly see in the unaccustomed light, and did not recognize each other. It was terrible. What seemed particularly dreadful was that doves were flying over the fire in the smoke; and in the tavern, where they did not yet know of the fire, they were still singing and playing the concertina as though there were nothing the matter.

" Uncle Semyon's on fire," shouted a loud, coarse voice.

Marya was fussing about round her hut, weeping and wringing her hands, while her teeth chattered, though the fire was a long way off at the other end of the village. Nikolay came out in high felt boots, the children ran out in their little smocks. Near the village constable's hut an iron sheet was struck. Boom, boom, boom! . . . floated through the air, and this repeated, persistent sound sent a pang to the heart and turned one cold. The old women stood with the holy ikons. Sheep, calves, cows were driven out of the back-yards into the street; boxes, sheep-skins, tubs were carried out. A black stallion, who was kept apart from the drove of horses because he kicked and injured them, on being set free ran once or twice up and down the village, neighing and paw-ing the ground; then suddenly stopped short near a cart and began kicking it with his hind-legs.

They began ringing the bells in the church on the other side of the river.

Near the burning hut it was hot and so light that one could distinctly see every blade of grass. Semyon, a red-haired peasant with a long nose, wearing a reefer-jacket and a cap pulled down right over his ears, sat on one of the boxes which they had succeeded in bringing out: his wife was lying on her face, moaning and unconscious. A little old man of eighty, with a big beard, who looked like a gnome — not one of the villagers, though obviously connected in some way with the fire — walked about bareheaded, with a white bundle in his arms. The glare was reflected on his bald head. The village elder, Antip Syedelnikov, as swarthy and black-haired as a gypsy, went up to the hut with an axe, and hacked out the windows one after another — no one knew why — then began chopping up the roof.

"Women, water!" he shouted. "Bring the engine! Look sharp!"

The peasants, who had been drinking in the tavern just before, dragged the engine up. They were all drunk; they kept stumbling and falling down, and all had a helpless expression and tears in their eyes.

"Wenches, water!" shouted the elder, who was drunk, too. "Look sharp, wenches!"

The women and the girls ran downhill to where there was a spring, and kept hauling pails and buckets of water up the hill, and, pouring it into the engine, ran down again. Olga and Marya and Sasha and Motka all brought water. The women and the boys pumped the water; the pipe hissed, and the elder, directing it now at the door, now at the windows, held back the stream with his finger, which made it hiss more sharply still.

"Bravo, Antip!" voices shouted approvingly. "Do your best."

Antip went inside the hut into the fire and shouted from within.

"Pump! Bestir yourselves, good Christian folk, in such a terrible mischance!"

The peasants stood round in a crowd, doing nothing but staring at the fire. No one knew what to do, no one had the sense to do anything, though there were stacks of wheat, hay, barns, and piles of faggots standing all round. Kiryak and old Osip, his father, both tipsy, were standing there, too. And as though to justify his doing nothing, old Osip said, addressing the woman who lay on the ground:

"What is there to trouble about, old girl! The hut is insured — why are you taking on?"

Semyon, addressing himself first to one person and then to another, kept describing how the fire had started.

"That old man, the one with the bundle, a house-serf of General Zhukov's. . . . He was cook at our general's, God rest his soul! He came over this evening: 'Let me stay the night,' says he. . . . Well, we had a glass, to be sure. . . . The wife got the samovar — she was going to give the old fellow a cup of tea, and in an unlucky hour she set the samovar in the entrance. The sparks from the chimney must have blown straight up to the thatch; that's how it was. We were almost burnt ourselves.

And the old fellow's cap has been burnt; what a shame!"

And the sheet of iron was struck indefatigably, and the bells kept ringing in the church the other side of the river. In the glow of the fire Olga, breathless, looking with horror at the red sheep and the pink doves flying in the smoke, kept running down the hill and up again. It seemed to her that the ringing went to her heart with a sharp stab, that the fire would never be over, that Sasha was lost. . . . And when the ceiling of the hut fell in with a crash, the thought that now the whole village would be burnt made her weak and faint, and she could not go on fetching water, but sat down on the ravine, setting the pail down near her; beside her and below her, the peasant women sat wailing as though at a funeral.

Then the stewards and watchmen from the estate the other side of the river arrived in two carts, bringing with them a fire-engine. A very young student in an unbuttoned white tunic rode up on horseback. There was the thud of axes. They put a ladder to the burning framework of the house, and five men ran up it at once. Foremost of them all was the student, who was red in the face and shouting in a harsh hoarse voice, and in a tone as though putting out fires was a thing he was used to. They pulled the house to pieces, a beam at a time; they dragged away the corn, the hurdles, and the stacks that were near.

"Don't let them break it up!" cried stern voices in the crowd. "Don't let them."

Kiryak made his way up to the hut with a resolute air, as though he meant to prevent the newcomers from breaking up the hut, but one of the workmen turned him back with a blow in his neck. There was the sound of laughter, the workman dealt him another blow, Kiryak fell down, and crawled back into the crowd on his hands and knees.

Two handsome girls in hats, probably the student's sisters, came from the other side of the river. They stood a little way off, looking at the fire. The beams that had been dragged apart were no longer burning, but were smoking vigorously; the student, who was working the hose, turned the water, first on the beams, then on the peasants, then on the women who were bringing the water.

"George!" the girls called to him reproachfully in anxiety, "George!"

The fire was over. And only when they began to disperse they noticed that the day was breaking, that everyone was pale and rather dark in the face, as it always seems in the early morning when the last stars are going out. As they separated, the peasants laughed and made jokes about General Zhukov's cook and his cap which had been burnt; they already wanted to turn the fire into a joke, and even seemed sorry that it had so soon been put out.

"How well you extinguished the fire, sir!" said Olga to the student. "You ought to come to us in Moscow: there we have a fire every day."

"Why, do you come from Moscow?" asked one of the young ladies.

"Yes, miss. My husband was a waiter at the

Slavyansky Bazaar. And this is my daughter," she
said, indicating Sasha, who was cold and huddling
up to her. "She is a Moscow girl, too."

The two young ladies said something in French
to the student, and he gave Sasha a twenty-kopeck
piece.

Old Father Osip saw this, and there was a gleam
of hope in his face.

"We must thank God, your honour, there was no
wind," he said, addressing the student, "or else we
should have been all burnt up together. Your
honour, kind gentlefolks," he added in embarrass-
ment in a lower tone, "the morning's chilly . . .
something to warm one . . . half a bottle to your
honour's health."

Nothing was given him, and clearing his throat he
slouched home. Olga stood afterwards at the end
of the street and watched the two carts crossing the
river by the ford and the gentlefolks walking across
the meadow; a carriage was waiting for them the
other side of the river. Going into the hut, she described to her husband with enthusiasm:

"Such good people! And so beautiful! The
young ladies were like cherubim."

"Plague take them!" Fyokla, sleepy, said spitefully.

VI

Marya thought herself unhappy, and said that
she would be very glad to die; Fyokla, on the other
hand, found all this life to her taste: the poverty,
the uncleanliness, and the incessant quarrelling.

She ate what was given her without discrimination; slept anywhere, on whatever came to hand. She would empty the slops just at the porch, would splash them out from the doorway, and then walk barefoot through the puddle. And from the very first day she took a dislike to Olga and Nikolay just because they did not like this life.

" We shall see what you'll find to eat here, you Moscow gentry ! " she said malignantly. " We shall see ! "

One morning, it was at the beginning of September, Fyokla, vigorous, good-looking, and rosy from the cold, brought up two pails of water; Marya and Olga were sitting meanwhile at the table drinking tea.

" Tea and sugar," said Fyokla sarcastically. " The fine ladies ! " she added, setting down the pails. " You have taken to the fashion of tea every day. You better look out that you don't burst with your tea-drinking," she went on, looking with hatred at Olga. " That's how you have come by your fat mug, having a good time in Moscow, you lump of flesh ! " She swung the yoke and hit Olga such a blow on the shoulder that the two sisters-in-law could only clasp their hands and say :

" Oh, holy Saints ! "

Then Fyokla went down to the river to wash the clothes, swearing all the time so loudly that she could be heard in the hut.

The day passed and was followed by the long autumn evening. They wound silk in the hut; every-one did it except Fyokla; she had gone over the

river. They got the silk from a factory close by,
and the whole family working together earned next
to nothing, twenty kopecks a week.

" Things were better in the old days under the
gentry," said the old father as he wound silk.
" You worked and ate and slept, everything in its
turn. At dinner you had cabbage-soup and boiled
grain, and at supper the same again. Cucumbers
and cabbage in plenty: you could eat to your heart's
content, as much as you wanted. And there was
more strictness. Everyone minded what he was
about."

The hut was lighted by a single little lamp,
which burned dimly and smoked. When someone
screened the lamp and a big shadow fell across the
window, the bright moonlight could be seen. Old
Osip, speaking slowly, told them how they used to
live before the emancipation; how in those very
parts, where life was now so poor and so dreary,
they used to hunt with harriers, greyhounds,. re-
trievers, and when they went out as beaters the peasants were given vodka; how whole waggonloads of
game used to be sent to Moscow for the young mas-
ters; how the bad were beaten with rods or sent
away to the Tver estate, while the good were re-
warded. And Granny told them something, too.
She remembered everything, positively everything.
She described her mistress, a kind, God-fearing
woman, whose husband was a profligate and a rake,
and all of whose daughters made unlucky marriages:
one married a drunkard, another married a workman, the other eloped secretly (Granny herself, at

that time a young girl, helped in the elopement), and they had all three as well as their mother died early from grief.   And remembering all this, Granny positively began to shed tears.

All at once someone knocked at the door, and they all started.

" Uncle Osip, give me a night's lodging."

The little bald old man, General Zhukov's cook, the one whose cap had been burnt, walked in.   He sat down and listened, then he, too, began telling stories of all sorts.   Nikolay, sitting on the stove with his legs hanging down, listened and asked questions about the dishes that were prepared in the old days for the gentry.   They talked of rissoles, cutlets, various soups and sauces, and the cook, who remembered everything very well, mentioned dishes that are no longer served.   There was one, for instance — a dish made of bulls' eyes, which was called " waking up in the morning."

" And used you to do cutlets *à la maréchal?* " asked Nikolay.

" No."

Nikolay shook his head reproachfully and said:
" Tut, tut!   You were not much of a cook! "

The little girls sitting and lying on the stove stared down without blinking; it seemed as though there were a great many of them, like cherubim in the clouds.   They liked the stories: they were breathless; they shuddered and turned pale with alternate rapture and terror, and they listened breathlessly, afraid to stir, to Granny, whose stories were the most interesting of all.

They lay down to sleep in silence; and the old people, troubled and excited by their reminiscences, thought how precious was youth, of which, whatever it might have been like, nothing was left in the memory but what was living, joyful, touching, and how terribly cold was death, which was not far off, better not think of it! The lamp died down. And the dusk, and the two little windows sharply defined by the moonlight, and the stillness and the creak of the cradle, reminded them for some reason that life was over, that nothing one could do would bring it back. . . . You doze off, you forget yourself, and suddenly someone touches your shoulder or breathes on your cheek — and sleep is gone; your body feels cramped, and thoughts of death keep creeping into your mind. You turn on the other side: death is forgotten, but old dreary, sickening thoughts of poverty, of food, of how dear flour is getting, stray through the mind, and a little later again you remember that life is over and you cannot bring it back. . . .

"Oh, Lord!" sighed the cook.

Someone gave a soft, soft tap at the window. It must be Fyokla come back. Olga got up, and yawning and whispering a prayer, opened the door, then drew the bolt in the outer room, but no one came in; only from the street came a cold draught and a sudden brightness from the moonlight. The street, still and deserted, and the moon itself floating across the sky, could be seen at the open door.

"Who is there?" called Olga.

"I," she heard the answer —"it is I."

Near the door, crouching against the wall, stood Fyokla, absolutely naked. She was shivering with cold, her teeth were chattering, and in the bright moonlight she looked very pale, strange, and beautiful. The shadows on her, and the bright moonlight on her skin, stood out vividly, and her dark eyebrows and firm, youthful bosom were defined with peculiar distinctness.

" The ruffians over there undressed me and turned me out like this," she said. " I've come home without my clothes . . . naked as my mother bore me. Bring me something to put on."

" But go inside! " Olga said softly, beginning to shiver, too.

" I don't want the old folks to see." Granny was, in fact, already stirring and muttering, and the old father asked: " Who is there? " Olga brought her own smock and skirt, dressed Fyokla, and then both went softly into the inner room, trying not to make a noise with the door.

" Is that you, you sleek one? " Granny grumbled angrily, guessing who it was. " Fie upon you, night-walker! . . . Bad luck to you! "

" It's all right, it's all right," whispered Olga, wrapping Fyokla up; " it's all right, dearie."

All was stillness again. They always slept badly; everyone was kept awake by something worrying and persistent: the old man by the pain in his back, Granny by anxiety and anger, Marya by terror, the children by itch and hunger. Now, too, their sleep was troubled; they kept turning over from one side to the other, talking in their sleep, getting up for a drink. Fyokla suddenly broke into a loud, coarse howl, but immediately checked herself, and only uttered sobs from time to time, growing softer and on a lower note, until she relapsed into silence. From time to time from the other side of the river there floated the sound of the beating of the hours; but the time seemed somehow strange — five was struck and then three.

" Oh Lord! " sighed the cook.

Looking at the windows, it was difficult to tell whether it was still moonlight or whether the dawn had begun. Marya got up and went out, and she could be heard milking the cows and saying, " Stea-dy! " Granny went out, too. It was still dark in the hut, but all the objects in it could be discerned.

Nikolay, who had not slept all night, got down from the stove. He took his dress-coat out of a green box, put it on, and going to the window, stroked the sleeves and took hold of the coat-tails — and smiled. Then he carefully took off the coat, put it away in his box, and lay down again.

Marya came in again and began lighting the stove. She was evidently hardly awake, and seemed dropping asleep as she walked. Probably she had had some dream, or the stories of the night before came into her mind as, stretching luxuriously before the stove, she said:

" No, freedom is better."

VII

The master arrived — that was what they called the police inspector. When he would come and what he was coming for had been known for the last week. There were only forty households in Zhukovo, but more than two thousand roubles of arrears of rates and taxes had accumulated.

The police inspector stopped at the tavern. He drank there two glasses of tea, and then went on foot to the village elder's hut, near which a crowd of those who were in debt stood waiting. The elder, Antip Syedelnikov, was, in spite of his youth — he was only a little over thirty — strict and always on the side of the authorities, though he himself was poor and did not pay his taxes regularly. Evidently he enjoyed being elder, and liked the sense of authority, which he could only display by strictness. In the village council the peasants were afraid of him and obeyed him. It would sometimes happen that he would pounce on a drunken man in the street or near the tavern, tie his hands behind him, and put him in the lock-up. On one occasion he even put Granny in the lock-up because she went to the village council instead of Osip, and began swearing, and he kept her there for a whole day and night. He had never lived in a town or read a book, but somewhere or other had picked up various learned expressions, and loved to make use of them in conversation, and he was respected for this though he was not always understood.

When Osip came into the village elder's hut with his tax book, the police inspector, a lean old man with a long grey beard, in a grey tunic, was sitting at a table in the passage, writing something. It was clean in the hut; all the walls were dotted with pictures cut out of the illustrated papers, and in the most conspicuous place near the ikon there was a portrait of the Battenburg who was the Prince of Bulgaria. By the table stood Antip Syedelnikov with his arms folded.

"There is one hundred and nineteen roubles standing against him," he said when it came to Osip's turn. "Before Easter he paid a rouble, and he has not paid a kopeck since."

The police inspector raised his eyes to Osip and asked:

"Why is this, brother?"

"Show Divine mercy, your honour," Osip began, growing agitated. "Allow me to say last year the gentleman at Lutorydsky said to me, 'Osip,' he said, 'sell your hay . . . you sell it,' he said. Well, I had a hundred poods for sale; the women mowed it on the water-meadow. Well, we struck a bargain all right, willingly. . . ."

He complained of the elder, and kept turning round to the peasants as though inviting them to bear witness; his face flushed red and perspired, and his eyes grew sharp and angry.

"I don't know why you are saying all this," said the police inspector. "I am asking you . . . I am asking you why you don't pay your arrears. You don't pay, any of you, and am I to be responsible for you?"

"I can't do it."

"His words have no sequel, your honour," said the elder. "The Tchikildyeevs certainly are of a defective class, but if you will just ask the others, the root of it all is vodka, and they are a very bad lot. With no sort of understanding."

The police inspector wrote something down, and said to Osip quietly, in an even tone, as though he were asking him for water:

"Be off."

Soon he went away; and when he got into his cheap chaise and cleared his throat, it could be seen from the very expression of his long thin back that he was no longer thinking of Osip or of the village elder, nor of the Zhukovo arrears, but was thinking of his own affairs. Before he had gone three-quarters of a mile Antip was already carrying off the samovar from the Tchikildyeevs' cottage, followed by Granny, screaming shrilly and straining her throat:

"I won't let you have it, I won't let you have it, damn you!"

He walked rapidly with long steps, and she pursued him panting, almost falling over, a bent, ferocious figure; her kerchief slipped on to her shoulders, her grey hair with greenish lights on it was blown about in the wind. She suddenly stopped short, and like a genuine rebel, fell to beating her breast with her fists and shouting louder than ever in a sing-song voice, as though she were sobbing:

Peasants 315

"Good Christians and believers in God! Neighbours, they have ill-treated me! Kind friends, they have oppressed me! Oh, oh! dear people, take my part."

"Granny, Granny!" said the village elder sternly, "have some sense in your head!"

It was hopelessly dreary in the Tchikildyeevs' hut without the samovar; there was something humiliating in this loss, insulting, as though the honour of the hut had been outraged. Better if the elder had carried off the table, all the benches, all the pots — it would not have seemed so empty. Granny screamed, Marya cried, and the little girls, looking at her, cried, too. The old father, feeling guilty, sat in the corner with bowed head and said nothing. And Nikolay, too, was silent. Granny loved him and was sorry for him, but now, forgetting her pity, she fell upon him with abuse, with reproaches, shaking her fist right in his face. She shouted that it was all his fault; why had he sent them so little when he boasted in his letters that he was getting fifty roubles a month at the Slavyansky Bazaar? Why had he come, and with his family, too? If he died, where was the money to come from for his funeral . . . ? And it was pitiful to look at Nikolay, Olga, and Sasha.

The old father cleared his throat, took his cap, and went off to the village elder. Antip was soldering something by the stove, puffing out his cheeks; there was a smell of burning. His children, emaciated and unwashed, no better than the Tchikildyeevs, were scrambling about the floor; his wife, an ugly,

freckled woman with a prominent stomach, was winding silk. They were a poor, unlucky family, and
Antip was the only one who looked vigorous and
handsome. On a bench there were five samovars
standing in a row. The old man said his prayer to
Battenburg and said:

"Antip, show the Divine mercy. Give me back
the samovar, for Christ's sake!"

"Bring three roubles, then you shall have it."

"I can't do it!"

Antip puffed out his cheeks, the fire roared and
hissed, and the glow was reflected in the samovar.
The old man crumpled up his cap and said after
a moment's thought:

"You give it me back."

The swarthy elder looked quite black, and was
like a magician; he turned round to Osip and said
sternly and rapidly:

"It all depends on the rural captain. On the
twenty-sixth instant you can state the grounds for
your dissatisfaction before the administrative ses-
sion, verbally or in writing."

Osip did not understand a word, but he was satisfied with that and went home.

Ten days later the police inspector came again,
stayed an hour and went away. During those days
the weather had changed to cold and windy; the
river had been frozen for some time past, but still
there was no snow, and people found it difficult to
get about. On the eve of a holiday some of the
neighbours came in to Osip's to sit and have a talk.
They did not light the lamp, as it would have been

a sin to work, but talked in the darkness. There
were some items of news, all rather unpleasant.
In two or three households hens had been taken
for the arrears, and had been sent to the district
police station, and there they had died because no
one had fed them; they had taken sheep, and while
they were being driven away tied to one another,
shifted into another cart at each village, one of them
had died. And now they were discussing the question, who was to blame?

"The Zemstvo," said Osip. "Who else?"

"Of course it is the Zemstvo."

The Zemstvo was blamed for everything — for
the arrears, and for the oppressions, and for the
failure of the crops, though no one of them knew
what was meant by the Zemstvo. And this dated
from the time when well-to-do peasants who had
factories, shops, and inns of their own were mem-
bers of the Zemstvos, were dissatisfied with them,
and took to swearing at the Zemstvos in their factories and inns.

They talked of God's not sending the snow; they
had to bring in wood for fuel, and there was no
driving nor walking in the frozen ruts. In old
days fifteen to twenty years ago conversation was
much more interesting in Zhukovo. In those days
every old man looked as though he were treasuring
some secret; as though he knew something and was
expecting something. They used to talk about an
edict in golden letters, about the division of lands,
about new land, about treasures; they hinted at
something. Now the people of Zhukovo had no

mystery at all; their whole life was bare and open in the sight of all, and they could talk of nothing but poverty, food, there being no snow yet. . . .

There was a pause. Then they thought again of the hens, of the sheep, and began discussing whose fault it was.

"The Zemstvo," said Osip wearily. "Who else?"

VIII

The parish church was nearly five miles away at Kosogorovo, and the peasants only attended it when they had to do so for baptisms, weddings, or funerals; they went to the services at the church across the river. On holidays in fine weather the girls dressed up in their best and went in a crowd together to church, and it was a cheering sight to see them in their red, yellow, and green dresses cross the meadow; in bad weather they all stayed at home. They went for the sacrament to the parish church. From each of those who did not manage in Lent to go to confession in readiness for the sacrament the parish priest, going the round of the huts with the cross at Easter, took fifteen kopecks.

The old father did not believe in God, for he hardly ever thought about Him; he recognized the supernatural, but considered it was entirely the women's concern, and when religion or miracles were discussed before him, or a question were put to him, he would say reluctantly, scratching himself:

"Who can tell!"

Granny believed, but her faith was somewhat

hazy; everything was mixed up in her memory, and
she could scarcely begin to think of sins, of death,
of the salvation of the soul, before poverty and her
daily cares took possession of her mind, and she
instantly forgot what she was thinking about. She
did not remember the prayers, and usually in the
evenings, before lying down to sleep, she would
stand before the ikons and whisper:

"Holy Mother of Kazan, Holy Mother of
Smolensk, Holy Mother of Troerutchitsy. . . ."

Marya and Fyokla crossed themselves, fasted,
and took the sacrament every year, but understood
nothing. The children were not taught their prayers, nothing was told them about God, and no moral
principles were instilled into them; they were only
forbidden to eat meat or milk in Lent. In the
other families it was much the same: there were few
who believed, few who understood. At the same
time everyone loved the Holy Scripture, loved it
with a tender, reverent love; but they had no Bible,
there was no one to read it and explain it, and because Olga sometimes read them the gospel, they
respected her, and they all addressed her and Sasha
as though they were superior to themselves.

For church holidays and services Olga often went
to neighbouring villages, and to the district town,
in which there were two monasteries and twenty-
seven churches. She was dreamy, and when she was
on these pilgrimages she quite forgot her family,
and only when she got home again suddenly made the
joyful discovery that she had a husband and daughter, and then would say, smiling and radiant:

" God has sent me blessings ! "

What went on in the village worried her and seemed to her revolting. On Elijah's Day they drank, at the Assumption they drank, at the Ascension they drank. The Feast of the Intercession was the parish holiday for Zhukovo, and the peasants used to drink then for three days; they squandered on drink fifty roubles of money belonging to the Mir, and then collected more for vodka from all the households. On the first day of the feast the Tchikildyeevs killed a sheep and ate of it in the morning, at dinner-time, and in the evening; they ate it ravenously, and the children got up at night to eat more. Kiryak was fearfully drunk for three whole days; he drank up everything, even his boots and cap, and beat Marya so terribly that they had to pour water over her. And then they were all ashamed and sick.

However, even in Zhukovo, in this " Slaveytown," there was once an outburst of genuine religious enthusiasm. It was in August, when throughout the district they carried from village to village the Holy Mother, the giver of life. It was still and overcast on the day when they expected *Her* at Zhukovo. The girls set off in the morning to meet the ikon, in their bright holiday dresses, and brought Her towards the evening, in procession with the cross and with singing, while the bells pealed in the church across the river. An immense crowd of villagers and strangers flooded the street; there was noise, dust, a great crush. . . . And the old father and Granny and Kiryak — all stretched out their hands to the ikon, looked eagerly at it and said, weeping:

"Defender! Mother! Defender!"

All seemed suddenly to realize that there was not an empty void between earth and heaven, that the rich and the powerful had not taken possession of everything, that there was still a refuge from injury, from slavish bondage, from crushing, unendurable poverty, from the terrible vodka.

"Defender! Mother!" sobbed Marya. "Mother!"

But the thanksgiving service ended and the ikon was carried away, and everything went on as before; and again there was a sound of coarse drunken oaths from the tavern.

Only the well-to-do peasants were afraid of death; the richer they were the less they believed in God, and in the salvation of souls, and only through fear of the end of the world put up candles and had services said for them, to be on the safe side. The peasants who were rather poorer were not afraid of death. The old father and Granny were told to their faces that they had lived too long, that it was time they were dead, and they did not mind. They did not hinder Fyokla from saying in Nikolay's presence that when Nikolay died her husband Denis would get exemption — to return home from the army. And Marya, far from fearing death, regretted that it was so slow in coming, and was glad when her children died.

Death they did not fear, but of every disease they had an exaggerated terror. The merest trifle was

enough — a stomach upset, a slight chill, and Granny
would be wrapped up on the stove, and would begin
moaning loudly and incessantly:

" I am dy-ing!"

The old father hurried off for the priest, and
Granny received the sacrament and extreme unc-
tion. They often talked of colds, of worms, of
tumours which move in the stomach and coil round
to the heart. Above all, they were afraid of catching cold, and so put on thick clothes even in the summer and warmed themselves at the stove. Granny
was fond of being doctored, and often went to the
hospital, where she used to say she was not seventy,
but fifty-eight; she supposed that if the doctor knew
her real age he would not treat her, but would say
it was time she died instead of taking medicine.
She usually went to the hospital early in the morning, taking with her two or three of the little girls,
and came back in the evening, hungry and ill-tempered — with drops for herself and ointments for
the little girls. Once she took Nikolay, who swal-
lowed drops for a fortnight afterwards, and said he
felt better.

Granny knew all the doctors and their assistants
and the wise men for twenty miles round, and not
one of them she liked. At the Intercession, when
the priest made the round of the huts with the
cross, the deacon told her that in the town near
the prison lived an old man who had been a med-
ical orderly in the army, and who made wonderful
cures, and advised her to try him. Granny took
his advice. When the first snow fell she drove to

the town and fetched an old man with a big beard, a converted Jew, in a long gown, whose face was covered with blue veins. There were outsiders at work in the hut at the time: an old tailor, in terrible spectacles, was cutting a waistcoat out of some rags, and two young men were making felt boots out of wool; Kiryak, who had been dismissed from his place for drunkenness, and now lived at home, was sitting beside the tailor mending a bridle. And it was crowded, stifling, and noisome in the hut. The converted Jew examined Nikolay and said that it was necessary to try cupping.

He put on the cups, and the old tailor, Kiryak, and the little girls stood round and looked on, and it seemed to them that they saw the disease being drawn out of Nikolay; and Nikolay, too, watched how the cups suckling at his breast gradually filled with dark blood, and felt as though there really were something coming out of him, and smiled with pleasure.

"It's a good thing," said the tailor. "Please God, it will do you good."

The Jew put on twelve cups and then another twelve, drank some tea, and went away. Nikolay began shivering; his face looked drawn, and, as the women expressed it, shrank up like a fist; his fingers turned blue. He wrapped himself up in a quilt and in a sheepskin, but got colder and colder. Towards the evening he began to be in great distress; asked to be laid on the ground, asked the tailor not to smoke; then he subsided under the sheepskin and towards morning he died.

IX

Oh, what a grim, what a long winter!

Their own grain did not last beyond Christmas, and they had to buy flour. Kiryak, who lived at home now, was noisy in the evenings, inspiring terror in everyone, and in the mornings he suffered from headache and was ashamed; and he was a pitiful sight. In the stall the starved cows bellowed day and night — a heart-rending sound to Granny and Marya. And as ill-luck would have it, there was a sharp frost all the winter, the snow drifted in high heaps, and the winter dragged on. At Annunciation there was a regular blizzard, and there was a fall of snow at Easter.

But in spite of it all the winter did end. At the beginning of April there came warm days and frosty nights. Winter would not give way, but one warm day overpowered it at last, and the streams began to flow and the birds began to sing. The whole meadow and the bushes near the river were drowned in the spring floods, and all the space between Zhukovo and the further side was filled up with a vast sheet of water, from which wild ducks rose up in flocks here and there. The spring sunset, flaming among gorgeous clouds, gave every evening something new, extraordinary, incredible — just what one does not believe in afterwards, when one sees those very colours and those very clouds in a picture.

The cranes flew swiftly, swiftly, with mournful

cries, as though they were calling themselves.
Standing on the edge of the ravine, Olga looked
a long time at the flooded meadow, at the sunshine,
at the bright church, that looked as though it had
grown younger; and her tears flowed and her breath
came in gasps from her passionate longing to go
away, to go far away to the end of the world.   It
was already settled that she should go back to Moscow to be a servant, and that Kiryak should set off
with her to get a job as a porter or something.   Oh,
to get away quickly!

As soon as it dried up and grew warm they got
ready to set off.   Olga and Sasha, with wallets
on their backs and shoes of plaited bark on their
feet, came out before daybreak: Marya came out,
too, to see them on their way.   Kiryak was not
well, and was kept at home for another week.   For
the last time Olga prayed at the church and thought
of her husband, and though she did not shed tears,
her face puckered up and looked ugly like an old
woman's.   During the winter she had grown thinner and plainer, and her hair had gone a little grey,
and instead of the old look of sweetness and the
pleasant smile on her face, she had the resigned,
mournful expression left by the sorrows she had
been through, and there was something blank and
irresponsive in her eyes, as though she did not hear
what was said.   She was sorry to part from the
village and the peasants.   She remembered how
they had carried out Nikolay, and how a requiem
had been ordered for him at almost every hut, and
all had shed tears in sympathy with her grief.   In

the course of the summer and the winter there had
been hours and days when it seemed as though these
people lived worse than the beasts, and to live with
them was terrible; they were coarse, dishonest,
filthy, and drunken; they did not live in harmony,
but quarrelled continually, because they distrusted
and feared and did not respect one another. Who
keeps the tavern and makes the people drunken? A
peasant. Who wastes and spends on drink the funds
of the commune, of the schools, of the church? A
peasant. Who stole from his neighbours, set fire
to their property, gave false witness at the court
for a bottle of vodka? At the meetings of the
Zemstvo and other local bodies, who was the first
to fall foul of the peasants? A peasant. Yes, to
live with them was terrible; but yet, they were human beings, they suffered and wept like human beings, and there was nothing in their lives for which
one could not find excuse. Hard labour that made
the whole body ache at night, the cruel winters, the
scanty harvests, the overcrowding; and they had no
help and none to whom they could look for help.
Those of them who were a little stronger and better
off could be no help, as they were themselves coarse,
dishonest, drunken, and abused one another just as
revoltingly; the paltriest little clerk or official treated
the peasants as though they were tramps, and addressed even the village elders and church wardens
as inferiors, and considered they had a right to do
so. And, indeed, can any sort of help or good
example be given by mercenary, greedy, depraved,
and idle persons who only visit the village in order

to insult, to despoil, and to terrorize? Olga remembered the pitiful, humiliated look of the old people when in the winter Kiryak had been taken to be flogged. . . . And now she felt sorry for all these people, painfully so, and as she walked on she kept looking back at the huts.

After walking two miles with them Marya said good-bye, then kneeling, and falling forward with her face on the earth, she began wailing:

"Again I am left alone. Alas, for poor me! poor, unhappy! . . ."

And she wailed like this for a long time, and for a long way Olga and Sasha could still see her on her knees, bowing down to someone at the side and clutching her head in her hands, while the rooks flew over her head.

The sun rose high; it began to get hot. Zhukovo was left far behind. Walking was pleasant. Olga and Sasha soon forgot both the village and Marya; they were gay and everything entertained them. Now they came upon an ancient barrow, now upon a row of telegraph posts running one after another into the distance and disappearing into the horizon, and the wires hummed mysteriously. Then they saw a homestead, all wreathed in green foliage; there came a scent from it of dampness, of hemp, and it seemed for some reason that happy people lived there. Then they came upon a horse's skeleton whitening in solitude in the open fields. And the larks trilled unceasingly, the corncrakes called to one another, and the landrail cried as though someone were really scraping at an old iron rail.

At midday Olga and Sasha reached a big village. There in the broad street they met the little old man who was General Zhukov's cook. He was hot, and his red, perspiring bald head shone in the sunshine. Olga and he did not recognize each other, then looked round at the same moment, recognized each other, and went their separate ways without saying a word. Stopping near the hut which looked newest and most prosperous, Olga bowed down before the open windows, and said in a loud, thin, chanting voice:

"Good Christian folk, give alms, for Christ's sake, that God's blessing may be upon you, and that your parents may be in the Kingdom of Heaven in peace eternal."

"Good Christian folk," Sasha began chanting, "give, for Christ's sake, that God's blessing, the Heavenly Kingdom . . ."

1897